Journal of Allen Brock

QUENTIN CANDELA

Journal of Allen Brock
Copyright © 2023 by Quentin Candela

ISBN: 978-1639455720 (sc)
ISBN: 978-1639455737 (e)

All rights reserved. No part of this publication may be reproduced, distributed, or transmitted in any form or by any means, including photocopying, recording, or other electronic or mechanical methods, without the prior written permission of the publisher, except in the case brief quotations embodied in critical reviews and other noncommercial uses permitted by copyright law.

The views expressed in this book are solely those of the author and do not necessarily reflect the views of the publisher, and the publisher hereby disclaims any responsibility for them.

Writers' Branding
(877) 608-6550
www.writersbranding.com
media@writersbranding.com

Contents

Writing by Candlelight vii
Acknowledgement ix
Introduction xi

Junipero's Wall 1
HEXAS 4
Endless Wars 7
Knob Noster 9
Mosaics 13
Lysander & Dagne 15
Cataclysm 18
Rift Space Effect 20
Instructor 22
Advisory Council 24
Ností 26
Prophet 29
Whisperings of Elohi 33
Hegira 36
Visions 39
Novo Ceres 42
Seaton Polytechnic 44
Proxies & Coolies 47
STASA 50
Willoughby 53
Moira 56
Apron of Hœff 60
Madame De Farge 62

Salton Basin	66
Highland Spring	69
Patriot	71
Expedition	74
Road To Aguijón	76
El Flaco	79
A Hexas Femme	84
Hexas Politics	91
Crag Rat	93
Cairo Coalman	95
Hunters Lodge	98
Hammering Matt	103
New Directorate	105
New Paradigm	109
City by the Bay	111
Fayean Speak	114
Ruthian Faye	117
"Heard through the Grapevine"	120
Sunrise Over the Bay	124
Only the Best for Faye	127
Of Sennists & Rods	130
Hook Line & Sinker	134
Timeless Whisper from Bon'aire	136
A Prince in Court	138
Tread not on Faye	142
Coeur d'Faye	144
Sororan	145
The Recruit	148
Strategy	151
Tactics & Feigns	155
Banfield Rout	158
Onward to Victory	163
Prince of Knaves	166
Dubious Prize	168
Staff	170
Eno Kelvin	172
The Matris	176

The Quahog	179
Lander Oberon	181
Bursa Pastoris	183
Justice	188
Drawing the Strings	190
Quilty	194
Reproached	196
Plains of Takk	198
Osprey	201
Lander Gly	204
Tragedy	206
Philo Grünfal	209
A Loss	212
By the Blood Stones!	214
"Pax Sui Generis"	222
Night Shadows of Brindal	232

Writing by Candlelight

The soft glow of candlelight suits my needs. It adds an ambiance of tranquility to my room. At the closing of the day, my mind comes to peace, and I think clearly. As I review the day, I recall with vividness those events that both disturbed and amused me…

Allen Brock Benitez

To Esteban

Acknowledgement

Thanks go to Joseph Francis Dessert for his hard work polishing this manuscript. It's his wordsmithing that makes Brock's narrative flow so well.

Introduction

I am Allen Brock. Before coming to Junipero Heights, I didn't know who I was. It's not because I suffered from amnesia, but because who I am is the result of present circumstances.

Natives, meaning the people of Highland and the Mosaics, are not Hexas, and no, the word "Native" does not imply a group of primitive people living on some faraway island. The term Native, when capitalized, is the group of hominids who evolved on this world, on Terra Firma, meaning Earth. Hexas and Natives share the same DNA, but they come from a different "tribe" of hominids.

Hexas are unwelcome guests in our lives. They established themselves here long before I was born, more than a century before my father was born actually, and to say they are guests would not be correct, nor can they be regarded as foreigners either. Hexas have gone to great lengths to set themselves apart because they are aliens but not in the traditional sense. Hexas, for example, didn't come to our world in starships or "beam" from a mother vessel orbiting Earth. Their zygotes didn't drift in the currents of space to land on Earth to snatch human bodies and overwrite their personalities. That's to say, Hexas didn't steal people's souls, although one can reach a conceptual similarity there. Nonetheless, some Natives admire the Hexas.

To the proponents of the alien theory, Hexas came from–"somewhere out there." Again, I've never subscribed to the notion that Hexas are space aliens. But if they are aliens, they are exceptional aliens indeed since their genome mirrors our own. Hexas are considered Earth's "fourth racial group." The current belief is that race is a construct. I intend not to argue this point or suggest that human evolution continues. What I'll point out is that it was Hexas' sense of timing that led to their ascendancy in the northern half of the continent.

Hexas rose to prominence in the north during the end of the fourth millennium. The old global empire was in tatters, ripe for disintegration. It was a time of chaos and destruction. People claimed it was the end of days. The Biblical "Cup of Wrath" was poured over the surface of the Earth, etc.

This idea, the end of time theme, is familiar to many cultures and faiths. It justifies our "just deserts" in the minds of religious crackpots. It is what we humans merit as a consequence of our inequity. Aye, we received in the form of final judgment what is due. Insanely as this sounds, the notion lends comfort to those who believe in a higher being. Such judgment usually comes from the heavens. They open up and pour brimstone and fire down on hapless humans. God's fury obliterates everything: modern metropolises, horse and buggy, a girls' soccer team, a ten-month-old infant in a perambulator, and the tadpole in the pond.

A worldwide flood, too, is a shared disaster theme. These are deluges of such proportions that mile-high waters inundate the entire surface of the Earth.

What changed the Earth, or Aerth, as Hexas speech enunciates the blue-green planet of our birth, was geological devastation. I imagine if you stretch the metaphor, it might fit into the category of divine retribution turned on its head.

Recorded history speaks of conquest eras wherein mass murder and thievery were the norms when one group of men and women took advantage of the circumstance to dispossess others. For instance, Europeans took the Americas, not necessarily through the force of arms. More advanced technology and weaponry did help, though. The sad fact is that the native population was decimated through the use of germs.

Fast-forward several millennium. Early history conquerors were not aware they harbored lethal weaponry, but the Hexas certainly did. How could they not?

The plagues following the Hexas arrival were different, however. They didn't come in the form of smallpox, typhus, or influenza. Those agents gained subtler functions, so taking longer for their effect to run the course. The sterility plague was the most devastating of these.

As Hexas numbers began to increase, they launched the second phase of their power-grab. In the north, they became the principal heads of state. Hexas honchos took control of the markets and banks, of communications and politics. Proxies, pejorative for Native turncoats, helped Hexas immensely. That's not just my opinion. Hexas seized the reins of power through the proxies and put their designer boots on the Native's neck.

As for the rest of the world, I can provide no information. But in the southern continent, we are confident that people also survived Gaia's fury. Except it wouldn't be wise to extend a hand across the sea to them.

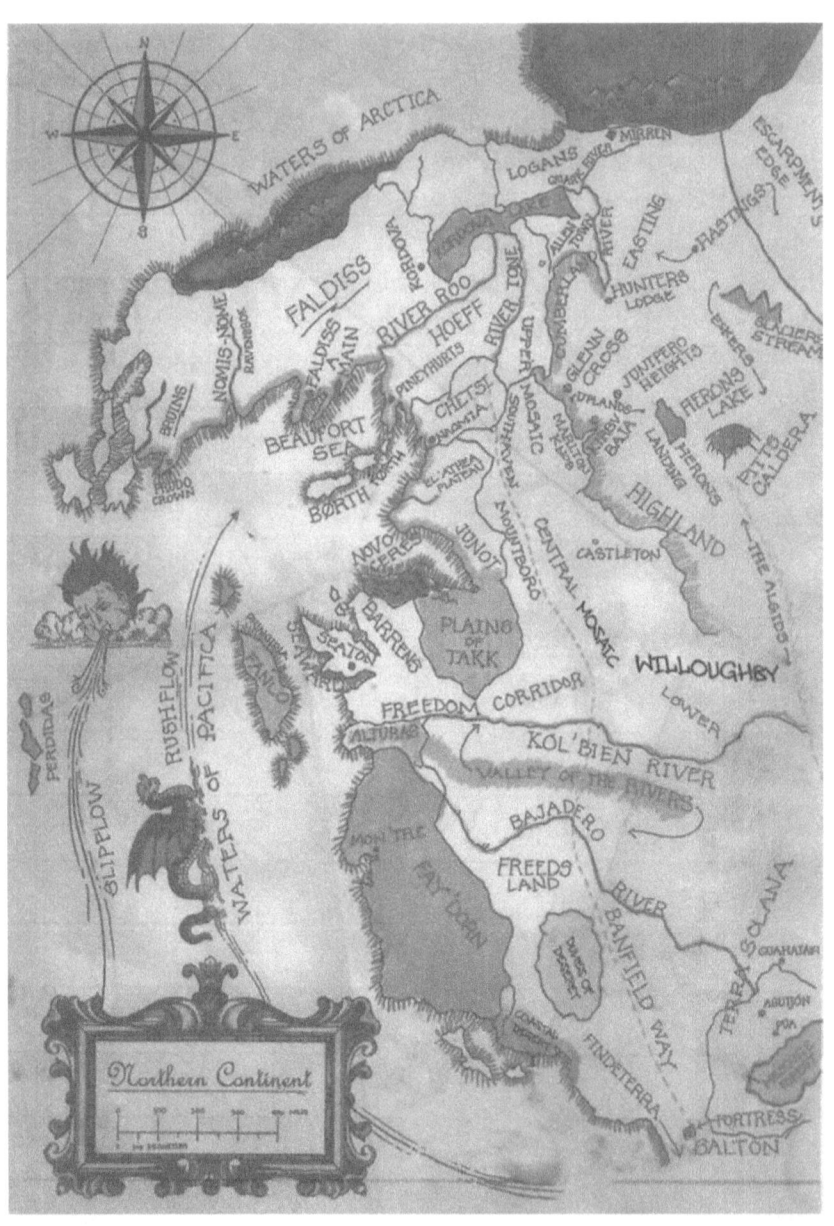

Junipero's Wall

When the sun casts longer shadows across the western foothills, the workday in Junipero Heights is done. After ten hours of labor, it's time to call it a day. Sighs of relief are heard from the work crews. Even though we use heavy equipment, cranes, backhoes, and bulldozers, the work is backbreaking at times. It's summer too, and in this part of Highland, the days are long, and the weather is hot.

To the east, the gray tips of the Escarpment belt are still visible in the twilight. The "Belt" is the zenith of the Escarpment, while the Escarpment itself is an endless wall of granite soaring high into the clouds. It's impressive, to be sure, and even if it's hundreds of miles distance, it's confining, and its effects are wide-ranging.

Today more so than others, I feel exhausted. We work six days a week, and the rate of pay is as low as it comes. Even so, I'm glad to find myself here, moiling among the brothers of Junipero Abbey. In the past, I've engaged in dangerous tasks for a pittance.

Elliot Madigan, Junipero Heights' abbot, has plans to fortify the northern and westernmost approaches to the abbey. I doubt, though, that the Logans will ever attack Junipero. However, in the north is Hunters Lodge, Easting's township. It's a place the Logans raid frequently. I'll explain the Logans in another entry, so for now, I'll get on with what's on the abbot's mind. He wants to build a wall that stretches across Junipero's northern approach. If Logans take Easting, but that's an assumption I disagree with since I'm an Easter, meaning I was born in Easting. As long as there are Easters,

Logans will never take Hunters Lodge. We both agree, though, that the Hexas army is the number one threat.

It's the belief of the people of Junipero that stockpiling supplies and upgrading our equipment is a good idea no matter what. Hence the reason Abbot Elliot Madigan had the township's cistern system enlarged and more generators brought online.

That's not all of it. Abbot Madigan wants Junipero Heights to be independent of the rest of Highland, and he wants this accomplished before the year's end.

"Brock, Highland has been fighting the Hexas military tooth and nail for generations. One out of every eight Highland-born males falls in battle before his thirtieth birthday as a result. The glacis of Glenn Cross' Citadel remains stained with the blood of the patriots. Do you recall the battle? It was the first Hexas offensive to take Glenn Cross."

What could I say? My father was the locum-teneris or "leftenant," meaning the officer holding in place to lead the fight in the same glacis. Lieutenant Lysander Benitez ordered a charge against an entire company of Hexas grenadiers. His force of forty-three men drove the Hexas from Glenn Cross Citadel. He was only twenty-two at the time. Yet, he understood the workings of war better than the colonels above him.

In the evenings, the brothers gather for a customary end of the workweek festivities. This results in copious drinking of home-brewed beer, seasonal ale. But, of course, there's enough food for everyone too. The members of the Junipero Order are unlike those monks of the past. They drink a great deal, and they revel. They commune with women also. These Juniperos believe that God means for a man to seek the company of the opposite sex. God frowns at a man who is attracted in this drive to another man. I, on the other hand, don't care whatever company a man prefers. That is his business, you see. Having said that, I find certain practices and behaviors unwholesome.

Junipero Abbey is different in other aspects as well. It opens its doors to everyone. A Junipero monk can practice Buddhism or be a Jew, a Zoroaster, or a Muslim. He could be a Bible-thumping nut—even an atheist like me. Though I've told the abbot that I'm in Junipero to become a friar, this doesn't mean I must be religious.

Abbot Elliot Madigan explains to the initiates that God's works are ubiquitous. In other words, they're seen everywhere. A man only needs to take a moment and observe his surroundings. Yet, God will never force his will on anyone. At times God seems indifferent, cruel, and unloving, but God is just. His actions must be measured in that context. God lets man find his own way. No matter if a man is heading in the wrong direction, God will not revoke his free will. When you ask God for his advice, He will send his reply, not with a crack of thunder from above, but straight into your heart. I, for one, have never asked God for anything.

HEXAS

Abbot Madigan suggested I should acquaint myself with my fellow brothers. So it was that I joined the weekend's feast in Junipero Abbey.

I heard one of the brothers say that Hexas were people just like we Natives. True enough, Hexas are people, but they don't view themselves as being the same as us. Hexas have made that point clear for some time. They are apart because they are better than us. To Hexas, we Natives are only useful when we further their aims.

Hexas deem themselves without physiological flaws, too, a salient point that the particular brother failed to mention. It's Hexas opinion that their race is perfect in physical design. The men and women are supposedly taller than average height. Their hair is dark–no question of that. Their skin is very fair too, but that's a general observation.

It's the opinion of several of the brothers too that Hexas women are lovely. They claim that these femmes' tawny eyes flux in the light and can mesmerize a man. A Hexas femme, meaning lady, need not apply makeup because her cheeks bear a natural blush. Her lips are full, and again, no glossy lacquer is required to enhance their allure. Those observations are partly correct. Hexas women are fetching, no argument there, but so are the fair ladies of Highland.

Supposedly Hexas are endowed with superior intellect. Then I say, by what metric? That is, who chooses the batteries of IQ tests to validate that fact? Any schoolmarm worth her salt knows that tests can be skewed to benefit or undermine a given target group.

When you speak to a Hexas gent or a femme, they are attentive. As a rule, their manners are refined. They are not argumentative. Seldom do they show opposition to your ideas or to your point of view. That's to say, they tend to accede to your opinion rather than argue the point. Instinctively, though, you sense their disdain for you. To them, we Natives are a step up from anthropoids. Non-Hexas are referred to as Faschones. The word is derived from a Hexas dialect, meaning outsider. When used as a verb, faschone infers something shoddily made, second-class wares. A blend of Native and Hexas is called a hafū, choné, and other derogatory terms. Chonés are despised by the Hexas. To the Highland folk, race or ethnicity makes no difference.

By the way, Hexas is a collective noun; singular and plural forms are the same. You wouldn't say, for instance, she is a Hexas. Simply stated, she is Hexas. Neither would they say they are Hexases; no, they are Hexas. One-word fits all.

Today these people live in the northern part of the continent, of course. This land is referred to as Upper and Lower Icenia. A Hexas might also be known as a Faldissi, Junotine, Chet, or correspondingly from the Barony' he or she hails from. More to the point, Hexas don't partner with us, and we don't seek their company either. Then enough of all that, I think by now you have an idea of the situation–a social divide.

Hexas are at war with Highland's people for three reasons: land, freedom, and fear. Hexas live in fear of the "Highland Animal," meaning anyone who looks like me, and who also thinks independently. Unfortunately for the Hexas, they've been unable to tame the millions of "trogs" in Highland. We are fierce people, and we are stubborn as well. Although they have persuaded others, Hexas haven't convinced us of their superiority, whether by charm or sword.

To write all this is quite boring, but there's no other way to go about it. If I'm to give you a complete picture of our "world," this is the only way. I'll stop for now.

Deciding to take Elliot's advice, I selected a handful his books for study. His library is filled with books on science and literature.

Printed books are a treasure because they're inalterable. It's not so easy to revise history when there are books, much as Hexas and their proxies would like.

I'll add that the Hexas are sharp and also devious. With the support of turncoat city officials of the Upper Mosaic, an area Hexas control, a bill striking down the right to own firemarms was forced through the sub-Legas. Citing public safety, the ownership of firearms was no longer a legitimate right. Not everyone in the Upper Mosaic, many of which are of Highland stock, went along with the decree. In Highland, we watched the gradual curtailment of the people's rights with a stern eye. The point is that a police force can't protect everyone. If a man is not allowed to arm himself, how does he protect his hold from criminals and raiders like the Logans?

I was born and raised in the northern Highland township of Easting. Easters, the term for the men and women who live there, are steadfast. One of our sayings goes this way: "When you're big and bad, it's easy to ask an unarmed man to crawl on his hands and knees and kiss your boots, but it's not so easy to ask that man when he's armed with a shot-pistol to do the same.

Endless Wars

Abbot Madigan explains his concerns while we share a few drinks from a bottle of sherry. "Hexas Faldissi are wooing the Logans," he says. "It's yet one more reason we need to fortify the northern approach to Junipero."

Elliot Madigan means that the Hexas want to strike an alliance with the Logans. Such an alliance would be dire news for Highland and Junipero because the enemy would be able to hit us from two directions.

The Land of the Logans, or simply Logans as we refer to the area, lies north of Easting. It's a cold, brooding place, not well suited for agriculture, but Logans manage to grow some crops, mostly winter vegetables. They raise sheep and miniature cattle; hunt caribou, moose, and harvest shellfish from Lake Kordova. Logans are big, belligerent, and uncouth.

Like my father and his father, I, too, grew up fighting Logans. I detest them.

Logans want Hunters Lodge, Easting's largest township. Hunters Lodge is the gateway to the Upper Mosaic. They've never been able to take "The Lodge" from the Easters. In bloody battles after bloody battles, they've failed. Abbot Madigan says that this is one reason why Logans might be amenable to striking an alliance with Faldiss.

Meanwhile, the land of our Hexas enemy is divided into Upper Icenia and Lower Icenia. I believe I've mentioned this. Their ceaseless attempts to invade Highland always originate from Upper Icenia. They come at us from the Upper Mosaic or south across Central Mosaic, violating that land's neutrality. They hit Glenn Cross or

Kirby Baja's knobs, but it does not matter from which direction. We've always repelled them.

I'll relate some history again to make a point. Hexas army, which numbered tens of thousands, invaded Glenn Cross. In their way stood the Citadel. The enemy could not afford to bypass this fortification, and so orders were given to storm it. What ensued was a debacle for the Hexas. As I mentioned, to this day, the stones of the Citadel's glacis remain stained with the blood of Hexas and patriots alike.

Knob Noster

Easting, Glenn Cross, Kirby Baja, Junipero Heights, Herons Landing, and Pitts Caldera are the Highland core. These areas comprise more than sixty percent of Highland's population.

The latest target of the Prince of Icenia, he's our Hexas enemy Meres Ma'tann, is Kirby Baja. His military advisors tell him that its most salient landmark, Knob Noster, must be taken before Highland proper is invested. From the Knob, one can see as far as the township of Marlton in the Central Mosaic. From this high hill, we can spy enemy movements in the valley.

Highland, as the name suggests, is no romping ground. Her terrain is rugged, filled with natural barriers perfectly suitable for defense. Further, and here are a few not so complimentary remarks of its people from the courtesy of our enemy: "Highland is a place teeming with 'troglodytes' that have recently emerged from the caves. Kill a 'Trog,' and two more take his place. They breed like rats."

I am thankful to Elliot for much, particularly for providing me a home. I'm impressed too by the extent of his knowledge. Abbot Madigan is not just a historian; he is a geneticist as well. Since I also studied biology at Seaward Seaton Polytech, we share common interests. Nevertheless, this evening we discussed neither history nor science but the ramification of a widening war. After decades of fighting Highland, Hexas High Command has opted for the final solution-the eradication of the "Highland Trog."

Abbot Madigan says, "If we can't protect Glenn Cross, Highland's cradle, and if we can't secure Junipero Heights, its spiritual center, then we're done for."

The reality is we're all but fighting alone because a cowardly group called the Mayoralty governs the Central Mosaic. These mayors run a Keystone Cops security that's laughable. Highland, though, has partisans, rogue elements around Freedom Corridor in Marlton, Castleton, and Mountboro. We train and arm these men. Most of them are hassims. I'll explain who these men are later on. Yet we need more allies, and although our defeat is not a forgone conclusion, victory over the Hexas remains a dream.

I expressed my sentiments. "Abbot, I don't believe in destiny, but when I weigh the strength of the forces arrayed against us and our lack of a unified effort, I say the Hexas will eventually wear us down. Highland's Directorate of Military Operations must change with the times."

"Call me Elliot," Abbot Madigan says. "When we have to deal with titles, we can't express our thoughts clearly for fear of offending."

I smile at him. "Using your first name would be out of line in front of the brothers, don't you think?"

"Brother Elliot would be apt," he replies. "That is while we're in the company of others–only a slight familiarity in the term brother, no? But to my point, this conflict is about land and about putting ideas in people's minds. You would know about the latter, about putting ideas in people's minds, right?"

Ah, so there it is, I realize. Brother Elliot knows about Willoughby. It's still talked about.

"You can grow a beard in an attempt to hide your face, but it's more challenging to obscure other aspects of you."

How well I know.

"When I heard you speak to your work crew the first time, and seeing how you walked amongst those men, I knew who you were. So, tell me, Allen Brock, alias Burton Black, what would change the Faldissi Meres Ma'tann's mind about going at Highland again?"

As he waits for my reply, the abbot pours me another glass. I wondered why he was interested in my opinion. Though my father raised me Roman Catholic, I'm not religious. And in my estimation, not very bright. I figure that my usefulness to Junipero is my knowledge of construction and my skills in managing people. I can fight too. Oh, I'm also a criminal, and I think the abbot knows that as well. Maybe he wants me to kill someone. I could do that, but it depends on who it is.

"I'm not sure I follow exactly," I reply, addressing his question. "Is Brother Elliot asking what we can do to change the mental fix of the Hexas people, or how to make the Hexas change their strategy of war?"

"Allen Brock of Easting, your presence here is no accident," he declares.

It's my turn to request a preference. "Call me Brock."

He nodded. "Very well, Brock. So when I heard your rousing speech in Willoughby, as many people have, I knew that at some point, you would find your way to Junipero. You can project your thoughts with great clarity, Brock. That's why your words reverberate still throughout the Mosaics. It's clear you aren't a simple man, no drunkard lashing out impotently at Hexas tyranny or at the corrupt mayors. That's the reason the Hexas came after you with such determination."

I wasn't aware there was a spark of interest of my actions other than from the people of the Apron of Hœff and, of course, the Stasa. "The Stasa came after me only because of the riots in the Apron."

Elliot differed with that opinion. "Brock, they came at you because they realized the danger that a man like you poses. The words you spoke made the Hexas recoil. While at the same time, your actions made Natives realize that their enemy is not invulnerable. For a century now, the Hexas psych labs and social engineers have attempted to squelch Native initiative throughout the Mosaics. Then there you go, and crap on those decades long works in a single night. You're such a blight, Brock, that you're to be shot dead on sight, except they don't know what you look like exactly."

I didn't ask him how he knew all this, but it was a fair assessment. I had committed crimes, sabotage, ignited riots, and committed murder.

I study him closer. Elliot Madigan has a handsome face. His nose is straight, and his chin, which he keeps clean-shaven, is firm. His hair is auburn and is tonsured, while his eyes are emerald green and sharp. Being above average in height and stout of form, he reminds me of one of Von Grützner's monks with ample belly holding a tankard of ale.

"What would make the Hexas military adopt a new strategy, Brock?"

"I'm no military strategist, Brother Elliot. All I did during my short stint in the army was to fulfill my obligation."

His eyes peer at me. "You were an infantry officer. You come from a military family."

Okay, Elliot knows who I am. He knows I'm from Easting. I don't question him about how he got this knowledge because it doesn't matter. His question is straight forward, though—is it possible to make Hexas regret invading Highland again?

I begin by saying, "To change the enemy's tactics and allow you to gain an advantage over him, you have to kill more of his than he kills of yours. You weaken his capacity to move against you by forcing him into tactical mistakes. You try and destroy his weapons and equipment while incurring as little expense to yours. You make everything that's possible to demoralize the enemy. When you put all those components together, it's called a strategy. The most important part of any strategy is to plant in your enemy's mind the seed of his defeat."

Mosaics

The Mosaics are not countries but lands governed by Mayoralty Council. The councilmen are city officials coming together in assembly. Hundreds of townships of varying sizes merged to form a loosely held confederation. In other words, Central and Lower Mosaics townships are quasi-independent entities.

I lived and worked in the Central Mosaic in townships like Castleton, Southaven, Marlton, Mountboro, Ventura, and others. During my residence in Marlton, I was never asked to attend any publicus–a general town meeting. This quarterly event occurs in Castleton, Marlton, and other townships on the last Wednesday of the month. The purpose is to alert the public of new policies from the mayor and gather input from the people.

This is the skinny from one of the men who attended the last Mayoral meeting on Wednesday evening. The mayor of Castleton Township is under the microscope. The other mayors are not too happy because of a lack of support for Hexas projects in her principality. Discussion of the Hexas war on the people of Highland, by the way, is now considered taboo.

Hexas proxies monitor these public gatherings. They are zealous too. The number of attendees will be such, no more of these people or less than those others. We don't want to hear from this person or shills from this other group, etc. The size of the audience is set, and speakers deemed hostile to the Mayoralty are disinvited.

I can't remember if I've written this on previous pages, but I'll write it just the same. The Mosaics are divided into three regions, Upper, Central, and Lower Mosaics. Terra Solana lies in the Lower

Mosaic, but it's an independent country. While Fay'dorn and Fin de Terra, just like Highland, are countries apart too.

This is it; I won't write about this boring stuff anymore. I heard the evensong, the time for evening prayer. I'll fold my journal. Before I do, I'll tell you this. I am an atheist. Yet, I admire people of faith. People like Elliot are not greedy or shallow. This is one of the reasons I attend prayers. I like hearing Abbot Madigan's words of wisdom. The man has given me a job and a home. I owe him loyalty.

Lysander & Dagne

I was born to a proud family, that is, on my father's side. Lysander, my father, was a busy man, yet he always found time for me. He explained his roots.

One of his ancestors was Victoria Rojas. She was the daughter of a Boricua from the colonized island of San Juan Bautista. While his great grandfather was Diego Benitez Duero, born in Novo Cadiz de Las Floridas. Highland's people, you see, are a blend of immigrants from the world over, a world that once was.

After marriage, the couple set roots in Santa Fe. This was a city in the Southwest. In her essays, Victoria described the natural beauty of the Painted Desert where she lived. Her writings are unique in their descriptive details. I'm speaking of the entries in her diary written hundreds of years ago. No matter that, it's hard to imagine the places she so vividly described. Like many other wondrous places of Old Earth, her "Fabled Santa Fe" no longer exists.

When I was a child, Lysander explained it this way: "Gaia became hungry. Her churning jaws devoured two-thirds of the world in a fraction of geological time. Our own continent was severed. The land running from the Logan North to Fin de Terra was separated from the other half of the continent.

"It's a time of turmoil," Victoria described in her diary: "As the Escarpment rises, east is divided from west. This is the beginning of the end."

Massive earthquakes, volcanic eruptions, and hundred-mile windstorms wreaked havoc. So many devastating events visited humanity during those decades that I wonder how it is that anyone exists on the surface of this planet.

What spurred this geo-seismic violence remains a mystery. For the time being, there is tectonic quiescence. No giant windstorms, tornadoes, or massive earthquakes are in the forecast. Then one never knows...

As usual, I awake early, but I lay in bed thinking about what the day will bring. I'm expected to be in the field grounds a half-hour past dawn. Little would come of this effort I'm afraid. The security force is simply too small to accomplish what it's being asked, to become an army. It lacks training, and no seasoned officers are at hand to lead it.

In time, I make it to the window and take a quick peek at the sky. A halo surrounds the moon. The nimbus radiates various colors: violet, pink, yellow. It's beautiful to see. Primitive people, lacking knowledge, would undoubtedly have interpreted this as an omen, a sign of ill tidings.

As I pass by the mirror, I see my reflection. I don't often look at my face unless I'm shaving. This time is different. I stare into my reflection, and for a moment, I don't recognize myself. An unfamiliar face looks back at me. Is this someone else? No, it's me, naturally. The hair is dark, and the eyes are blue. The jaw is firm, and its square outline is the same. I'm still Brock, the boy who grew into a man in the snowy hills of Easting. Yet, there is something different in that visage. It's an unsettling feeling because I can't define what there is about me that has charged. Has that ever happened to you?

In affirmation, I say, I am a man from the northern hills of Highland. I know who I am, what I've become, and know there is a purpose to my existence.

I will go on to a new subject, lest you begin to think I'm rounding the bend.

Lysander let my mother choose my name. She said she liked Allen, yet her father's name was Brok. She was conflicted. I'm not sure precisely what Brok means, maybe rock or boulder. It comes from one of several dialects spoken by her kin. The short story is that she searched for a like-sounding name, finally settling on Brock as my middle name. I've never cared for either name, even if Brock is Highland name.

Meanwhile, Allen is a name befitting a scrawny kid who gets beaten up daily in the schoolyard. To me, Brock sounds like a label on a hardy pair of footwear, which isn't too bad, but I wished she had settled on Brok as my first name. But you become your name no matter.

My facial looks are primarily those of my mother, unfortunately. Dagne is her name. Her forbearers came from the eastern part of Finland, a land similar to Northern Easting–cold, snowy and uninviting. She told me that her paternal grandfather was born in Helsinki and that her mother hailed from Stockholm. Those cities, like Santa Fe, are no longer found on the map. Two giant glaciers spanning across the northern half of the globe swallowed them. Fortunately, my forebears made their escape to the Highland.

I inherited the color of my eyes and my nose from Dagne's side of the family.

Lysander was Dagne's opposite. He was stocky, dark-haired, with olive tone skin. From him, I inherited dark hair and high cheekbones. He passed on to me my skin's ability to tan like that of a Solano.

I loved my father very much. I can't say the same feeling extends to my mother. Growing up, I found Dagne to be cold and distant. Mostly she kept to herself. From the way she talked, I figured she begrudged having married Lysander. He was a professional soldier, not a lawyer or politician, not a man of "Standing."

Dagne played the piano and sang soprano. She had an excellent singing voice known as coloratura. However, she was quarrelsome, a true virago. My mother found purpose in opposing Lysander's decisions even when she knew he was right. Although I grew to dislike Dagne, not once was I disrespectful to her. She is still alive, and I've avoided seeing her for quite some time. I do drop her a letter now and then and send a gift on her birthday. That's about the extent of our connection. In her last letter, she wrote that she had at last found the truth. "I am no longer lost." I have no idea what she meant. As far as I can remember, Dagne was never lost. That cold Finn always knew where she stood.

Cataclysm

On my nightstand sits the only source of light, a vintage candelabra. The abbey is wired with an up-to-date power grid, of course. But candlelight suits my purpose, though. Its luminescence is soothing and sheds all the lighting I need.

Victoria Rojas wrote her thoughts and ideas in her diary. I suppose I'm doing the same now. Of course, I'll never be as good at writing as she.

Some believe that people in the Southern continent didn't survive the cataclysm. The southern continent, to put it simply, broke apart like a salt cracker. The teeming millions who peopled the tropics are presumed to no longer exist. And if some did survive, why would you want to meet them? I'll explain it. The last transmission heard from the southern continent came from Caracas. A journalist delivered her final report: "Plagues haunt the land. Animals and men die in their tracks. Women have stopped bearing children, the day has turned to night, and the air is hard to breathe. Massive quakes, volcanoes, floods make their call. Millions perish. People say this is God's doing. It's his way of cleansing the land. The tectonic plate where the edge of Brazil strides has tilted. We have little time left. An immense tectonic force will push part of our country to the north. Before that happens, tons of molten rocks will bury our city. "Ora pro-Nobis."

When translated, the journalist's last words mean—pray for us. Their northern cities were going to disappear. Being a good Christian, she clung to her belief that God had willed the plagues and now the impending destruction. This was happening because people lacked faith. Catholics, in particular, place blame on themselves when things go wrong. I know this because my father was one.

Any attempt to sail to the southern continent is a violation of the law. Not to worry, no one is stupid enough to go there. Equally, any ship approaching from those southern waters would be destroyed miles before reaching us. Again, no vessels from that direction have ever been sighted. It's possible, too, that those waters are "mined" by the Scylla, a mountain rage hidden by sea swells. Another theory is that the cataclysm created enormous whirlpools south of the equator. This region is termed the Charybdis of the Antipode. It's the watery graveyard of thousands of ships. In any event, how could any sensible people, no matter how heart- wrenching the decision is, will allow a Typhoid Mary, let alone a thousand of them, to set foot on their land?

Plagues have visited mankind throughout history, wreaking havoc in their wake, causing myriad sorrows to man and animal alike. The sterility plague the woman journalist in Caracas mentioned is known in the northern hemisphere also. This pestilence is subtle, hides its maleficent effect for decades. Women of the Mosaics, for example, are not as fertile as those of yesteryears. Generations ago, a new virus was introduced into the population. It infected women's ovaries, increasing aneuploidy. Unlike a man's gonads, which can create millions of sperm cells every day, women are born with a finite number of ova; damage to the ovaries, the woman becomes barren. The Native's birthrate began to decline with the arrival of the Hexas. Instinctively the people know that the sudden appearance of the Hexas and the cataclysm are related.

Rift Space Effect

The most significant change in the planet's environment is the RSE, an abbreviation for Rift Space Effect. RSE is a negative electromagnetic anomaly, a force with similar qualities to an EMP but with some differences. The RSE impacts electronic equipment naturally, but it also affects mental and physical energy, including a person's mood. RSE changes ambiances by subtle means. It can cause ripples in the still waters of the pond, tease a candle flame, even disturb one's dreams.

There are two sets of theories for the RSE, one that it affects molecules or molecular cohesion. This is an increase in quantum freak incidents where things that should happen in Newtonian space fail to occur. For instance: Explosives or combustible material fail to react or burn at times. Weapons, shot-pistols, and carbines, for example, lose their effectiveness when the RSE index is high. A bullet fired from a high-powered rifle drops off yards before reaching its intended target. An artillery shell is equally affected. The explosive potential of a bomb is dampened.

The other theory is that the RSE is brought about by the effect of light-matter interaction with dark matter material, mere wisps that bleed in. The combination makes a failed bond in our reality, leading to a negating impact of a given reaction.

This whole process could be fueled by micro wormholes, inserting the tiny parts of dark matter material into Rift Space. Not explained is how it has all come into being. What is causing energy and matter to interact in this manner is unknown. Then this is all theory, after all.

In the grip of RSE disturbance, you feel heaviness all about you but not consistently ponderous: still, it can become exhausting. RSE brings about mental lethargy too. When RSE is in full swing, it's called The Dampening. During a heavy Dampening, you quickly grow tired, moody, and irritable.

The RSE goes beyond what I've just described. When the Escarpment rose from the continental divide, we entered a new era. Air travel was no longer possible. It's not difficult to see why. Think of what will happen when the RSE flares, and you're in a plane thirty thousand feet high? The airplane drops from the sky like a lead balloon. Then where would anyone hurry to and fro in today's world?

Instructor

The three companies of recruits muster early in the morning on Junipero's grounds. They are drilled, marched for miles, taught to turn left and right, about-face, present arms, and so on. After a quick lunch, they are mustered again and trained in the use of weapons. The recruits are singularly young men in their teens. Except for a handful, none are Highland-born. Nearly all are sons of immigrants from the Mosaic, having come to Highland seeking a better life. Not to cast these young fellows in a bad light, but much can't be expected from them. Their fathers fled the Upper Mosaic while they should have stood their ground against the Hexas.

To train civilians, you need NCOs to forge them into soldiers. A recruit must be vetted to see if he has what it takes to go into the fight. He has to be indoctrinated, instilled in the tradition of the unit he serves. Junipero has not raised an army before, which is what Brother Elliot wants me to do: "Raise a fighting force to stand against the forces of evil. Like the Jesuits of old, Brock, our men must be steadfast. They must never waiver from the mission."

Brother Elliot, although pragmatic, will have his moments of drama. DMO, the brass in Glenn Cross, in answer to our request, sent two graduate cadets to assist our developing forces. The DMO, or Directorate of Military Operations, fully supports Abbot Madigan's plan to establish a defensive force. Unlike the rest of Highland's townships, Junipero only has a tiny home guard. It's more a constabulary than a fighting force. However, the colonels in Glenn Cross suggest that Junipero's Home Guard should raise two regiments.

When DMO's directive was read, Brother Elliot plopped onto the nearest chair and declared, "Where in God's Green Earth will we find the men?"

Advisory Council

I got nothing useful done from the moment I awoke until the sun finally set. The news from the front is dismal. I'll start with its worst. A large Hexas force with maniples is attempting to breach the outer defenses of Kirby Baja. It's hammering Knob Noster nonstop, and Brigham Square, its trans-line station, is about to be taken. Kirby Baja is a mere six miles from Junipero Heights. If Kirby Baja falls, then Junipero is in the crosshairs. Not that Junipero Heights is a pushover. Even though the home guard is small, every Junipero will fight to defend his home. Nonetheless, it makes sense to the Hexas to take Junipero Heights because Outer Hastings is their objective. The Knob, all of Kirby Baja and Junipero have to betaken before a drive to Outer Hastings can become a reality.

Having listened to words of caution from Elliot for an entire afternoon, it is difficult to hear more of the same the following day. Elliot, I should point out, heads Junipero's Advisory Council. No matter, the councilmen fretted, wrung their hands. What's to be done? They could not come to an agreement, any agreement.

When at last, the council members run out of things to say, they look toward Elliot, who then turns his eyes on me and says, "What's your opinion, Brother Brock?"

Every village has an idiot, and people stop if, for a moment of amusement, to watch his antics. But I am not going to play the role.

"Our neighbors are fighting tooth and nail against our enemy," I tell him. "It's the abbot's doctrine to fight behind a wall. I can understand the tactic. It's safe, puts a formidable barrier between you and the enemy. Hexas, after all, have armored maniples with deadly Belcher cannons. I say make Kirby Baja our southern wall. We join our brothers and fight behind that wall and give it all we've got."

Ností

I'm drinking my morning brew when the orderly informs me of an emergency meeting. Whenever I hear the words "emergency meeting," I cringe, but I'm disabused of my hasty notion. A lieutenant by the name of Emilio Lawson is the bearer of great news. The Hexas siege of Knob Noster is broken. With the bolstering forces from Junipero, the defensive lines held. That's extraordinary. In terms of numbers and equipment, we are no match against the Hexas military might. But why is this news considered an emergency?

Ha! Sometimes you kick the can down the road until you don't see it again because it set off a minefield.

In defeat, the enemy forces under Master Eduord Lyon Ností de LeBey took out their anger on the people of Marlton Township. This city was in the path of Hexas retreat. As Ností forces withdrew to the northwest, hundreds of civilians, mostly men, were massacred. Thousands of people were evicted, and their homes were destroyed. Entire city blocks of that fair township vanished in the conflagration.

"Justice calls for a response," says Judge Wilkes. Wilkes is the judicial head of the Ad-Council. "The enemy under the command of Edourd Ností," he adds, "has violated the rights of non-combatants. Hexas Ností permitted his soldiers to do harm to the civilian population of Marlton."

The councilmen look toward me. The question on their faces is a familiar one. What am I going to do about all this?

"There's nothing to do, gentlemen." I go on to explain my reasoning. "Hexas maniples roam at will in the western hills. That force is five times our own. We're not strong enough yet to challenge them."

A spy of ours embedded in the Hexas camp relates this: "The young Master Eduord is noted for his use of foul language. When his dinner is late or not to his taste, or when his Gineff, Hexas liquor of choice, is not served correctly, he explodes into a frenzy and rants the foulest invectives imaginable. Eduord Ností shouts at his servants and spits on their faces. This is a matter of course. During one particular event, Ností had a Native female caned savagely in the buttocks, claiming she glared at him."

Eduord Ností is the favorite nephew of Tallos Bay, who is the Baron of Hœff. That's why he carries the Surname–LeBey. No, the last name is not misspelled; it's a slight variation meaning he's not a direct heir. Tallos sired only two daughters, so Edourd, his sister's son, is heir presumptive to the Duchy of Hœff.

Since Hœff is a duchy, Baron Tallos Bay is soon to become a duke. A bit of background information here about Eduord Lyon Ností LeBey, which I will simply call Ností. I don't like long names since there's no reason for having one. Ností is a dandy, but he's also a soldier who has led men into combat. His officers admire him. He's courteous, they say, except that of late, he's developed a despicable habit, which has stained his polish. Captured young women are paraded on all fours before him. They are forced to wear choke collars and made to bark like seals. If a given one does not perform accordingly, she is severely punished. The Cetrons in higher echelons look at this behavior with disapproval, but given Ností's rank, they will not make an issue of it. One of Ností's quotes goes this way: "I prefer the musk of Native wenches over the fine perfumes of Hexas femmes."

Young Hexas Ností loathes Natives, yet at the same time, he's drawn to them. This is an example of how twisted our enemy is. That's why the men of Highland fight on.

I've forgotten to mention a point, Ností's title Master is the customary title bestowed to the firstborn son of a Hexas nobleman. Ností is such. He is Master Eduord Lyon Ností LeBey, but again our record knows him as simply Ností.

To the point, Judge Wilkes was speaking as the judicial arm of Junipero. As judge, he upholds the jury's decision–a council in this case. His words: "Hexas Ností was the military commander while a massacre occurred in Marlton Township. He did not kill prisoners of war or civilians personally, but it was his responsibility to ensure that no crimes be committed while he was in command. I realize this is difficult to do. No commander is all knowing. Yet, this council persuades me that Ností, in fact, encouraged his men by his words and actions to behave with brutality toward the people of Marlton. Therefore, Cetron Eduord Ností is declared a war criminal. As such, Hexas Ností is sentenced in absentia to death by hanging for the crimes committed by troops under his command."

Prophet

After Castleton and Mountboro, Marlton is the third largest township in Central Mosaic. Marlton, I'll point out, is a beautiful place despite the damage Ností's troops inflicted. It has tree-lined avenues, well-cared residential areas, parks, and plazas. But, like all townships, Marlton has a lower end too. That would be the trans-line district. First, let me point out that Central Mosaic is teeming with millions of people. It's the largest and is more ethnically diverse than the other two. It has industry, technology, and resources. In my wanderings in townships like Midland, Ventura, and the others, I got to know many people, including Abolafia. I should say I know about him since I've not met him personally.

A Latter-Day Prophet arose from the slums of Freedom Corridor. I think that an apt term. Well, no matter, I'll go straight to the point. This prophet's name is Abolafia Hassa, and he's a concern to the Hexas. Hexas have seen seedy, ratty-dressed preachers come and go, stirring trouble in their spheres of influence. This is one reason Stasa goons keep a close watch on Hassa.

Freedom Corridor is the narrowing stretch of land south of Junot that allows Central Mosaic access to the sea. Moreover, access to Pacifica, the western ocean, is essential to everyone.

Again, to my point, most prophets are fakes, smooth-talking quasi-religious conmen. However, Hassa is not one of those. He's truthful and articulate, and he knows how to deliver his message. So it is that his words have spread throughout Central Mosaic.

Hassa's philosophy, resist unfairness but confront it peacefully, makes little sense. If a man hits you, you hit him back harder. If he spits in your face, you kick his teeth in. That's the Upland way. I'll point out, though, that not all of Abo Hassa's followers subscribe fully to his philosophy of non-vi olence. We have Abolafia's piccolos in the Highland army and in the ranks of partisans. They are steady and dependable.

Around the eastern borders of Junot, Chetsí, and Upper Mosaic, Abo Hassa's followers make their presence known by staging riots and shooting proxies. Those "thugs," according to the Barons of Icenia, must be exterminated. Ah, but that's not so quickly done. Abolafia's men are everywhere. Even more critical, this Native element has managed to tie up two Hexas legions around the l communities from their borders, Abo ignores them.

Lest I forget, Abolafia Hassa, the great communicator, shortened his first name to Abo. Regardless, what Abo Hassa has to say is interesting. I'll get to that.

First, Abo Hassa is an ascetic. He drinks a cup of tea instead of a well-crafted pint of ale. That's his loss. Though he's a pacifist, Abo is defiant. He agitates, creates havoc, blocking roads, and shutting down trans-lines across the Mosaics.

The Hexas public view is that Abo is a crackpot. I suppose there are some aspects of Abo Hassa that lend credence to that. Outwardly he's more the Gandhi than the skull-bashing Highland man we'd like him to be. Yet, I believe that the presence of Abo and his hassims is why the Hexas have not pushed into Central Mosaic.

Unfortunately, since his return from a trip to the Escarpment, Abo's energies are directed toward a new mission. He'll no longer resist the Hexas or quarrel with the mayors of Central Mosaic. He declares that he is done with sit-ins, boycotts, and demonstrations because this practice has become irrelevant. Nothing he's tried has brought about a change in the plight of his people. He is, after all, only a man.

Abo says this: "Unless the Hexas are flushed into Pacifica by a flood from the Highest, they will not take leave from our lives. The mayors will continue to rob you and extort you with unfair taxes. These evil beings will hold steadfast unto the Mosaics, and in time, will consume your lives. The men of the Highland will continue their fight, yes, but in time they too will vanish. The tyranny of the Hexas Barons will persist, oh blessed hassims. In the end, natives will be uprooted and displaced, and nothing can be done. The tyrant's boot is too firmly placed on the Native's neck. This is to Hexas satisfaction and to the corrupt Mayoralty, who serves them."

That's one frightful vision, no? Ah, but there's more. Abo adds this: "Oh, hassims, do you want to serve, or would you rather be free, own your hold and live in peace?"

Abo promises his people that he will take them far away from that tyranny. Elohi has enlightened him, and he knows the way.

Physically, Abo Hassa is tall and dark. He is handsome and distinguished. His eyes have the power to mesmerize, and he speaks with a distinct voice. But, even though he's a striking piccolo, women are suspicious of him, and for good reasons. I'll explain later.

Piccolo is a Highland term to describe a man or woman of dark complexion. The term is widespread, though. Don't know how "piccolo" became a reference; regardless, it's not derogatory. To Natives, it's equivalent to calling pasty redheads ginger or a blonde girl a waxy tassel. Brunettes are called stoats, and so on. Highland girls used to call me Piccolo Brock. As I've said, I sunbrown easily, and my dark hair, although not curly, has a slight wave.

Back to my point, I've read the Bible. As a boy, Dagne made me read it from cover to cover. To this day, I think of the Bible as another form of mythology, a horrible one at that. The Bible, particularly the Old Testament and Koran, are books replete with strong points of view. One of these is the concept of "Chosen People." By its very definition, to be chosen implies that those who aren't selected fall into an inferior category for whatever reason. Such points of view are not limited to religious fundamentalists. Hexas, for example, view themselves as superior to the people of the Mosaics. To them, Hexas, Highland men are the lowest in that evaluation, little more than anthropoids. Worth mentioning is Hexas' objection to people of sun brown skin. A man or woman from Terra Solana is subject to a head tax if they decide to work in a Hexas city. This amounts to taxation on melanin. After all, a fine Hexas gentleman or lady doesn't allow the sun to touch the skin. The "highborn" prefer to live in the north, clothes themselves in white gossamer sheets during summer. They look like walking mummies wrapped in gauze.

Natives don't look very different from each other, but they aren't anything like the Hexas, not in looks, dress, or manners. But let me get back to Abo Hassa.

Abo went on a spiritual journey to the Escarpment. Supposedly spent sixty-five days and sixty-five nights in the "Icy Wilderness," meaning he climbed the Lower Shelf and camped there. A climb to reach that up-thrust rock is virtually impossible experienced mountain climbers say. So whatever motivated Abo Hassa onto a spiritual journey is unclear.

"It's his Road to Damascus," Elliot supplied. But with Elliot, it's not easy to tell when he's being facetious.

Whisperings of Elohi

When Hassa returned to Marlton, he gathered his people on Counsel Butte, the highest point in that township. Wearing a full-length kaftan, "as white as snow," according to the olam–that would be the spiritual translator. "Abo Hassa, blessings to him, begins his message: "I have scaled the Escarpment and found the truth."

This "truth" is supposedly explained in a manuscript, which chronicles Abo's experience. At times the narrative text gives way to poetic prose, and frankly, after reading it, I'm still left in wonder about this "truth." However, I did find some parts of his chronicles quite interesting.

Here's an excerpt: *"For days I climbed. The meager rations I packed were spent. I was beset by the elements. The cold, hunger, and intense fear were my constant companions, yet I climbed steadily. The Escarpment is HIS creation. I acknowledge HIM. I survived only through the divine intervention of His agent, an angel who guided my way through the snowbound wilderness."*

Abo calls this angel Elohi. This "unearthly being" sustained him during his perilous quest for the "Truth." I had to read some of Abo's oras, meaning chapters, several times, yet I failed to make much sense of them. What I figure, and no ridicule, is intended by the way, is that Elohi must have imbued Abo with incredible stamina via a serum or drug because it seems there was no obstacle or perilous encounter the man can't overcome. Abo gained more than strength and vigor, though. He was endowed with the gift of glossolalia. He can speak in "tongues." The olam is readily there to interpret the meaning of his words to his hassims. Call me a cynic, but I don't see why you should use any other language than the one people speak if you want to get your message across.

"He's speaking Elohi's tongue," Elliot said.

"Everyone speaks variations of English, including the Hexas," I replied. "What's the point of a new tongue?"

"It's as God will have it, Brock." This is Elliot's way of saying that maybe Abo and Elohi have a scam in mind.

Here's more from Abo: *"Elohi, Elohi, Elohi, rang the far-off whisper. It bled in the night through the bleakness of snow-covered buttresses and frozen plains.*

Elohi! The whispering echoes emanated from the frozen waste. It is the voice of the Devine. He made me see through the gathering 'Blind.' I walked deep into the frigid darkness but did not turn into a pillar of ice. "Ohalahhh, alho'm, shah, Elohi lavatis hassim! Thou hast called.

"Though exhorts the people to rise above their plight. I know this. I am but a servant of thee, and before Him, who is High, oh Elohi. I abjure thee to let thy hand shape thy servant like clay in the turn-wheel. Mold me into a vessel so I might carry the words of Him who is Most High.

"After a day of absence, Elohi revisits. The Messenger Elohi— laudations unto his name— alights upon a massive boulder covered in glistening frost. He folds his wings. His form is ethereal, surrounded by a silvery halo, which sheds shimmering particles resembling diamonds. The wind takes the diamonds aloft, and they crown the frozen heights in the fullness of the moon. And in the ghostly shimmer, I see Elohi's words written boldly across a silvery sky.

"Elohi's smoldering eyes fixed on mine. He spoke: 'He who is above all things has heard thy plea, Abo Hassa. Abo Hassa has found grace in HIS eyes. He that is Most High has opened his heart to the affliction of Abo's people. Abo Hassa shall bring His message to them. Abo Hassa shall bring his people forth.'"

Abo's book, *The Whispering of Elohi*, goes into a disjunction at this point, setting aside the spiritual aspects of the journey to describe the Escarpment's fauna. He's like a modern-day explorer, giving names to the animals and plants in this frozen wonder.

"I strike the flint to light the oily gray lichens clinging to the rocks. A faint smoke emanates, and soon the lichen clump is ablaze. It is then that I see groundhogs the size of cats."

Here, Abo's description conjures large, furtive rodents running out of snow caves, but these, according to him, are not rats. Instead, they are small herbivores that resemble hefty capybaras. Elohi calls them plopos. Supposedly their meat is tender and delicious, even when uncooked.

"Plopos are clean because they feed on lichens and nuts. They eat the nutritious carrot-like roots and green-gray crest that grow ubiquitous in the high rocks. In the evenings, birds ghost in the clouds, and you hear their nesting coos during the night. At sunrise, they take flight, scoop up vast amounts of insects that thrive in the narrow, deep caverns of the Escarpment shelf."

I continued to read: *"Large flightless birds roost on the lee side of the glacier. I took some of their eggs, cooked them. They were delicious. However, the meat of those birds was gamy, tough, and unpalatable.*

"On the upper shelf, by the jagged icy rocks, mountain goats climb and scamper. Those creatures have a fleece whiter than newly fallen snow. The males, whose coats are gray, are endowed with thick, wicked horns. They fight by smashing into each other. Rams are constantly seeking ewes in estrus. How those bucks remind me of my young hassims. Lavat feloquin, chovat!"

The latter words, as translated by Abo's olam, means, arise and propagate! I could go on with Abo's fantastic tale, but it will distract from the point. Before I end this entry, though, here is a fact worth noting. When found, Abo Hassa was wandering in Highland's eastern foothills, delirious, half-starved, and suffering from hypothermia.

Hegira

In my room, I watch the flicker of the candle flame. Dark thoughts creep across my mind. How much more difficult would it be to kill again, I wonder.

Marlton is less than a hundred miles from Knob Noster. I can slip into Abo's enclave wearing a keffiyeh. I don't have to darken my face. The Highland sun has done that already. I've grown a thick beard as well. So dressed I'll blend in the Ol'assim—meaning those who believe—and wait for my chance. I can send Abo Hassa to his promised land ahead of schedule.

Ah, but killing a man in a fight is one thing; assassinating is a different matter altogether. An assassin gets paid, while a man confronted by his enemy kills because he must. What Abo Hassa says sounds bizarre, yes, but he is a man on a mission. I could never bring myself to murder a man who has done me no wrong.

The reason I've devoted so many pages to Abo Hassa is that he has called for a hegira. That's what Elohi demands, and Abo is emphatic about it. The separation must occur; removing the Ol'assim from the Trochi—the unbeliever—is a must.

Here is the problem. Two out of twelve soldiers in Kirby Baja and a tenth of men-at-arms in Glenn Cross are followers of Hassa. That's a significant portion of men in a military unit. The hassims are disciplined and skilled in fighting. Replacing them is going to be difficult.

The Advisory Council deliberates for hours to finally wash the matter from their hands, deferring the decision to the DMO in Glenn Cross. Three days later, the DMO and DCA issue the order.

No one would be stopped from joining the hegira. The people of Highland believe in individual rights.

The hegira begins. Family members holding different views shake hands and part from each other. Fathers stand straight and show no emotions; even if their wives weep before their son or daughter, they might not see again.

In one fell swoop, Hexas have scored an unplanned victory. The resistance movement in the Upper Mosaic is as good as dead. In the Central Mosaic, the mayors are in a panic. North Central Mosaic is ripe for the picking, and the Hexas Barony is waiting to pounce.

I walk to Junipero Crest at dusk. This hill rises above others. The usual winds from the east sweep across, and so its top is bare, except for tenuous grasses clinging to its sides. From there, the entire township of Junipero and beyond is seen. Kirby Baja is to the south, and the lights of Glenn Cross Citadel glimmer in the north. Herons Landing to the east is visible through strobes of blue light. Townships place beacons on towers and higher ground. It's an old custom that dates back to the days of airliners. From the Crest, I watch the Ol'assim, those who are faithful, as they wind relentlessly around the tall boulders toward the east. It is a host, thousand upon thousands of people, trudging through the barren plain of eastern Highland. Looming in the east is the forbidding foothills of the Escarpment—"By Elohi!" the multitude clamors. "By Elohi!" Except for vehicles, which would not function under a heavy dampening of the RSE, the Ol'assim take all the possessions they can tote or tow along, animals, house goods, yurts, and building materials.

Abo Hassa is a solitary figure galloping ahead of the host on a bay stallion. Outriders carry banners. I put the binoculars to one. The banner displays an emblem of a large gray ram perched on a high snowy ridge. Rams are stubborn and unafraid. Rams usually lead the herd. It is a suitable symbol for Abo Hassa.

The Directorate of Military Operations is apprehensive about permitting a hundred thousand people, many of whom are soldiers, to cross into Highland. It needn't. Abo Hassa had given his word: "Ol'assim will pass through the land in peace. The Ol'assim will always look on the people of Highland as benefactors. Elohi, laudations to his name, whispered that our two peoples would remain long apart but come together as one in the latter days. That is what Elohi has decreed. We share a destiny."

As the sunlight fades and deeper shades bathe the land, Abo Hassa and the Ol'assim disappear in the snowy foothills.

The scouts who have been following at a respectful distance report: "Abo Hassa and his fellows disappeared. They climbed the high foothills, and then, well, they vanished."

I look at the two soldiers narrowly, but I know they are seasoned scouts. "How exactly did they vanish, sergeant?" I asked.

"They must've found a pass, a gap somewhere up there,' said the junior scout. "We sure as hell, eh, sorry about that, sir," he amends quickly. "There was no trail to follow, and that's God's truth, sir. We galloped up to where we last saw their banners. When we reached the spot, we saw only a solid wall of ice."

The lead scout, SSGT Mullins, corroborates those words. "We kept the distance as ordered, sir. We always made sure we saw the tail end of Abo's caravan, though. Well, sir, here's what happened. One moment we saw a few trailing piccolos, a mile or so ahead. Suddenly the wind picks up with a scream, and the snow blinds our way. When we gain visibility again, Abo's men weren't there."

I look from one scout to the other. My eyes fastened on Mullins. "So you're saying that the solid rocks of the Escarpment parted like the Red Sea and that tens of thousands of people just, uh, slipped through?"

Mullins chuckles. "Well, sir, Abo must've figured Ali Baba's password, 'Open Sesame,' or something, because that's what I'm thinking must've happened."

I had to laugh. Obviously, Mullins understood my allusion and lobbed back a better one.

Visions

I can't explain how I find myself in the chapel this night. A moment before, I was in the abbey's courtyard, chuckling about Mullins' Ali Baba reference. I guess I got cold and decided to come inside.

No one is there, not a sacristan or monk fussing, not even the usual mourner widow. My eyes sweep across the roomy expanse. Its design is different than I remember. There is planned avoidance of harsh corners and obstructions, even in the long, ovate nave. The vaulted ceiling slopes, blending with the walls, creating an ambiance of serenity. There's sparkle from polished pews set in neat rows along the hardwood floor. Then the vanilla scent of the votive candles drifts from the altar, and my eyes are drawn to the dedicated assembly of multi-colored candles. It's all very beautiful.

"Why am I here?" I ask in a voice that, for a reason, has an odd ring. It's my voice, yes, but it seems to be that of another person.

Moonlight flashes across the nave and sweeps down the chapel. What I see next stuns me. Men at arms gather there. Their heads are bowed. Then the moonlight fades, and the chapel is empty once again. What does this mean? Is it a hallucination?

My eyes return to the votive candles. I approach the altar and kneel. I don't know why I'm doing this. I don't pray; I haven't done so since I was a boy.

Troubled, I relate to Elliot the apparition I saw in the chapel and how strange it was. "Elliot, I say to him, "I've never experienced anything like it. It was so vivid, so real."

Elliot nods. "You had a vision. People experience them now and then, but nearly all deny the fact. These insights occur only once or twice in a man's life. If it happens more frequently, where he can't understand what he's seeing, well, then it's likely he'll lose his marbles, so to speak."

"Elliot, what I saw was real, tangible," I begin to explain. "I read the sullen faces of the men. Everything about those men was detailed finely against the backdrop of the chapel. It was like looking at you right now. I tell you, Elliot, that I could've walked down the aisle and touched those men. Here's another thing, their heads were bowed over the pommel of their swords as though praying. They seem like knights of old, except that these men wore modern body armor."

After I'm done, Elliot relates one of his own visions.

"I was a boy eight years old," he began. "My parents, my two younger siblings, and I went on a picnic to the beach. It was during a truce period, as I recall. It was a hot day, perfect for such an outing. The wind on the beach was calm, not blustery as it usually is in the Sound. My smaller brother had wandered too close to the shore, and my mother told me to get him. As I pulled Andrew back from the waves, I saw a startling sight. This can't be real, I told myself. It can't be! Before my eyes was a great herd of seagoing animals. They swam in unison, like dolphins, dipping into the water and out again, cavorting. Except these weren't porpoises. Not fish either, mind you; instead, they had long blue necks and sleek bodies that bore orange and purple and green colors. How large they were, I couldn't be sure, maybe the size of a horse, I suppose. They had brilliant eyes, which suggested intelligence, and I had no reason to doubt such ability because they were communicating with one another all the while. These aquatic beings, travelers or animals, call them what you will, were not from Earth. I don't know whether they saw me standing on the shore. If they had, they decided to ignore me.

"I told no one about it, of course, fearing that if I did, my parents would think I'd gone bunkers. Later on, I composed several explanations for it, an overly active imagination for one, the stress placed on me in school and at home. I was the oldest, needed to set an example for my brother and sister. The event remained vividly clear in my mind, and I came to accept it. It was no hallucination. I was permitted to peer into one of God's realms, a view of another world. What you saw in the chapel, Brock, is also real, just as those sea traveling beings on the beach were too."

"Yes, but what does it all mean, Elliot?"

"God allowed you to see a glimpse of your future, Brock. You will understand its significance in time. Trust me on this."

~~~

Tonight, I feel a strange cold flowing into my room. It's the Rift wind filtering through, driven from an unimaginable distance into my chamber. How far has it traveled to reach me? Its touch is like that of icy tentacles.

Novo Ceres

The Escarpment's birth changed Earth's geography. Its advent altered the wind patterns and sea currents. We now have the phenomena known as the Flows, alterations of wind and water currents. The Slipflow sends northern, moisture-filled air streaming south, transforming the once arid land into rain forests. The Rushflow speeds warm water from the south, creating a cradle of fertility in the coastal waters of Upper Icenia.

In one area of the coast, the land extends two hundred miles northwest from where it laid. The Hexas refer to this area as a "Novo-Ceres," meaning newer lands created. I've never traveled there to see this geological event, but I'm told that Novo-Ceres is a simmering vastness wherein geothermal gouts burp up from Earth's bowels to explode on the surface without warning. Two expeditions taken by Sci-Wizards and Technissi from Seaton Polytechnic perished. It was reported that they were scalded, boiled away by the fury of Novo-Ceres. If it were within my power, Novo-Ceres is the place I would send the Hexas.

As I briefly mentioned, the Escarpment is a soaring wall of granite. Nearly all of it is covered by ice. That's the best way to describe it. The phenomenon emerged from the rumbling ice shelves of Arctica. Its incredible quick pace toward the south was frightening and devastating. Its growth continued, taking a southeasterly track. It was violent, changing everything in its path, including the old mountain ranges. The birth of the Escarpment cut our continent in half, as I pointed out.

Journal of Allen Brock

It's several centuries since last we heard a word from the other side of the Escarpment. A theory proposed, a bleak one, is that the eastern half of the continent is entombed under massive glaciers. Naturally, there is no way to confirm this since we're unable to crest those soaring heights, or as one of Mullins' scouts facetiously remarked: "call on Elohi to beam us over."

I'll conclude by giving you a brief account of a man who lived during the birth of the Escarpment. Fulton Pitts was a trained geologist turned prospector. His notes are very detailed, as well as his observations. Pitts Caldera at the southern end of Highland is named after Fulton Pitts. In his writings, Pitts mentioned that it was a peculiarity of his to measure, with the most care, the width of cracks in his basement's floor. After one long road trip, he returned home, and to his amazement, gaps that had measured no more than one sixteen of an inch before had grown in size to three-quarters of an inch. Two months later, when he again visited his basement, he could not set foot on it. The floor was gone. He stared instead into a bottomless yawning pit. How the house remained standing was a miracle, but he didn't stop to praise the Almighty. He loaded provisions, and Percival, his dog, into the back of his truck and high-tailed it, but not before warning everyone in the area of what was to come.

After having done careful research, Fulton Pitts fled to Salton Basin. Salton was a geologically stable area. He was proven right. That's why the Hexas selected Salton for their magnificent project. Now the Salton Basin a restricted zone. I used to work there.

Seaton Polytechnic

I've accomplished more today than any other day I can recall. I promoted Cadet William Edward Bartlett, also Cadet Josephine Areu, to First Lieutenants.

Sergeants Devlin and Mullins are appointed top NCOs. Junipero's force is growing, and it has the beginnings of a command.

The defensive wall in the north is complete as well. It stands twenty-two feet high. The last capital stone on the central tower was, in fact, mortared and firmly set by Elliot.

From St. Junipero's Crest, the abbey resembles a castle. It's a stone structure surrounded by bastions with crenelated walls. I recall a different wall during my time as a teenager.

In Easting, there is a boulder-strewn height called the Crags. This geo-formation provides a defensive height against the Logans. More often than not, though, Easters defend their lands against the Logans in the open. They always outmatch Logans.

When I tell my father that I had joined Easting's force, volunteered as a Crag-rat instead of going to a summer workshop, he is struck mute. Finding his voice, he asks me this: "Allen Brock, have you become my idiot son?"

"Sir, I'm the only son," I remember saying to him.

Lysander's eyes stare down. "Next, you'll tell me you want to be a Wolverine or a Snow Ghost," he says. He remains outwardly calm even as those implacable eyes show otherwise. I know my father well; he is seething inside.

"Yes, sir, I've thought about that also," I say softly, a whisper actually. Never would I want to disappoint my father, but I realize I had done so.

Men of the Wolverine Battalion comprise an elite warrior class. Logans and Hexas fear them because they will die fighting rather than surrender. A Snow Ghost is a warrior trained to fight in the high snow. Logans fear them more than any other opponent.

"Three generations of soldiery in the Benitez family is enough," my father says. "You have two years of formal schooling ahead of you, and after that, YOU WILL ATTEND HIGHER EDUCATION!"

That is an order, and no one, as far as I can remember, ever prevailed against Lysander. Such was the power of the man.

So to Seaward Seaton Polytechnic, I am sent. There I acquired a degree in biochemistry with a minor in physics. I also learned while attending this prestigious science and engineering university that educated idiots abound.

SSP is exclusive, admitting only the most gifted Natives from the Mosaics. Its faculty is predominantly Hexas, yet its best professors are Natives. Seventy percent of the student body is Hexas, naturally, because Hexas significantly influence Seaward Seaton's township and control all of the Upper Mosaic. As for Hexas students and professors, I grow to despise them.

After four years in SSP, I earned a degree. I don't outclass my peers, not in grades or awards, but simply accomplish what I promised my father-earn a degree. When I present my resume and credentials to prospective employers, their authenticity comes into question. Interviewers tell me politely that I would be notified about their decisions. Plain enough, I needn't pursue this line of work further. I can't find a job in my field of study, not because I lack skills, but because I look too much like the Highland "troglodyte."

Hexas, as I've explained, have influence in the Central Mosaic also. They can direct the forging of new laws. They buy off the hundreds of mayors in the largest area of the continent. Hexas plan is to control the continent. They're in no hurry to accomplish this. They're known for their patience. As long as Native proxies are helping them, they'll take their time. I'm thinking then that the Native men of this Mosaic who trudge through life in a trance and disillusionment need to be awakened. I'm not unique in thinking this way. Some Natives have tried to do so, tried and been betrayed by proxies.

Why do we Highland people fight so stubbornly against Hexas? Why don't we work out an arrangement with the Barons? That, you see, would be impossible. Highland people are proud, and we will fight to remain free. It's not in our nature to compromise or beg for scraps from the Hexas table. We will not exit from the stage, take to the wilderness, and hide. We people of Highland will not be dictated to, and we'll fight to the end to expel the Hexas from the Upper Mosaic and to keep what's ours.

Days run, become weeks, and weeks become months. I wind up living on the shallow end of the economic pool, short on money, doing odd jobs here and there. I eat only one meal a day. Figuratively speaking, I shuffle my way with an empty bowl in hand toward the nearest soup kitchen. I didn't want to return to Highland since that would be admitting failure.

Proxies & Coolies

As I said before, I needed steady employment, preferably in a sector that would allow me to ply my scientific and technical skills. Obviously this was impossible in the Upper Mosaic.

Jobs in Central Mosaics are available, however, but only if I become a bootlicker, in other words, a proxy. As mentioned, these are Native traitors. Men mostly, but women also, well no matter, they're all turncoats who have gone over to the Hexas. Without exception, Proxies are mean-spirited. They practice being meaner and nastier than their Hexas masters. A proxy's heart is missing, see. They feel no compassion or empathy for their fellow Natives. Proxies ape their Hexas masters in speech and also in mannerisms. Proxies go about filled with self-importance. They play the role assigned to them by Hexas with eagerness.

For a man of the Highland, as you might understand, the nature of a proxy is difficult to bear. It boils my blood to know that given a chance, men from Marlton, even today, even after the massacre perpetrated by Ností, would queue up to become his proxies.

~~~

It dawned on me after a time that my education at SSP– Seaward Seaton Polytechnic– was a pointless pursuit, a waste of four years of my life. I gained no valuable insight or practical knowledge I couldn't have acquired by reading books without a professor's guidance. None of that matters now. I'll write about something different, the RSE.

The RSE is another phenomenon associated with the Escarpment rise. I've set down the effect of the Escarpment on Earth's energy flow. Before going further, I'll take a relevant detour.

Salton Basin lies to the south, very far from the Hexas capital of Faldiss-a-Main. It's in Salton that a massive project has been under construction for decades. Hexas recruit throughout the Mosaics seeking the best minds and workers too. Their goal is to create a Rift Space Project, a machine and technology system that will accomplish wonders. The Salton Project's area is vast. Its nucleus is a mile long in diameter.

It's hard to imagine, no? Still, this enormous effort requires an army of workers, engineers, masons, and heavy equipment operators. It needs men and women who can direct coolies. In Salton, coolies are the ones who perform the dangerous digging in the multi-tiered pit called the Belly of the Beast. A coolie will use a shovel or a digging bar if that's what's needed to get the job done.

It's out of the question that a Hexas gent, those perfumed-haired fops dressed in the finest togs, should think of doing an honest day's work. To them, the notion of engaging in manual labor is abhorrent.

So I become one of the ten thousand coolies in the Salton. I am hired as a coolie-first-class. Quaint designations that don't you think? That's the rank of an entry-level "digger." I bust rocks, excavate, and push wheelbarrows when ordered to. Even though I know how to handle heavy equipment, a coolie cannot operate a backhoe, front loader, or tractor. In the diminished RSE of the south, motorized equipment gain efficiency and are therefore in use. These positions, heavy equipment operators, are exclusive and assigned to senior lackeys and longtime proxies. Now that I've given you a brief synopsis of what the job was like, I'll resume my former narrative.

The Rift Space Matris, which was not yet completed when I worked in Salton, is the first part of a dual system. The Escarpment is the other, and the two will tandem to seine or capture RSE energy; meanwhile, the core of the Matris stores that energy. The MMS, or Matris Main Stem, is the central brain. The process is programmed by computers and is used for multiple applications. Engineering, the surface of the planet, is one.

Journal of Allen Brock

The MMS's energy-gathering towers orient the minerals inside them using nano formation techniques to counter RSE energy. In other words, they convert negative energy. There are hundreds of these towers surrounding the Pit. The pit is the heart of Matris.

Supposedly this system will be capable of drawing in, capturing matter from space, decelerating its speed during reentry, and landing it safely back on Earth's surface. All this remains to be seen since no "dry runs" have been made. At any rate, that's the Hexas explanation why the Rift Space Matris is being built. The cost of the project, by the way, is unknown.

Have the Hexas conceptualized the RSM? I'm in doubt here. Their technissi are smart, but they're not, in my opinion, innovators. I wish I could've remained in Salton longer, learned more about the project. That became impossible. I worked under the supervision of a woman by the name of Moira Ney. She was the section-overseer and I murdered her. I had to flee from Salton.

STASA

As the crows fly northwest from Highland, Hexas cities are found. These cities are not part of the Mosaics but are located in Icenia, a land apart. Hexas Baronies number six in all. Their towns, like the townships of the Mosaics, are connected via underground trans-lines. Hexas' central city is Faldiss-a-Main, meaning Faldiss by the Sea, as you might have guessed. Faldiss is also the largest, most populous of all Hexas Baronies.

Hexas gents don't like doing manual labor, as explained. This is beneath them, so the sweat of others maintains their cities. I'm referring to roadway maintenance, sustaining the structural integrity of buildings, keeping grounds, and managing water treatment plants. Streets need to be swept from dirt and debris; streetlights replaced. There's also the thankless task of garbage disposal. You wouldn't want tons of garbage in your backyard, alleys, or the streets. Everything that makes a city a suitable place to live has to be done by machines or laborers.

Municipal bosses are hard-pressed to meet the demands of their wards. Should the expected standards of aesthetics demanded by the people not be met, they'll be canned and out of a job. That's the reason why Natives, by the tens of thousands, are hired to do the jobs Hexas gents and femmes refuse to do.

Prisoner labor was tried, but this experiment fell flat. You can't expect criminals to do what's right, what's expected of law-abiding men and women. That's one of the reasons they're criminals in the first place!

Native laborers in the Hexas cities have to tread carefully. Proxy guards will card them at the gates. Transline pods, those carrying

Journal of Allen Brock

laborers, must stop short of the city itself. Workers have to get off and walk a five-hundred-yard distance to the city's checkpoint." Ha! Why make life easy for inferiors, eh?

Native peons are asked why they've come, even though the question is pointless. Do you have an entry pass? Do you hold a current work permit? The questions are asked in a hostile manner too. How else would you treat a worthless Native from the Mosaic? Never are proxies civil in tone. This is their game to play. It's a sadistic form of control, and they love it.

But wait, carrying only one proof of identification with your entrance admission is not sufficient. You must provide, when ordered to, a biometrics card. This document tags you, your height, weight, hair color and eyes, blood type–don't know why they need this–ethnicity, and where you reside.

Obtaining a biometrics card is a bureaucratic nightmare. Only a third of Native workers can acquire them, not that they're unwilling to pay the cost, but because the rotten Hexas system makes it difficult for them. It's policy.

If you happen to be a peon that provides a biometric card that's not been updated, you'll be placed on hold. Hold means spending time in a guarded room with about the same comforts of a hoosegow. Being detained also means loss of wages.

Jackbooted thugs patrol all avenues in Hexas cities, not to check on unruly Hexas, never would such a thing occur, even if you're an annoying Hexas sot. The thugs are there to keep eyes on Natives, especially those that might be found in the street loitering or annoying the Hexas femmes.

Checkpoints abound. The agents in charge of these are usually proxies, but sometimes there's a Hexas goon or two behind the counter, hidden somewhere like the cockroaches they are.

Proxy thugs are on the "qui vive" for Natives that have delayed leaving the city too. They are easily spotted because laborers must wear uniforms.

The security apparatus in Hexas cities is layered. Overseeing the various organs is the State Security Agency, better known as STA.S.A. This force functions independently from local jurisdiction.

These gangsters make Hexas feel safe in the streets and in their abodes.

There's always a Stasa sadist lurking behind all checkpoints, so never mind proxies. To Natives, that man is not just unfriendly but overbearing and can ruin your day. He is also dangerous.

The Stasa is an instrument of terror, and its members are gangsters. One facet of their uniform I need to point is the insignia on the tunic's collars. Natives know that the more pips on the collar or lapel on a Stasa man's uniform, the nastier he is. The look in Stasa goon's eyes is cold. The sneer of his face perpetual. One of these thugs at the gates adds to the anxiety.

When a Stasa thug demands entry documents, the laborer must surrender the certificate of entry instantly. When a Stasa gangster is done examining it, he doesn't hand it back to the worker; the bastard tosses it to his face.

I decided to become a coolie in the Salton instead of a day laborer in a Hexas city, because I know that the moment I was insulted by a Stasa punk, I would strangle him with my bare hands.

I am Allen Brock Benitez, son of Lysander Benitez. My father was a man of honor. Never has the virus of cowardice tainted a Benitez.

Willoughby

Willoughby is a stop along the Banfield Way. The Banfield is a thousand-mile Trans-railway line. It originates in Chetsí, Icenia, and runs south to the Salton Basin. I used this high-speed trans-line to commute from Marlton to my job in the Salton Basin once a week. I would travel to Salton on Sunday night and return to Central Mosaic on Friday evening. The Bullet-Trans, as it's called, runs underground, except in Kol'bien and Bajadero, where it has to surface to cross those water spans. These rivers are not only wide but very deep.

No food is served on the passenger pods of the Bullet Trans, so you have to bring your own or go hungry on a long trip. If you need water, then you have to purchase it from the steward at an exorbitant price. Coolies are tight with their money, so they bring along what they need. Yet, they don't mind spending silver doubloons in Willoughby after a week of work in the Basin.

Willoughby Township is hyped as "Our Mecca of Sin." It's a drinking town, sure enough, also gambling and whoring paradise. That's why coolies gravitate to it. After a week of backbreaking work, where else can broken men forget their misery?

The neon signs in Willoughby's avenues are spectacular. Gambling halls abound. You find one on every street corner. Queans and painted doxies walk arcade boulevards. Con men roam the alleys behind taverns and casinos, offering get-rich-schemes. It's not uncommon for a neophyte–young coolie barely out of his teens–to be taken in by practiced conmen: "There is a vault with gold buried in the eastern sands of Terra Solana. I know its location. A Doncella

—a maiden— from a prominent family of Aguijón is held for ransom in a desert station somewhere in a remote region of Guahataki." Or for that matter, deep in the Sonora lands of Fin-de-Terra, etc... "You and I can rescue her. You're a young, good-looking fellah. You seem the type that can handle matters in a fight. What'd you say?"

Here's another creative fabrication: "A high-placed Hexas femme was kidnapped in the Transbridge station of Seaward Seaton. She's been taken south, and now she's languishing in a prison in the Lower Mosaic. The police in Puá will do nothing about it. Solanos hate the Hexas presence. But let me point out that this femme's Papá– meaning the paterfamilias–is an Upper Hexas Legas. He will pay whatever amount is asked to get his daughter back. A former sergeant from a Wolverine battalion in the Highland devised a clever plan to get her out, except we'll need starting capital to execute his plan. You can triple the amount of silver in your pocket."

Willoughby is where my life takes a turn. I am drinking in one of its many beer halls. I recall the sun-browned girls from Terra Solana dancing on stage and the video screens jutting from rounded walls. Every so often, the screen flashes the face of a lucky fellow who won the latest jackpot.

On those screens, I can also see people in other drinking establishments. The usual stuff is taking place: arm-wrestling contests, dart throws, drinking bouts, arguments and fights.

I observe all this as I drink a pint of red ale. I see in the faces of the men a look that I had failed to see before. It is a look of defeat, and one man after the other owns it. The spirits of these men have been broken. They've succumbed to the circumstances of their lives without a fight. These men, unlike their cousins in Highland, have given up hope.

Lysander told me once that when a man begins to doubt his ability to change his life circumstances, that man is defeated. I feel outraged, and a fit of dark anger wells from within me. I pound my fists on the table and kick it away. I straighten. My head pans across the rows of gambling tables, and I scream. "I don't see men, not one! Your balls have been taken from you! You've been made coolies in your minds too." I rage on. "You sit there, guzzle cheap beer and watch the dancing girls you can't afford while your Hexas masters rinse their mouths with the finest wines from Fanlo. Hexas, piss on your hopes. They serve your table with leftovers, and they expect your gratitude. You are less than coolies because at least coolies serve a function. You are a waste. A Hexas gold doubloon will buy your daughters. You serve men who are of less worth than you, and why? Because you have no balls!"

I look at the ocean of gaping faces and say, "I'll show you how to acquire a pair. I'm a man from Easting in the Highland, and I've killed more Hexas than the fingers on my hands. Tonight, I'm in a mood to dispense justice, and if I die, so what. It's not the life of the individual that matters, but that of the homeland! I need men of stout hearts, men brimming with the anger and hate I feel for Hexas. If you're a man whose knees knock when you see a Stasa thug on patrol, remain seated. Now, if you're a man of action, a man who wants to bash in the head of that Stasa thug, stand up and rage!"

I bring up my fists. "I need men who want to crack a proxy's skulls in the name of justice. I'm heading to the Apron to the Lower-Legas slum. I'm going to haul out the first rat I see sitting in his plush bench, and I'm going to guillotine him. I'll do it by myself if I have to. Who among you Natives is a man? Grope down and feel if the pair between your legs is still there. God, I hope Hexas haven't robbed you of those too."

An immense roar from the sea of faces rises, and in unison, their anger rings loud: "Death to proxies! Death to the sewer rats in the Lower Legas! Down with the Hexas!"

Moira

To Moira Ney, I am yet another "maggot." Maggot is one of several terms she uses to refer to the men of the Mosaics she manages. Following my entry interview, Moira who interviews, all prospective coolies tells me I should be grateful. After all, I am employed to work on one of the most ambitious projects ever devised by the Hexas' mind. No mention of Native's contribution here because her contempt of Natives, particularly coolies, is enormous. In her words, Natives have the brains of tapeworms, one of the reasons she loathes them. The irony here is that Moira is a Native, but she is a proxy too, and being one, she's a bully.

The glint in her eyes, the wry twist of her lips as she smiles, composes a sadistic expression. If I were an artist, I might have captured that part of her nature on canvas. I wouldn't be able to capture her soul, though, because there's not one to be found. Moira is arrogant and sharp of mind. Anyone who figures the system's inner working and secures herself a niche within its power structure has smarts.

Although she knows how to handle Natives, especially those under her, she doesn't know what to make of me. I show no fear of her. Clearly, this is a mistake on my part. I should appear humbler. The problem is that I can't show what I don't feel. Then maybe that aspect of mine is the reason she decides to hire me in the first place. In any event, I don't worry. That's how things go in Salton.

To Hexas, non-affiliated Natives, meaning non-proxies, are potential troublemakers. Moira has her sub-leads keep an eye on me for that reason. I maintain a low profile. In her gaveta, that's a Hexas term for a military unit or work division, Moira wields absolute authority.

Journal of Allen Brock

The personnel under her snap to her every command. The Hexas apparatchiks encourage this style of management. So, Moira has a carte blanche, that is, as long as she produces the expected results. Oh, and the men refer to Moira by several monikers: "The Eater of Coolies, Nut Cruncher and the Royal Queen of the Pit."

~~~

It's a hot and windy afternoon in the basin, the worst conditions to work in. The dust is in my clothes, hair, and pores. I walk to the farthest bivouac. Fundamentally bivouacs provide a measure of privacy to coolies, where they can relieve themselves, wash up, or bathe after a day's work. Unfortunately, bivouacs are the huts where the disposal machines are housed. From one end to the other, bivouacs smell worse than a sty. Why should that matter anyhow? Coolies are on par with chimpanzees in a zoo.

In Salton, a coolie is given a number, and that number is who he becomes. The pit bosses address him by the number stenciled in large numerals on his work vest. When a man decides to become a coolie, he gives up his name.

Now to the point: It's hard to work the six-hour morning shift without respite. You're not sitting behind a desk in an office. You're rushing in every which direction, avoiding drop-offs the flakes of rocks have covered. You're ducking the swinging scoops of the power shovels digging down into Satan's Pit. The ear protection you wear is barely adequate to muffle the blasting noise from jackhammers and whirring drills. If a coolie is killed or maimed while doing the job, it is of little concern. Coolies are a dime a dozen, as the old saying went. This stew goes on while you're trying to listen to the Pit Master's muffled orders in your earpiece. Half the time, you can't hear what the boss is shouting. Call it Highland vigor, but I can manage all the havoc with little or no trouble or injury.

As I wash the salt and sand from me, I'm thinking of the mindless creature I've lived with for a time. That would be my child's mother. The vile woman packed her bags and posted the reasons why she was leaving. I read the note and tossed it onto the cluttered kitchen counter. The woman never kept the house in order. I chuckled, thinking of a dozen choice ripostes to her grievances. Then the realization struck— where's Bristol? Where's my daughter?

"Aha! There you are, Coolie 6404. Think I haven't been keeping an eye on you?"

My head comes up from the water basin, and there is Moira. She closes the distance between us and stops within a foot of me. To Highland men, this is personal space. I ask her if she's always this forward.

"I can be what I want, coolie," she says, adding a careless shrug. "You are relegated to your station in life. You are a coolie who is paid to do a simple task. Yet you idle. Here you are, doing a skive while the rest of the crew draws in your slack."

She knew better. Pitmasters provide performance evaluations on every coolie in their gaveta. I decide to annoy her. "Moira, are you in need of a man?"

Her eyes flare momentarily, then the corners of her lips rise, creating twin dimples on her cheeks. I must admit it touches off an attractive look.

"A man's hand on me feels repulsive, coolie. I don't care for sweaty palms on me or a man's breath on my face. Ugh!" She draws away from the thought. "It's all disgusting!"

I grin. "I don't like men touching me either."

"Think you're amusing," she replies.

Of course, I say to myself, why should she be amused since the normal drives and desires that govern healthy individuals will not be found in her.

"I'm not here to amuse," I add with indifference, "But I wonder if you're here to inspect the latrines?"

"I am Cetron Moira Ney, coolie. You will address me precisely. Is that clear?"

I almost laugh. To become a cetron in the Hexas military, a man would first serve as a foot soldier, rise through the ranks, become a grenadier, crawl on elbows and knees with his head down across bloody battlegrounds, thus proving his worth and courage before he's considered for promotion to a subaltern. That's four ranks below a cetron.

I indulge her fantasy, however. "Very well, but I'll remind, uh, Cetron Ney, that as a coolie I'm allowed a ten-minute break."

She stares at me with unblinking eyes, obviously trying to make me squirm. She strokes her chin, continuing her stare. I notice her fingers are long and graceful.

"Do you want to know why I hired you, Coolie 6404?" She says.

I am flippant. "You were taken by my charms."

"Coolie, wasn't your charm that drew me, but your voice. It gave you away. You've been smoked out from the bogs, Highland Trog."

Bogs? I wonder why she uses the term because I know of no Highland bog. Rain is not prevalent there, snow is, but it comes at the wrong time of the season to form fens or swamps. I stick to my story. "I'm Burton Black from Marlton."

Her head swings slowly from side to side. "A Burton, you're not. Many men living in the Central Mosaics have dark hair and clear eyes like you, but the Central Mosaic accent you affect is not good enough. You're from Highland, the criminal trog who incited the riots in the Apron. Yours is the voice in Willoughby who called for insurrection." Her eyes twinkle with a smile. "Are your knees shaking now, Highland Trog?"

I'm not sure why she refers to my knees; they are steady enough. I don't feel like a cornered rat either. She had mentioned the voice in Willoughby, which by inference meant the call to action I delivered there.

"Proxies are Quislings," she shouts in a solid voice, squaring up. "They work with the Hexas to keep the Native in chains," she continues. "Ask yourselves, what have the Legates done on behalf of the Natives made refugees by the Hexas infringements? What bills have the Lower Legates members introduced to address income disparity or bring Hexas war criminals to justice? You are second-class citizens in your own land. What are the Legates doing about all the unfairness and the poverty stalking the land they represent? I'll tell you what those paper-chewing rodents in the Lower Legas have done for you–Squat! Natives of the Mosaics, the Legas have written you off!"

That was my speech she quoted, word for word.

Apron of Hœff

I'll return to Moira later. First, I need to explain the Apron and what it signifies. This area on the western bank of the River Tone is the underbelly of Hexas' Hœff. In fact, Hœff annexed it two decades past. It's the only area of Icenia where Natives, proxies that is, are allowed to live.

One wears an apron to protect from the splash of smelting dross, dirt, or cooking grease. Proxies are so deluded that in their minds is the belief that in the proximity of Hexas, they will gain acceptance, that in adopting Hexas custom and manners, they too will become Hexas. They are like a troupe of apes looking through the confining fence, mimicking their keepers in the hope that one day they will be set free. I stoked the banking anger inside the Native men in Willoughby, and I lit a fire in their bellies. I'm a man born and bred in Easting, like my father, his father, and great grandfather. I would first die than to live in dishonor. Yes, that's how proud we Highlandmen are. It is our fighting that has kept the Central Mosaic from being swallowed by the Hexas. My rage exploded in Willoughby because the men of the Mosaics have done nothing to protect their heritage.

That's what ate at me at the time. I wanted to tear down the system, cause mayhem, and I could think of no better way to start than to smash the head of a Legas. In Willoughby, I gave words to my rage: "How long will you men stomach tyranny?"

Well, you heard the rest. Moira quoted what I said accurately. So in Willoughby, we hijack the connecting trans-line heading not to Hœff's Apron Station but to the west end of Upper Mosaic, just outside the annexed areas. A cordon sanitaire exists within eastern

Hœff. As my allusion of the Fence indicates, no Native is allowed passage beyond the Apron, that is, except for Sub-Legas heading to the famous Capitol Drive of the Barony of Hœff. This wide avenue is where the Sub-Legas assemble to kiss the rear of their Hexas masters. It is here where they craft laws to keep Upper Mosaic's Natives in line.

There is more to explain, but I'll be succinct. Presiding over the Lower Legas is the Upper Legas. Those Hexas hold power over the Lower Legas proxies. It's, as always, bigger rats in charge of the nest. So I muster the men on the eastern bank of the Tone. They are screaming and urgent for action. I hold them back, not with words of reason but by smashing the head of an idiot who tried to steal my thunder. I promised that I would tear out the throat of the next man who disobeyed. I didn't want a mob.

I sent out scouts, and soon they report proxies are guarding the two crossings to the Apron and a gated post to Capitol Drive. Having been a front-line soldier, I am familiar with tactics. I know what I am doing. It was simple enough—two strike teams take the crossings and the post. When our approach is cleared of sentries, I give the order to cross the Tone, and we take the Apron. It's not long before the chamber of the Sub-Legas is surrounded.

We find rats busily crafting more laws still, more appeasement efforts, and ways to satisfy the never-ending demands from their Hexas masters. Like those high priests of old, who sacrificed humans as offering to appease their idols' wrath, the rats of Lower Legas were doing the same.

I wonder why society continues to elect people with no scruples or values whatsoever. Is this an inherent flaw in us? If the extinction of the human race is inevitable, as we're told, I think it will be sped along, not by the works of nature but by politicians' tireless efforts to undo what's right.

Madame De Farge

The trip to the Apron sobers the men, but in no way had the ride diminished their passions. They arm themselves with chains and lash–the symbols of slavery.

The shackles have been struck from their minds, and the whips are now theirs to snap. These men of the Mosaics have at last severed the bonds of servitude. For sure, this contagion would spread.

Why should we stop at the Sub-Legas? I think. Why not go fry the parasites in the underbelly too? They are evil. They lick Hexas boots and victimize their own with zeal.

When compared to the drabness of most cities in the Mosaics, Hœff is splendorous. Yet every city, no matter how fabulous, has a slum area or enclave. Quartered in the annexed lands, Apron is one of these.

The Hexas baron of Hœff is Tallos Bay, uncle of the butcher Eduord Ností. I don't know the man personally, but I hear he's ill-tempered, a man of a sour disposition. However, Tallos, the martinet, is not home in his magnificent wooded retreat known as Piney Hurst. He's on "campaign" or rather on his way south to Terra Solana.

Amid much fanfare, and with the Hexas Crown Prince's secret directive, the Baron marshaled two-thirds of his garrison, and into the Lower Mosaic, he went.

The Lower Mosaic, peopled mostly by Solanos, is a region wealthy in natural resources. Large mineral deposits exist there due to the uplift of superheated groundwater and the irregularity of its geology. Precious minerals have been deposited in large quantities

Journal of Allen Brock

as a result of meteor impacts too. Avid of exploiting these, Hexas established an enclave in the high hills to the southwest, an area with cooler weather. Vast amount of wealth has been spent on infrastructure, damns, bridges, railways and mines. The government of Terra Solana refuses to pay debt accrued for the past two decades through dubious business dealings. Hexas claim that the Faldissi National Bank is owed billions in Silver Doubloons.

Ah, but I digress. Let me get back on track. A list of proxies, the most flagrant ones, is put together before our assault on the Apron. The men on that list are irredeemable bottom feeders. These men are known as "Judases." They are the shopkeepers who mark up wares, the food merchants who refuse to extend credit to families in need, even when the household heads have creditworthiness. We target bank managers who jump to foreclosures on a property in the blink of an eye. We raid their business establishments and homes. On the second day of our occupation, we erect a guillotine.

Charges are brought, defense arguments are heard, and the accused are sent to the guillotine. Their toadies don't face Madame DeFarge's vengeance, but instead, they are flogged in public. I don't want a bloodbath. I seek justice.

Why the guillotine? Ah, guillotining is the preferred Hexas' method of executing criminals, that's to say, Native criminals.

Guillotining strikes terror over all other forms of executions. Hexas studied its psychological effect and applied it, but only to Natives.

Admittedly, beheading a person is a less painful ordeal than electrocution or hanging. Or is it? Hexas are skilled in many ways, and when it comes to extracting the last moments of dread from a man to be executed, they are experts. The condemned man or woman–seldom is a woman guillotined–is forced to wait with his neck inside the locking board's lunette. As he looks down, he stares at the "receiving basket" below, sees severed heads. Are those brains aware of what's happened? I think so. The human brain lives past the trauma for a time and understands its time is done. Do you wonder what thoughts are contemplated during those final moments?

The executioner, stifling a yawn of boredom, at last decides to release the hanging blade above. Swish! Done!

Again, the guillotine is not used on Hexas criminals, only on the Natives in the Hexas dominion.

My words ignite the long-simmering resentment of the men of the Mosaics. The fire is fanned, and the streets of the Apron run red with the blood of proxies. Although no Hexas is harmed, their places of business are set ablaze. There is no looting. I forbid it. We are not thieves; we're avengers.

The Legas label the seizure of the Apron an orchestrated uprising by the "Anomy." Anomy is another confounding Hexas term I need to take a moment to describe.

Anomy is a person who is the architect of anarchy. The term Anomy can also refer to a criminal enterprise, a syndicate presided by a Mafiosi. So it is that Anomy's display of violence in the Apron excites fear throughout Hœff: "Will Trogs cross the River Tone to pillage and rape again and again," Legate Petronil rages.

Whipped into a panic, the people of Hœff demand protection from its Baron. Tallos Bay is on a campaign, as mentioned. So the Upper Legas asks Prince Meres Ma'tann to intervene.

They needn't have because from the instant the riots began Meres Ma'tann knew this was his moment. His propaganda machine spews his message day and night throughout Hœff and those parts of the Mosaics under the Hexas sway. I'll quote one of his appeals: "The lawlessness in Hœff, my good people of Icenia, would not have been possible without the incitements, the arming and succoring from the Highland. Highland is a sanctuary. The Anomy, like a termite queen, makes its nest in Junipero Heights."

If this is so, if indeed this Anomy is in hiding in Junipero, I can't imagine where or who he, she, or they might be.

From loudspeakers booming all across the plazas of Upper Mosaic and North-Central Mosaic, the people pause to listen to Meres Ma'tann's propaganda: "Meres Ma'tann of the House of Royce is a benevolent ruler." Running the Propaganda machine is Legas Olmar Petronil, the top Upper Legas, and a rat I would love to find.

Here's another slice from the pie: "Our Prince always, no matter the demands imposed by his office, takes time to listen to the people of the Upper Mosaic. It's not the people he blames but the armed criminals from Junipero Heights. Those murderers of innocent people will be hunted down and brought to justice."

However, to Meres Ma'tann's chagrin, we slipped out of the Apron before his grenadiers got there.

Salton Basin

"**B**urton, I think that a better name for you would be Brad-Grog," Moira tells me. "How does Egg-Thu sound, hmm?"

She's in an upswing mood because today, as she doesn't refer to me as maggot, coolie, or shovelhead. She's being funny, see and, well, to Moira, people of the Uplands are anthropoids, simply higher apes, hence the reason for those guttural sounding names.

In Moira's mind, a myth exists. She is convinced that Highland people are savages, having taken but a few steps from Neanderthal ways. She is supremely confident in the knowledge bestowed by her Hexas coaches.

Naturally, Moira had deduced I am from Highland. But that's faulty logic, even if she is right. The Mosaics is a milieu. Uplanders live there too. Regardless, she assumes I am a danger, except she has no proof of this.

I'll take an aside for a moment. Having served my mandatory time in Easting's military as an infantry officer, I returned to Marlton's township in Central Mosaic. Again, it was a question of priorities. I had a family then, but not out of choice. Not to be sidetracked again, I'll explain how that came about at a later time.

Hunters Lodge in Easting is a township constantly beset by raiding Logans. When the snows of Mirren Glacier thaw, Logans raid. Like many Easters, I have misgivings about the Colonelcy in Glenn Cross. We know these men aren't running the war properly. The DMO demoted Easting to a secondary theater of action. This is the reason why Easters, Easting's people, are always in the thick of the fight. But, unfortunately, Easting receives little assistance from the Directorate of Military Operations. The DMO's focus is on the west instead. My anger flares whenever I think about this. All the same, this is my roundabout way of explaining that technically I am a resident of Central Mosaic and not of Highland. But I'm wandering off again; so let me resume my original point.

My actions in Willoughby frighten proxies like Moira, and for good reasons. If the vast number of men in Central Mosaic took up arms, the Hexas would be done away with, and people like Moira would walk the long straight path to the guillotine.

"You can ask me for mercy, Allen Brock," Moira suggests. "I might be in the mood to dispense some."

"I don't kiss anyone's rear, Moira," I retort.

Although she draws away from me, her smile remains as poisonous as ever. "You are a jewel, Allen Brock," she declares. "Your pillaging of the Apron has brought you fame, and you revel in the carnage."

"I didn't pillage, and I didn't murder." I give my head a definite shake. "No, Moira. What my men and I did was deliver justice. But what's that to you? Why would you care? You're not going to gain more laurels by going to your handlers. To the Hexas running the show here, you're just a pair of tits on heels."

Those words fire up Moira's ire, sure enough. She grabs hold of my shirt's collar and draws me towards her. "I will not remind you again, you Highland-bred-trog. I am going to be present when the Stasa interrogates you. I will see you piss your pants."

"You know nothing about me, Queen of Coolies," I reply. "I, on the other hand, know all there is to know about you."

"Know nothing, you say?" Oddly, her hand straightens my shirt collar that moment, supposedly to make me look more presentable to her. "Oh, on the contrary," she adds. "You've just confessed that you are, Allen Brock. You're mine now."

Her smile is a twisted one, full of venom. She is worse than any Hexas. She is a Native, corrupted by the vile ways of the enemy.

"Allen Brock, the anarchist who incited violence in the Apron. It is an honor to meet you," she declares.

By then, I'd worked in the Salton Basin for half a year. Throughout this time, my mind is in constant turmoil. Bristol is always in my thoughts. Understand that Moira's timing was poor.

As Moira brings up her quirt to whip my face, I seize her wrist before she can strike. My grip is firm. I hear the snap of bones breaking. I'm no sadist, but I feel a moment of satisfaction. My other hand comes up and closes tightly around her white throat.

This is a seminal moment for Moira as she realizes that her power over this coolie has vanished. Entering the bivouac to face a man by herself was a mistake.

My hand tightens around her windpipe. I see her eyes bulge as my hand presses. When her knees buckle, I loosen my hold. I don't want her to give up the ghost quite yet. "You might have walked away from this, Moira. You could have ignored me. Instead, you had to play the proxy's game."

As she gasps for breath, I activate the shredder. She is alive when I toss her body into the churning metal jaws of the compost bin.

Is this murder? Possibly, but think for a moment. Had I done nothing, Moira would have played, as I said, her proxy card and turned me in. I would've been tortured and then executed. My life meant nothing to her; why should hers mean anything to me?

A strange thought visits me at times, that of Moira's fingernails. She had long fingertips. I recall her nails were painted with a crimson lacquer wherein cleverly embedded diamond-shaped motifs resided. In one bizarre moment of reflection, I wondered what she had paid the manicurist for such excellent craftwork.

Highland Spring

Highland springs run behind those in St. Andrew Valley. Be that as it may, millions of migrating birds from the south darken the skies in the afternoons. They fly south to Mirren by the millions.

The reason birds fascinate men is because they fly. Birds, though, engage in fighting one another for mates and territory also. Those that migrate from very far are aggressive, and they try to evict resident birds from their hold. Resident birds consider their winged kin invaders. They are robbers, trying to filch from their food source. It's intolerable when these foreigners stake out a territory. Birds and men think alike.

In the spring comes an up-tic of fighting throughout Highland. Men try on their field uniforms again, clean and oil their weapons, and prepare to be called to arms in support of the armed forces. Neither the Logans nor Hexas are going to give up the fight.

Junipero Heights is, in large part, rural. In early spring, the people go about doing seasonal chores, tilling the land, selecting seeds, and figuring which field to rotate. There's farm animal husbandry, new calves to tend to, colts to be sized, sheep needing shearing. Goats are let loose on the lower meadowlands to rid the flats of invasive vines. As in olden times, these chores fall on women and teenagers, and neither enjoy it. Women are the most vocal in expressing their dissatisfaction. Tractors and farm implements need overhauling too. During this time, the smithies and metallurgists are tempering steel in a thousand shops throughout Highland.

Don't be mistaken in thinking Highland is a simple agrarian society; on the contrary. Highland has an advanced economy and high industry. Its townships are connected by trans-lines, like everywhere else. However, its largest population center, Glenn Cross, is no metropolis. It only has a population of over two hundred thousand people. Nevertheless, Highland has many townships and millions of people.

Ah, but I've veered from the topic again. Spring is the season of festivals, county fares also, and of course, the season of love. Ah, can anything compare with what you felt when you were seventeen? When the bold girls in town teased you? I'm way past that age, though, having celebrated my twenty-ninth birthday this month. I got drunk that day.

I became a father at an early age. I'm not married to Bristol's mother because I've never loved the woman.

Zee, that's how both Bristol and I referred to her mother, was from Bajadero River's uplands, more specifically from the Valley of the Rivers. Her father was a Native of the big island of Fanlo, and her mother was a Fayean from Alturas. I met the woman in Marlton while doing construction work there. She, Zee that is, was a barmaid in a Pub. Her straw blond hair and crystal blue eyes drew me. We hooked up for a time then went our separate ways.

One day, Zee shows up at my doorstep with a round belly. She tells me she's carrying my child.

The day Bristol was born I had her DNA tested. Unless the woman is his loyal wife, a man should never trust the word of any when she indicts him of paternity.

Patriot

When Meres Ma'tann hears of our escape from the Apron, he flies into a rage. It is reported that with his scepter, the Prince lambasted the Cetron he sent to capture us. Our getaway is a personal insult since he swore to bring the Highland brigands to justice.

Tallos of Hœff, Meres Ma'tann's favorite Baron, is doing his master's bidding in the south. The Prince tells his trusty Baron to ease his worries. Piney Hurst, Tallos' estate in Netisto Bay's shore, "is beyond the reach of those brigands." His communiqué to Tallos reads: "My finest uncle, my staunch ally. You, Tallos, who I rely upon, rest with ease."

This is a flattery-ridden directive, too lengthy to recount, but I'll give you the skinny. Baron Tallos is to establish a permanent Hexas military presence in the heart of Terra Solana until Solano's debt to Faldiss, specifically to the House of Royce, is paid off. We are told that the Baron of Hœff grins with delight as he read Meres Ma'tann's directive. His understanding is that this will be a quick incursion, collect what's owed, and pull out.

Officials throughout the municipalities of the Lower Mosaic lodge heated complaints. The very presence of Hexas forces in the Lower Mosaic is a blatant violation of the Banfield Accord. By sending Hexas troops into Terra Solana, Hexas are in flagrant violation of an established treaty. Meres Ma'tann ignores the collective outrage from the Mayoralty. To him the members of this body are third-rate politicians. I agree with Meres Ma'tann. The mayors of the Upper and Central Mosaics are flunkies. Solanos think the same. So it is that the people of Aguijón, the largest city in Terra Solana, take action on their own.

"Terra Noster! This is our land."

It is a fighting man who shouts those words. He is a patriot, and his name is François "Pico" Franx alias El Flaco.

When Pico Franx sees his countrymen hauled away in chains by the invaders, he is outraged. In the company of fellow patriots, he enters Presidio, a fortress being used to hold Solano prisoners by the Stasa. He shows his entry pass to the guard then shoots him and three others dead. Presidio's detainees are set free.

Pico's name is not whispered through the streets of Aguijón; it's shouted from rooftops: "Long live El Flaco!" He is the man to follow. Exhortations to surrender blast from Hexas loudspeakers throughout Aguijón. Even though Hexas forces only hold a quarter of the city, they're dug in.

El Flaco speaks: "We will flush the Hexas out of every street corner of Aguijón. We will make them fight mano-a-mano. If they drive us out, we will double our effort and fight them in the barrios and outskirts of the city. We won't give up the struggle."

"Terra Solana is Terra Noster!"

El Flaco furthers: "Solanos will fight for their land in the tangles of the Mesquite Forest if they must. In every rocky desert hill and every sand dune. We Solanos will continue our fight past the point of exhaustion. My people, you are called to endure the unbearable. We fight, fight and fight until there are no weapons left but our bare hands and the rocks at our feet. When no more ground remains, and when every breath is labor, and when fatigue threatens to drive us to our knees, we will find new strength and continue the fight. Only when no breath remains in our breast, then and only then will we resist no more because we will be dead."

"By the blood-stained stones of the Citadel!" I shout after the man signs off on the wireless. "Here's a man without fear, I say to Elliot. "I have few regrets, but there's one that crops up continuously–I'm doing nothing worthwhile to rid ourselves of the Hexas. As a Crag-Rat, I hoped that one day I'd become a Snow-Ghost or a Wolverine. One of those amazing soldiers is what I wanted to be more than anything, Elliot. A Snow-Ghost rises from the snow and slashes at the enemy with his poniard. He guards the snowy hills of Easting. Instead, I was ordered to attend school, and that was that. As a Highlandman, I performed my military service, yes, but I accomplished little other than killing Hexas. Now, thanks to my father, I know how to turn this fight around. I'm going to Terra Solana."

Expedition

From sunrise to sunset, Junipero's brigade hurries preparations to embark. Lt. Areu shows me a list with countless names. She tells me these are the names of the volunteer soldiers from every corner of Highland. "I don't know whether they heard El Flaco's call of duty or Abbot Madigan's call to the faithful," she says with a wide smile. "No matter, it echoed throughout Highland. I'm beginning to believe in miracles."

The news spread. Junipero Heights is putting together an expeditionary force to join fighters in Aguijón.

Today Lt. Bartlett, my second-in-command, also delivers a "must-read" message from Glenn Cross Headquarters. Its cover is stenciled in blue letters, C.I., or classified information. This is for my eyes only, and no one else has the need to know. It comes from the top DMO colonel, Mathew Weaving. "Hammering Matt" makes his point of view explicit:

> "According to my calculations, two regiments of seasoned soldiers are being removed from the battle line. I am hard-pressed to figure out how these men obtained open-ended furloughs. More surprising is that to a man, they have joined Junipero's home guard. So indirectly they are under your command.
>
> Sir, you have organized Junipero's forces very effectively. Junipero's force stood determinately alongside the defenders of Knob Noster. I am not sure which rank to use in the

address. I wonder if Captain of the Guard is apt? I realize that it's within Junipero's Advisory Council authority to appoint you as an interim commander-in-chief.

Nevertheless, I invite Captain Benitez to reconsider his planned mission to the Lower Mosaic. This move risks expanding the war into a new theater. This must not occur, for we would be unable to project this military effort through such a distance. I request from Captain of the Guard Benitez a parley. Let us meet in the Citadel and confer on this matter."

Yours Truly,
Col. Matthew Weaving DMO
Colonelcy

Weaving could not order me to attend his conference. Junipero Home Guard is not under the command of DMO.

Way back, the Colonelcy ignored Captain Lysander Benitez's advice, even though the high-ranking officers there knew, and in particular, Weaving knew, that Lysander was the finest tactician in DMO. So today, Lysander's son, Allen Brock, ignores the colonel's advice.

I strike the cover page of Weaving's document with a broad red X. Then I tell Lt. Bartlett, "Use a choirboy from St. Polycarp to deliver my reply."

I wanted to rub it in; Hammering Matt once referred to my father as a choirboy because Lysander was Catholic.

Road To Aguijón

We jump off from Pitts Caldera and take the Eastern Algid, the cold roads shadowed by the Escarpment. They run from northeast to south, and Junipero's brigade makes good time trekking along those barren twisting grades halfway to Terra Solana. The men are in good spirits itching for action, and some, no doubt, are also looking forward to meeting dusky-eyed ladies of the land graced by the sun.

Finally, we cross the Kol'bien River Bend, turn southeast to Guahataki, Terra Solana's northernmost city, and reach the Bajadero. Bajadero is the largest river on the continent. Its headwaters spring from Cerro Estribas in the Escarpment divide. The river runs through Púa and Aguijón, the unincorporated Freeds Land, and flows through northern Fay'dorn. Then a thousand miles away from its headwaters, Bajadero empties into Pacifica.

We arrive in Guahataki, one might say in the nick of time. Baron Tallos Bay had just launched his final offensive against Aguijón. We have only time to sort our gear before rushing to the front.

The term front is apt because the combat lines are set. The Hexas are north and west of Aguijón, while Solanos hold a precarious defense line in the rubble of the city's southern districts. The Bajadero River is to their backs.

After two days of fighting, the Hexas relent with their drive. Obviously, driving out men determined to die if they have to made Tallos Bay's cetrons pause. It's obvious where the Hexas are vulnerable, and I mention it to Captain Felix Montoya. He is the Solano officer commanding the front lines.

Captain Montoya agrees; unfortunately, we are not in strength to capitalize on that. Heck, we're hanging by our fingertips.

As Aguijón's defenders remain stubborn, Tallos Bay harangues his grenadiers ordering them to flush out the Mud-mix rabble–a derogatory term for Solanos–from the rubble.

No easy task. But it becomes clear what I have to do. The brigade skips the rubble and strikes at the Hexas rear. It is hard fighting, but we destroy the Hexas command post and take prisoners.

When Tallos hears Highland men attacked his Command Post and that we are fighting alongside Solanos, he rages. He takes a Hexas battle-ax and swings it repeatedly, wrecking furnishing and walls before the pleadings of his mistress can calm his fury.

"May piles grow on Philo's moldering ass!" he swears profanely. "Let the wombs of these sun-browned bitches wither and dry!"

Driven by malice, he offers a two-ounce doubloon with gold leaf for every head brought to him with fair skin and blue eyes–an inference to Highland men, of course.

It's June tenth and it's hot. The balmy days of May are long gone. There's no let-up in the savage fighting around Aguijón and in her streets. Our enemy shoots at us from a distance, and before a Highland soldier is prepared, a grenadier runs up and launches his explosive. If you're fast, see him first, and draw a bead, you might shoot him down. Not every Hexas grenadier is brought down, unfortunately.

The whistle of grenade trajectories are heard, and then the booming explosions resound across the line. There are skirmishes all along the line. Hexas infiltrators probe at night. We find ourselves fighting hand-to-hand in the give-ways and in the rubble-strewn streets. It's as personal and as fierce as any fighting I've seen.

In the mornings, Hexas artillery rounds burst overhead. Once again, shrapnel showers down on the dug-in defenders. Tallos Bay is determined to destroy the last vestige of resistance.

Behind armored maniples, the grenadiers are sent in once more. The war machines scramble over the rubble, bullying their way into what they know is the last pocket of Aguijón's resistance. No matter how brave and dogged our resistance, we are driven across the Bajadero, and at last, Aguijón falls.

What the birth of the Escarpment failed to accomplish in its fury, Baron Tallos' vengeance manages. His artillery leaves not a single building in the center of the city standing. Aguijón, the oldest city on the continent, is obliterated along with thousands of its inhabitants.

Words of praise from his nephew, Ností Le Bey, is sent: "Uncle, you will go down in Hexas history as a hero. Battle poems, like those of Latismo, will commemorate this epic battle."

A torrent of accolades follows from the members of Hexas Court and from the Upper Legas too. Every stooge had his say.

Meres Ma'tann awards Baron Tallos Bay the Illustrious Six Star Ring. Only the most distinguished, most valorous soldier is awarded one of those. No matter if Tallos didn't fire a shot in the fight, just the same, he now wears the Ring of Valor on his finger.

El Flaco

Baron Tallos Bay's advisors put an end to his strutting by nudging him back to the reality on the ground. No matter his victory in Aguijón, his army still hasn't destroyed the rag-tag Solano resistance after two months of fighting. Those men pulled back across the Bajadero. In fact, the ranks of Solanos are swelling.

Volunteers from Fanlo and as far as Perdidas/Perdue are joining the fight. What's to be done then? Does the Baron allow El Flaco and his gang of cutthroats to just slip away? Never! He will capture the man and take him to Faldiss to be guillotined in public.

Another difficulty presents itself. Now that the Baron has taken Guahataki and Aguijón, will he have sufficient forces to hold onto those cities if he sends his expeditionary force into Púa—which he must.

"El Flaco! El Flaco! I am surfeit! Seeing and hearing that swabbing name everywhere!" Tallos rages while speaking to Patrice Gambetta, the business and commerce liaison from the Hexas Barony. Unbeknown to the Baron, Gambetta, an ex-pat, detests Meres Ma'tann. Like many Faldissi who had long settled in Terra Solana's Austraneés, Gambetta is sympathetic to the Solano cause.

Here again, is a brief of a recorded conversation passed to us by the resistance: "I can understand why Baron," says Patrice. The graffiti is scrawled on nearly every wall in the city because El Flaco, you see, Gambetta replies. "El Flaco, you see, walks on water."

"El Flaco walks on water, you say?" Tallos exclaims with surprise. "What is this, another one of the cofounding beliefs of these brown-skinned primates?"

"Ha-ha-ha!" Gambetta is obviously driven to laughter. "It's an old legend, my good Baron. Supposedly Jesu, the principal deity here, did just that."

"Flaco, Flaco, Flaco!" I'm surfeit Patrice, surfeit!" Tallos exclaims again.

Incidentally, the word "flaco" refers to someone slim. François "Pico" Franx is tall and slender, hence the moniker. He orders us to dig in, throw up barricades, and fortify Púa's defenses as best we can. To our backs is the Mesquite Forest.

The conversation continues. "So, Patrice, will Pico Franx admit defeat and agree to pay was is owed to Faldiss?"

"Ah, but you see, Baron from Pico Franx's point of view, Terra Solana has already paid twice more than all Faldiss' loans combined," says Patrice. "Terra Solana has, in fact, been pilfered, exploited actually."

Tallos Bay scoffs. "That is not the Prince's opinion."

"True, but Pico Franx doesn't give one whit about Meres Ma'tann's opinion or for that of the Barony's either."

"Hexas grenadiers will flush Pico-the-Rat out of Púa," Tallos swears then. "The only place for that Fayean renegade to run will be the Mesquite Forest. If I have to, I'll set fire to it!"

Patrice gasps in amazement. "That's rather extreme, don't you think, Baron?"

"Patrice, in a war, there is no such thing as extremes," Tallos Bay suggests to the liaison. "I've given my word to the Crowned Prince to bring this so-called El Flaco to Faldiss in chains. I always keep my promises, Patrice."

However, Baron Tallos Bay is in no position, military speaking, to fulfill such a promise. First, the city of Guahataki, though in the rubble, remains unsecured. Solano snipers left behind target Hexas soldiers. Commando squads cross the riverbanks during the night and infiltrate. They raid Hexas command posts and slip back across the river. Booby-trap mines are strategically placed. Solanos know where not to go, but not so Hexas soldiers.

Terra Solana is seldom affected by RSE's. Explosives are very effective here. Still, the Baron manages to hold key positions, but it is a tenuous hold. The only way to strengthen that grip is to deal the enemy forces a final obliterating blow.

Finally, the decisive blow Tallos promised comes. He throws everything he has at us. Púa is subjected to a series of heavy bombardments. We are driven from Púa and into the Mesquite Forest. The fighting is hellacious. But it's there in the Mesquite that the Hexas grenadiers learn that they are not invincible. Solanos don't surrender; they have to be killed, and in the thousands of square kilometers of the Mesquite, they can be anywhere.

To wrestle the Mesquite from the Solanos, Meres Ma'tann sends in Legionnaires, a new concept, a regiment size unit comprising Hexas malcontents released from jails, Logans seeking plunder, and proxies, the lowest of the low. Tallos gives the command: "Flush the Mud-mix and the Highland scum into hells firestorm!"

The Mesquite, however, refuses to be set ablaze, much as the enemy tries. Torrential rains drench the land, and no matter how many incendiary rounds Belchers fire into the woods, they don't produce the desired result.

Felix tells me that the Solanos are calling the rains a miracle. "They'll be clutching crucifixes and going back to church or on pilgrimages to the statue of Jesu in Cerro Azul."

Montoya is educated, a hidalgo in this land. The man is as tall as me, muscular yet slender in form. Equally, his hair is as dark as mine, and his eyes are the color of slate. The sun has tanned his face, and he looks formidable.

"Felix," I say, "I'd walk on my knees to that mountain if that's what'll take to win this fight."

The fight goes on, but this time we have the advantage. Solanos know the forest well. They know where to stand and fight, what areas to run to, and the best places to set an ambush.

What was supposed to be a brief incursion into the Mesquite turns into a bloody, month-long, non-stop battle. We make Hexas soldiers pay a hefty price.

Pulling out of the Mesquite finds Baron Bay's troops in a pickle. Between Púa and the Mesquite, there's nothing but sparse meadows and scrub, basically open ground. Tallos Bay's men are stabbed and slashed by saber-wielding cavalrymen. They are blasted to pieces by exploding bolas, which the riders lob their way on the gallop.

Soon the fighting in Guahataki, Púa, and in the ruins of Aguijón resurges. The fight rages from building to building and throughout the rubble-strewn streets. The tide turns, and the beginning of the end for the Hexas expeditionary forces grows near.

Word from our agent is passed to El Flaco's HQ. This from a briefing, and I quote some of Tallos Bay's remarks: "Why is it, I ask, that the Mud-mix breed of this land is not brought to heel by the mighty Hexas sword? We've killed tens of thousands of them, yet they remain inflexible. Why do they fail to learn? I tell you, Patrice, if in my hands fell an atomic weapon, I would use it on them without hesitation. I would obliterate them all. "

"But my good Baron," Gambetta proposes, "you've tried the sword and the pen; you've waged a brilliant campaign. Maybe it's best to retire the debt. Call it a victory and withdraw."

Baron Tallos Bay realizes that without massive reinforcements from Meres Ma'tann, which will not be forthcoming, El Flaco would close all escape avenues. He takes Patrice Gambetta's sound advice, withdraws his forces from the cities and departs from Terra Solana.

Solanos win!

~~~

Under the light of a full moon in an impromptu fiesta, we celebrate the victory. Cooking fires are ablaze, and the young women and men dance. The breeze from the southeast carries the scent of Mesquite that blends with the cooking coals. That's the smell of victory. The camp tables are scrubbed and draped. They're ready to receive the product from the roasting pits.

After the feast, Pico, Montoya, and I drink late into the night.

Pico turns to me. "Brock, you and your men came to Aguijón and bolstered us. We thought our friends in the north had turned their backs to the Solanos." He downs a gulp of Ardiente, a favorite liquor of the area, and says, "Solanos won a victory because you and Junipero's brigade made it possible."

I look at him and shake my head. "No, the credit goes to the Solanos, to their courage, and to the sacrifices they made."

Felix Montoya has a different opinion. "Not entirely," he says. "You and your men traveled a thousand miles to fight alongside us. When my men saw that Highland fighters were with us all the way, they knew that victory was assured."

"I have to agree with Felix," says Pico. "But let's not crow too loudly," he cautions. "The Hexas used one-sixth of their army, and we had a devil of a time beating them. They'll return, and in larger numbers. Of that, I am certain."

A Hexas Femme

Dressed as laborers and holding fake identification documents, Felix Montoya and I stroll through one of Southaven's streets. Montoya is now the official liaison between Highland and Terra Solana, and he's an excellent choice.

"Southaven is a filthy town, Felix," I inform him. "It's the southernmost township in the Upper Mosaic, and the Hexas boot is firmly set on the neck of the resident Natives. I've never worked here, but I used to come this way via the Trans-Salton-Line to pick up freight."

Montoya sent narrow glances about. The man despises Hexas and for justifiable reasons. Hexas just got through killing tens of thousands of his countrymen.

"Southaven Township is rife with informants," I let him know that too. "So we've got to tread with care. An undercover Stasa goon is waiting in just about every street corner. We keep a low profile."

The Highland Brigade disperses for apparent reasons. Agents of El Flaco had heard that Meres Ma'tann ordered a Mosaic-wide seine in an attempt to capture the "Highland brigands," who aided and abetted Pico Franx and "his criminals." Our men, traveling in groups of twos or threes, and in some instances, as individuals, are slowly making their way back home.

~~~

As we cross the bridge to Township Center, I look up at Southaven Trans-Station Tower. A huge, old fashion clock with minute and hour hands hangs on its tower.

Journal of Allen Brock

"Felix," I whispered, pulling at his sleeve, "it's too early to go into the station. We're laborers see, and if we're being followed by chance, what's customary is to stop for a drink or quick bite. The next cargo tram, which we're supposedly here to load, isn't due for another hour."

While in the outdoor café, I look across the street to a Mo-wag crew unloading produce. I wonder what rural community it hails from. It has no markings.

When I lived in Marlton, I use to take fare in the Out Bound Trolley to see the countryside. This is a surface line that takes people on tours to the farming communities. The soulless woman I lived with didn't understand why I found enjoyment in doing this. She was nursing Bristol at the time, and that was the reason I brought her long. The woman, meaning Zee, of course, complained about how the baby would clamp onto her nipples, "hurting her." I told her to put up with it. I refused to buy Formula. Bristol needed her antibodies to ward off a range of infectious diseases and medical issues associated with an immature immune system. Zee didn't understand that basic concept.

Farmland communities surround Marlton. This is how the land lies throughout the townships of Central and Upper Mosaics. Farm buildings, stockyards, and grain elevators are all kept in top shape in the outbound areas. When it comes to commerce between farm communities, the townships of the Mosaics and Icenia, laissez-faire is the rule. Baron Tallos Bay's invasion, however, changed that. When the price of pork loin and cutlets in the market, which Hexas imported from Terra Solana climbed two hundred percent, opprobrium rose throughout Icenia.

Getting fresh meat or produce to market from the countryside to townships is done by Motorized-wagons. Mo-wags, as they are known, are midsize semis with kinetic engines. Most operate with the use of multiple gears. A Mo-wag engine has a cowling that's resistant, although not impervious, to the RSE. Their fuel is a mixture of binary hydrogen and crystalline coal compounds. This fuel is fed to the engine's combustion chamber via an aerosol pump. Little or no electricity is required for motility once the vehicle gets underway. Energy storage batteries are used as a backup. Mo-rigs can be harnessed and platooned together to save energy.

The ownership of vehicles is a luxury only top Hexas or proxy rats can afford. Public transportation is what's available to most. In the Upper and Central Mosaics, farmers, ranchers, or produce vendors are unable to own Mo-wags or powered farm machinery. These must be leased long-term or rented. The men and women who grow food pay an exorbitant price because of regulations. Natives of the Mosaics own neither nor have access to technology unless it's controlled by the Hexas.

No more about this stuff. I'll just add that these are the circumstances of the times.

Attached to the menu is a leaflet. I immediately see it's another rant from the High Muck, Legas Petronil.

"This is one for the books," I say, slapping the sheet of paper with the back of my hand. "Meres Ma'tann and his Legas are asking Natives for cooperation."

"Hexas asking us for help?" Montoya says in wonder.

I beam a smile his way. "Seems they want help in finding Highland 'anthropoids' and sun-brown types like you, Felix. Hexas are smarting from the defeat El Flaco inflicted."

Felix stirs his black tea and sends me a lowbrow stare. "I think they're keener on the Chief Trog's head rather than mine."

An old woman, mopping the floor, steals close and unsnapped the top of her work glove to show us a signet ring. "Both of you stand out," she whispers. "Soldiers you are. Everyone can see that."

With an asp-like motion, her index finger comes to her lips. She sends a gesture over her stooped shoulder, which I realized is a false effect, a disguise. My eyes follow her motion.

"Cloaks, two of them," she whispers in a raspy voice.

Cloaks are a Native term for undercover proxy agents. What I had warned Felix about is reinforced. Cloaks and snitches are on the prowl everywhere.

"Beat out of Southaven now!" the old woman adds with urgency. "A friend is near, but your enemies are getting close."

Journal of Allen Brock

Having said that, she moves on to mop another section of the floor. I am not going to engage her in further conversation. Her point is clear enough.

It's time to leg it out of Southaven. Felix and I split up. He'll head east, and I will take my chance in the crowded Trans line out of Southaven. The plan is to meet in Kirby Baja's Knob.

I wait in the trans-station, thinking of the old woman in the café. Is she part of the Anomy? I recall the emblem on her signet ring. It's that of a python girding the planet, like no ring I'd seen before.

A young Hexas femme startles me from my thoughts. She's in such a hurry to read the split-flap A/D display that she all but shoves me aside.

"My apologies for standing in your way," I say tightly.

She turns my way and seems to smile. "Altogether, my fault. Um, it appears that the passenger trans-pod to Faldiss-a-Main is late again," she adds, reading the screen. "Are you headed there?"

When I attended Seaward Seaton Polytech, I would occasionally run into a Hexas, but we would exchange only a few words. Of course, I was never invited to their fraternity functions, not that I would've attended any. One day a femme stops me to ask for directions to a lecture hall. After a minute or so, she offers me a broad smile and admits that she knew the hall's location. On her mind was the chance of running into a man of the Highland, and she has. She wants to have sex. She's been curious to know how a "Trog's uncommon penis" would feel inside her.

Did I oblige her? I'll let you wonder. So let me get back to my chance meeting with the Hexas femme.

"No, Hexas femme, Faldiss-a-Main is not my destination," I reply. She's standing too close, so I take a small step back, then another. But as though we're engaged in a bizarre dance. She follows my steps, draws closer still to where our bodies are touching. For a second, the lilac scent of her hair reaches my nostrils, and I find it pleasing.

The Hexas femme tugs at her green hood and looks at the split screen. Then again, her head turns my way. "The Stasa is circulating a sketch throughout Southaven," she says casually. "It is that of a Highland criminal on the loose."

Her words freeze me on the spot.

She places her trans-rail ticket back inside her purse and, in seeming frustration, exclaims, "rikkens!" This i s a Hexas expletive. Directly translated, it close to, well, damnation!

"I've missed my ride," she says. "It's always this way with this trans-line, early or late but never on time. It's as though this inconsistency is intended. Oh, as I began to mention." Her hooded head comes up. "These individuals are dangerous. Every Hexas citizen must watch for them and point them out to Stasa agents the moment they're spotted."

My hand moves to my knife, which is sheathed inside my sleeve. I can stab her in the heart, or cut her throat, or better still, toss her in front of the inbound trans. I have killed people before, as you know. Except this femme isn't threatening me directly, at least not yet.

I tell her, "A second ago, you said individuals, Hexas femme, but now you say there's a criminal on the loose, meaning one."

"Ah, then I must've misspoken," she explains, "because there is more than one, a list full actually, but it's a particular one that has everyone on edge. I understand that he's a true villain."

Her hood covers part of her face, so I can't make out her looks. Her voice, though, is that of a young woman.

"Every day, more names are added to the list," she continues in a calm voice. "I hear that this villain tops the list. He goes by the name of Allen Brock."

"Allen Brock, eh?" I say with a false air of imperturbability. The fact is I am desperately trying to think clearly.

She nods. "The criminal was spotted in the center of town, um, in the company of a sunbrown fellow believed to be a Solano. It's alleged that this Solano killed two Stasa agents and managed to slip from the cordon. To hear news of this nature is horrible, simply terrifying."

There's nothing more to say. I realize I am trapped. I figure that if I am going to kill this femme, I have to do it this instant.

As I start my move, she lifts a finger. "I am neither informant nor pursuer. Stasa suits guard all three exits out of this station," she says imperatively.

There is no hesitation or fear in her voice. I look around, still trying to hash out a plan of escape. Well, let's see. I can kill the femme here first, then the snide cashier manning the ticket screen, or the bored Suit standing by the turnstiles. This will provide a diversion . . .

She says, or I'm thinking that she said, "I believe this Allen Brock has a good chance of evading his pursuers. The first restroom on the upper level," she motions over her right shoulder with her head "has an emergency exit. This morning the cleaning crew forgot to reset its alarm."

Figuratively, my jaw drops to my chest. I don't know what to think.

"A Disposal & Waste Mo-wag with blue markings awaits in the backstreet," she goes on. "It's hidden from sight behind the power taper station. It will not wait for long."

Again, my instincts put me on the alert. "Why should Allen Brock, a man on the run, believe anything a stranger says, particularly when that stranger is Hexas?" I ask.

"What choice does he have?"

She tosses back her hood. Her face is oval with a delicate chin, straight nose, and the most amazing eyes. They are large, luminous, and the color of a dark whiskey. Her looks are striking.

"Allen Brock, you must take leave immediately," she whispers. "The noose is tightening."

I search her hands to see if she too has a signet ring, but she wears gloves. The doors of the arriving trans-pod slide open; she hurries past me and deftly slips inside.

I recall an old saying: "He that fights and runs away may live to fight another day."

The restroom smells awful, as expected, like just about every other rundown place in Southaven, you might say. Inside, two men are relieving themselves. They ignore me; after all, who strikes conversations in such a place? I see the door "my contact" mentioned. It has a wide metal push bar that reads: "EMERGENCY ONLY."

The instant I find myself alone, I push down on the bar and ease the door open. No alarm is set off. I walk out casually.

I'll get on quickly with rest. It's a dark alley, but the light from power tapers standing fifty or more meters away makes it possible to find my way.

The Mo-wag driver with a tank full of effluvia shows his ring. It's not dissimilar to the one the old woman was wearing with an emblem of a snake. This one, though, is coiled as though ready to strike.

The fellow's manner is tense, his instructions clipped. If stopped on the way, on a makeshift checkpoint, I'm to say nothing. I am his "pump-man," meaning lowly assistant. I'm to look dumb, which is easy enough. Hours later I am dropped off five miles west from Knob Noster.

I never saw the Hexas femme again. I often wonder what motivated her. To know I was Allen Brock, the criminal, and not warn Hexas authority, is a crime. It is, in fact, treason.

Hexas Politics

By now, it has occurred to you I don't generally cite dates or times of day on my journal. I'll provide the missing time components in this entry. It's a Thursday evening in late summer. I decided from the beginning to do, well, nothing. So I sit in the courtyard, watching the setting sun. My mind has been very active all day. I need to relax, and the best way to go about it is to write.

Meres Ma'tann, the Crown Prince of Faldiss, is on the fast track to becoming Magnus Royce, or Ruler of Icenia. In one form or another, he's eliminated the competition or opposition. He tried to have his half-brother declared incompetent due to a speech impediment. Then while on a fishing trip, his sibling's boat capsized and he drowned. One of Meres Ma'tann's three cousins was paralyzed in an equestrian match. The other two got the message. They fled, and no one knows where. After Guymon, the old Baron of Faldiss, died and his nephew, Meres, naturally, assumed his responsibilities, Meres decreed that Faldiss didn't need a Baron, a Duke, or a Count because now it has a Prince, he, Meres Ma'tann.

Needless to say, the Barons of Icenia are wary of the Prince. They basically do what he tells them, if grudgingly. Faldiss, after all, is the strongest and most populous Barony and would be able to impose its will if it must.

What Meres Ma'tann is pursuing, though, is the title, Magnus Royce. That office wields the power of a shōgun. In that event, all six Baronies of Icenia and the Upper Legas would be subordinate to his decrees.

Meanwhile, the Royal House in Faldiss-a-Main is the actual power in Icenia. It's here where the Hall Of Barons convene, meaning where the power brokers come together to decide policy. Only the Royal House of Royce can decree who's to be Magnus, or supreme ruler of Icenia.

Year's back, an emergent Faldiss invaded the Upper Mosaic. Col. James Castleton, a Native, enlisted the men of Easting. His army crossed the Cumberland River, engaged the Hexas Faldissi on the River Tone's east bank, and beat them back into Hœff. Unfortunately for Castleton he lost the subsequent fight for Hœff and also his life. Baron Manfred Royce of Faldiss killed him. To this day, this Royce lineage holds the rein of power over Faldiss and exerts significant influence over all of Icenia.

The notion that a given individual should be entitled to rule over others because he belongs to a royal household is absurd.

Crag Rat

I haven't written a word in days because I've had nothing worthwhile to say. I've been in low spirits too. The past is frequently on my mind, bringing me no joy, while little of it is worth remembering.

One day, as a crag-rat in Easting's militia, there was an event I'll take time to talk about. Several times I infiltrated Logan camps, watched and listened to the men singing and getting drunk. It seemed easy. Then one day I was surprised by a pikeman on duty. Luckily I was dressed in Logan buckskin, green jerkin, and flappy wool hat.

Assuming a Logan brogue, I cursed at the Pikeman. He laughed, slapped me upside the head, and told me to get lost. He thought I was a pederast's toy. Yes, some Logans are pedophiles, using boys when women aren't available. Usually the boys are paid for their services. It's a vile practice, unnatural. The Highland people are disgusted by it.

In physical characteristics Logans are not too dissimilar from the men of Highland. We share the same language and several customs as well. The critical difference between us is that the people of Highland know the value of freedom; Logans don't. That's one of the reasons why Meres Ma'tann employs Logan mercenaries.

I'll break away from the Logans and mention another significant group of people.

As the swallow flies south from St. Polycarp's belfry, you'll find Fay'dorn. Its central city is Mon'tre. Although Natives populate this country, few men from Highland visit it. Fay'dorn is a gynocentric society. Highland's men find that unacceptable.

I've not visited Fay'dorn, so I can't provide valid information about what goes there or what Fayeans think about, well, anything. A small cultural exchange center exists in Highland. It's located in Pitt's Caldera, and that's about the extent of Fayean presence in Highland. Fayeans don't like the people of Icenia and vise versa. Meres Ma'tann claims that Fay'dorn is uncompromising. Meanwhile, Fayeans say the same about the Faldissi, meaning the people of Faldiss. The Prince of Faldiss accuses Fayeans of wanting to carve out the Valley of the Rivers and Freeds Land from the Lower Mosaic. While Fayeans demand that the Hexas pull out of the Upper Mosaic. There's tension between them because Meres Ma'tann's plan is to expand Junot's border south to the Kol'bien River near Alturas.

In an Advisory Council meeting, Councilman Elliot Madigan said that Fayeans will not fight the Hexas because Highland is fighting for them.

How true!

Cairo Coalman

It's a hazy, windless afternoon in the Heights. I open the large window of my office, and the scent of rain is in the air. I hear the cadence count from the parade ground. The voice is that of Sergeant Mullins. He has temporarily assumed the duties of training instructor. Here's what he tells the recruits: "It's great to be a crackshot with the carbine, but it's just as important to know how to handle yourself with the long poniard and tomahawk. A carbine will do you no good in high RSE."

Sergeant Mullins molds civilians, men and women, into soldiers while Captain Montoya oversees the vetting of recruits. Felix has a sharp eye, sees the measure of a man straight away.

Young men and women from the Mosaics are flocking to Junipero. They come to join the "Grand Crusade."

We will not have proxies in our ranks. The process of vetting the right men and women is tasking and slow. Regardless, Junipero's army continues to grow!

Lt. Josephine Areu informs me, "Captain Coalman from DMO is in reception and would like a word. He has no appointment but says he is willing to wait."

Captain Cairo Coalman enters and stands at attention. "Thank you for seeing me, sir."

"Is your name, in fact, Cairo?" I asked with curiosity. It's an odd name for an Uplander, which obviously he is.

"Yes, sir, it is," he replies, and with a smile, he begins to explain how it came about. "You see, sir my mother wanted me named

Caylou. Father said absolutely not; he would have me named Kramer. After a back and forth tug of wills, or so my older sister told me, they agreed on Cairo. So I was named after the city that was once the Jewel of North Africa."

I like the man immediately. His jaw is firm. His eyes are clear, and he's plain spoken.

After he explains why he'd come, I go immediately to the point. "Captain, the Colonelcy opposed Junipero's decision to aid the Solanos, even though we are sworn enemies of the Hexas. Weaving and the others don't seem to understand that we can't continue to fight the Hexas individually. These are different times, captain. We're dealing with Meres Ma'tann, a Faldissi who knows strategy. He has a vast army, and he's aware that our disunion is our weakness. Once again we hear the rattle of musketry, the pounding of grenadier boots. Meres Ma'tann will come at us more robust and with more brutality than ever."

Cairo says, "Sir, Colonel Weaving understands he made a mistake. Your success in Terra Solana opened his eyes. After long deliberation, the Colonelcy agreed that the smart thing to do is to assist your effort. There's good reason to. Your forces are only six miles from Kirby Baja, so why not coordinate a defense? That's the essence of Weaving's dispatch."

Why not? I'm thinking, heck, I'd make a pact with the Devil himself if he helps me defeat the Hexas.

~~~

Several days after Cairo's visit, military units from Glenn Cross arrive in Junipero. My junior officers, lieutenants Bartlett, and Areu are awestruck.

"Sir, before you are some of DMO's best units," Cairo lets me know. He, Felix Montoya, and I stand together as troops pass in review. "Artillery batteries are under Chuck Raylock there." Cairo points at a lieutenant. "He's a graduate from the Citadel. Junipero is also acquiring an armored cavalry unit and a detachment of scouts. Best of all is the mounted infantry regiment. It's led by Captain Gioffre Guilfoyle." He turns and looks at Felix.

"Are you impressed, Captain Montoya?"

Felix, who is known for his economy of words, simply nods. I prompt him, "Well, go on. Let's hear your opinion."

At length, Felix says, "with Junipero's brigade, Kirby Baja's detachments and Solano volunteers, Junipero commands an army division. That's a larger force than Pico led when we fought in the Mesquite."

That's exactly right, as I recall. But would Junipero be able to use it to further its aims? I watch Cairo out of the corner of my eye. "As I recall Weaving's dispatch, it's DSO's plan to limit the deployment of these troops solely to Kirby Baja."

Cairo doesn't look my way; instead he continues to watch the troops passing in review.

"Yes, sir, that's correct," he replies after a moment. "However, the dispatch's orders don't specify the exact location or locations of deployment needed to shore up Kirby Baja, do they?"

I think he has a point, if a shaky one.

Hunters Lodge

It's the Ides of March, seven months since Baron Tallos Bay was driven from Terra Solana. It's on this day that Meres Ma'tann's offensive begins. Its first blow falls on Kirby Baja's salient known as Knob Noster, meaning "Our Hill," as you know. According to DSO intelligence, the assault on Knob Noster is the beginning of a full-scale offensive.

"Isn't officially spring," Cairo says to Lt. Areu. "You'd think the Crown Prince should've waited another week before launching his Spring Offensive."

Lt. Bartlett explains the need for haste: "Warm fronts are rushing from the western seaboard, pushing back the RSE Dampening. This weather front will prevail for two, three days at the very most. Regardless the positive energy will create a C-Front all the way to Mirren. Meres Ma'tann will capitalize on that."

The term C-Front implies low "Dampening." So far, we know this much. Hexas forces have forded the upper Cumberland and are heading straight for Easting.

Meanwhile, Logans are mustering near Hunters Lodge. Army Post Bellmore's commander in the Lodge is Major Pruska Spencer, a Citadel graduate, and she's a tough professional soldier. She'll hold the Lodge at all costs."

We lace our boots and reach for our weapons. Hours pass and we wait on the rocky hills overlooking Hunters Lodge. The Lodge, as it's commonly called, is Easting's heart.

Journal of Allen Brock

Waiting is almost unbearable. The men have been under arms for days. A soft drizzle impairs visibility, and we can't see beyond the lines of defense.

No matter the report from the meteorologist, I still feel a weight on my shoulders. It's a sure sign the Dampening hasn't dispelled as promised.

Major Spencer deploys two intersecting lines of defense. The mainline is arrayed across the north, while the other runs northwest from it. If Logans come straight at Hunters Lodge, they'll run into crossfire.

Gradually the warm breeze from the west drifts in. It dispels the rain, increasing my field of view. To the north I spot multiple flashes; the sound of thudding explosions follows in succession. Artillery!

The RSE is ebbing, and the explosive power of Belchers will increase. Soon, Hexas forward units begin to appear in the northwest. First come the sluggish maniples, armored vehicles with medium size Belchers on turrets.

Faldissi cannons are called Belchers because their recoil is reminiscent of a loud, prolonged burp.

The Hexas force is an overwhelming sight. Never before, to my recollection, have they fielded this much infantry. I shake with rage, but I'm resolved to fight no matter what. I instinctively know, though, that Pluska's Easters won't hold against this massive force. Fury wells inside me all the more. Highland's men are being killed unnecessarily. The Colonelcy hadn't imagined anything like this, so it falls on us to respond to that strategic shortsightedness.

Indeed, Weaving and his colleagues have insisted that the target is Kirby Baja. Granted, Hexas have always attacked there for good reasons, and so goes DMO's doctrine. Take Kirby Baja, Junipero Heights falls, Glenn Cross, and so on, like a row of dominoes ready to be thumbed.

Meres Ma'tann is ten times smarter than Weaving and the rest of the colonels of DMO. He knows the Colonelcy is fighting the old wars, and so he decides it's time for a drive all the way to Hastings, the manufacturing center of Highland, but not thorough Kirby Baja. No, he's going around it through the supposed impassable glacial roads of the northeast.

"Shuzzz-shpt, burrrrp, BOOM! Shuzzz-shpt, burrrrp. BOOM! BOOM! BOOM!"

The ground shakes; the noise is ear-splitting!

Belchers find the range, and the dreadful burp, burp, burping of Faldissi artillery intensifies. This tears gaps in the Pruska's northern lines and then rips them apart. Logan riders quickly rush through the breach. Hexas infantry follows. Under the onslaught, Pruska's first line of defense buckles.

A decisive battle is unfolding a scant two miles from us, and it doesn't appear to be going the way we figured.

"Let's get in there, shore them up," I shout.

"Impossible, sir. We can't help Major Spencer," Cairo yells over the noise. "We have to stick to the plan. We wait. Let the enemy think they have a clear road to Hastings. They've not detected us yet. When they reach Glacier Flats, we'll let our Mollies announce our presence. In the meantime, let's pray for clear skies and sunshine."

Our howitzers are referred to as Mollies. They aren't as accurate as Belchers, but they are powerful large-bore cannons, and in low SRE, they are deadly.

On the rippled plain, the troops from Bellmore are done for. Belcher fire blasts the two lines. Hexas infantry is outflanking the secondary line of defense. Grenadiers blast at the center, and down go Pruska Spencer and her fighting Easters.

I grind my teeth in frustration. Again we have to deal with the Logans. Those animals have cast their lot with the Hexas. They are in this not for a worthwhile cause but for the spoils. It's no longer a question of which group I detest most; I hate Hexas and Logans with equal intensity.

Thinking their Highland enemy is done for, the Logans hoop it up and race after Bellmore's soldiers. Ah, but not so fast, from rocky hilltops, our compound bows go into action.

In the Dampening of RSE, this time-proven weapon is useful. Arrows arc down on the Logan lancers and pikemen. Scores of riders are feathered and dismounted, but more come on. Logans are fearsome men.

Describe me by whichever pejorative you decide, but to me, Logans are on par with mindless savages. They know we are skilled fighters and better men, yet like unreasoning beasts, they continue to trek from Mirren to get killed.

The Hexas under the command of Entor Boski go all in. This decorated Entor of Maniples from far-flung Nomis-Nome is determined to become a hero at whatever cost to his men.

At long last Cairo gives the command. Our Mollies open fire, and canister rounds explode amid the Logans, blasting them. But the Hexas infantry continues its advance.

Heron's Terrapins, our light cavalry, and Guifoyle's heavies clash into Logans and Hexas infantry, stalling the advance. Sabers meet sabers. Men stab and slash at one another. More fire from Mollies explodes on the frozen flats of Hasting Glacier, hurling deadly shrapnel at the advancing enemy.

No matter, Boski sees that his maniples and infantry have the advantage. He orders his Cetron of Grenadiers to neutralize the artillery and sends in more infantry to bolster the grenadiers.

The primary armament of grenadiers is a multiple function launch-loader, which they call tubes. The individual grenadier will also carry either a shotpistol and, of course, a bandoleer for grenades. He also carries a short sword that can be attached to his launch-loader and used as a bayonet. I've never seen a bayonet charge by Hexas. In any event, Highland soldiers would mow them down if they try.

A Hexas grenadier is proud. This man is chosen for his strength and size; none of that matters to a Highland soldier. He can kill a big guy just as quickly as a smaller one.

Hexas grenadiers rush over the hills at us. Junipero's forces holding the higher ground make fair use of it. We've tiered our firing lines to provide another lethal crossfire, and so we kill more of our enemy.

Above us, Mollies continue their fire. Hexas grenadiers fall by the scores trying to reach those batteries. Hell has broken loose and spills across the hills and finds us.

We're in the middle of the fiercest fight I can remember. Hexas regulars rush up the gray hills toward us. Grenadiers are in front, and we fire point-blank into them. Grenadiers wear good body armor, and our shot-pistols and carbines can't stop them all. All the same, hundreds lay dead and wounded. Yet more Hexas run-up, and we kill those as well, but they kill our men too.

Numbers don't always swing the outcome of a battle, and this time the pendulum, which had been turning our enemy's way, swings ours. Still, we're beset from all sides, but we continue to hold, I don't know how long. During fighting like that, time is not perceived the same. I recall the noise, the explosions, the shouts of orders, and the screams. I hear all this long after it ceases, in particular the cries of the dying. Fighting is terrifying yet unaccountably exciting at the same time.

Aha! Finally it's here; it has appeared at last! From over my right shoulder, I see a flash of light. I feel the warm rays of the sun! The clouds part and the RSE is swept aside. Mollies begin to fire for effect, and then an unceasing clash of artillery thunders through the ice hills and into the flats. Molly batteries fire at will, hitting with precision. The Hexas are annihilated.

The after-battle report is brought to Cairo, and he reads it to us.

"Sad note, Maj. Pruska Spencer went down with half of her command. Montoya pulled Bartlett's company out from the low hills, but it's shot to pieces. The shape of Areu's company is no better. A grenade fragment hit Jo in the hand, a Purple Heart for her, I suppose. Regardless, the Hexas forces are hightailing it across the Cumberland. Raylock is rolling back his Mollies."

Cairo stops reading, looks up, and says, seeming surprised. "Heck, I guess this means we've won."

Hammering Matt

The Director of Military Operations, Colonel Matthew Weaving, is handed a battle report by his adjutant, Lt. Niles. It's an account of the fight to defend Hastings. Indeed, Meres Ma'tann's attack on Kirby Baja was a ruse!

Weaving reads: "Combined forces from DMO and Junipero under the dual command of Captain Coalman and Chief-of-Staff Allen Brock Benitez halted Meres Ma'tann's advance toward Hastings. This offensive by the Faldissi Prince was an intended stab at Highland's heart."

"A monk is now the Chief-of-Staff of Junipero." Weaving supposedly said, looking up and shaking his head. "Can the Colonelcy's cloak seem more threadbare, Niles?"

His adjutant presents an editorial piece from the *Highland Times Dispatch*, the home paper. "Sir, your skills as a military genius are being highlighted. Let me read this to you: 'Colonel, 'Hammering Matt' Weaving is proven to be a most skillful strategist. He feigns a defense of Knob Noster in Kirby Baja, then turns to attack the enemy in the right direction, Hunters Lodge. Colonel Weaving is a tactician without peers. As every colonel in the Directorate, every post commanding mayor, and field captain are aware, Hammering Matt is known not just for his doggedness, but also for his subtlety.'"

Weaving can't listen to any more of it. No matter what *The Times Dispatch* says, he has been made to look the fool by Allen Brock, Lysander's son! Every officer in the DSO knows it.

Living in his stupendous tower in Glenn Cross Citadel entertaining guests while being admired, Mathew Weaving, the top colonel in the DMO, had never imagined a military man smarter than he. Of course, he's wrong there. No matter, the Faldissi Prince had devised a brilliant plan. The Logans would attack Hunters Lodge as usual, and then under that cloak of confusion, his force would drive into Outer Hastings, take out Bellmore Army Post, and race to Inner Hastings. Had Meres Ma'tann's top officer, Entor Raoul Boski, succeeded, Highland would have been stripped from half of her capacity to produce weapons. This was a colossal blunder in strategy, and he owned it.

Here's a clip of a personal conversation between Weaving and his mistress that I'm privy to, and I quote: "Cora, the public thinks that it was my strategy that won the day. It's a hoax, but I must play along. I know the people responsible for the design of that victory."

No doubt you'd figured that Lt. Niles, adjutant to Col. Weaving, is a Junipero, and his alliance is not to the DMO but to Highland.

Yet no matter how significant a victory or whatever spin you give it, Junipero's losses in Glacier Flat were substantial. We spent munitions, military equipment, and more importantly, men. Men are not easily replaced.

In their retreat toward Mirren, Logans take reprisals on Northern Easting. Those vandals kill indiscriminately, making no distinction between soldiers and non-combatants, not even if that Easter from Hunters Lodge is a child. They murder, pillage, and burn. It's always like this in war. For every soldier that is killed, ten civilians suffer the same fate.

In his last Sunday sermon, Abbot Madigan said that a day will come, and this might not happen in our life when God will smite the Hexas and make them bite the dust. I was thinking then that the Logans should suffer the same fate.

New Directorate

I'm putting a gelding through a pace when I see Cairo coming my way. I halt to greet him.

"You've improved on your dressage since I last saw you on the saddle, sir," he points out with a wide grin.

I dismount and toss my troxle his way. He catches the helmet nimbly and examines it, then lobs back a remark. "My old lady bought me one of these when I learned to ride a bicycle."

"Rubbing salt on the wound, eh?" I reply.

Here is the story. On our way from Hunters Lodge, I am pitched headlong from the saddle, not sure why the horse decided to suddenly dig his hoofs. It's all inconsequential. I'm not hurt.

Today Cairo returns to Junipero, not as a captain but as a lieutenant. In a quick summation, Weaving demoted him for not following "standing orders." No good deed goes unpunished, as the saying goes. Regardless, Cairo is there, and I want to hear the latest from him.

"The DMO has a new plan in mind," he discloses.

Before I go into what he has to say, though, I have to delve into a bit of history. I know it's boring but bear with me. It has relevance.

Highland has fought the Hexas to control the River Tone and the Cumberland River since we've been at war. That's a long time, as you've heard. The story goes this way. Highland troops cross the Cumberland, drive west, and take the Banfield trans-lines in the Upper Mosaic. The Hexas cross the Tone and repel them. Then Highland's Wolverines Special Forces drive Hexas back across the River Tone and so forth. It was called the See-saw Campaigns, and it lasted years. Finally, a truce is brokered by the Mayoralty of Central Mosaic. The fighting is bad for business, the mayors declare. After all, the Upper Mosaic is a vital area for trade and commerce. It separates Highland from Upper Icenia. Goods from the Central and Lower Mosaics and Fay'dorn have to travel through it. Yet, like the low-bred legas, the Mayoralty never addressed the real issue, Hexas occupation of the Upper Mosaic.

As to the Mayoral Council, its task is to guide, coordinate, and assist in making decisions throughout the Mosaics' municipalities. The Mayoral Council has the power to quash local government decisions within the Mosaics. This council can censure public officials and can impeach, if need be, presiding mayors. The latter is seldom done since corrupt officials run the Mayoral Council.

Let me return to the original point. Highland's DCA, Directorate of Civic Affairs, signs the truce; Hexas Baronies do the same. The Seesaw Campaigns end. Incidentally, the Directorate of Civic Affairs is Highland's legislative branch of government. It prefers to set policy by consensus and is, for the most part, a useless institution. This is not just my opinion.

So it comes to pass that the mayors of the Mosaics agree to make the Banfield Way a neutral zone. The Hexas Chets, meaning people of Chetsí where the Banfield Way begins, don't like it, and frankly, neither do we in the Highland. Lest I forget, I'll mention that Highland doesn't have a permanent executive or president either. However, the DCA can appoint a president if the need arises. In that event, a colonel from the DMO would be that candidate.

The Colonelcy, whose members are from CMA (Citadel Military Academy) does not get involved in civil affairs. Its colonels are vintage or getting along in tenure, meaning they're old no matter how they phrase it. They've decided to give themselves quaint monikers. As you know, the privileged Matthew Weaving is referred to as "Hammering Matt." He is DMO's Chief-of-Staff. There's also Col. Bren Drummond, referred to as "Battering Bren." Not sure why this moniker was selected or bestowed. Bren hasn't battered his way into anything. His wife's maiden name, though, is Battering. She's from a very influential family, so maybe there's a connection.

DMO also has "Poker Face Pratt." That would be Col. Francisco Pratt, who is known for his skills at poker. While Col. Dashiell DeWitt is referred to as "Thundering Dash." Dash is not altogether right in the noggin.

According to the captains on his staff, Dashiell is a proponent of corporal punishment. In Thundering Dash's military, a soldier found to be AWOL would be shot. Under his direct command, officers and men must do half an hour of calisthenics three times daily, with no exception. DeWitt is also into the occult. He believes Atlantis will rise from Pacifica's bottom, and the ensuing Tsunamis will engulf all of Icenia. I'll round out this night's entry by describing the fifth man in the Colonelcy. He's James Oliver Tisdale, or "Tags Tisdale." He is so old that the current joke is that he died a while back and was mummified in an officer's uniform.

Col. Weaving and Col. DeWitt were contemporaries of my father. They made it possible for Bren Drummond, a less qualified officer, to be promoted over Lysander Benitez.

This was the most devastating day for my father. Weaving and DeWitt torpedoed his career. Dagne railed at my father, called him a failure. She only thought of herself. No woman in Highland's recorded history can compare to this unfeeling, vindictive viper that called herself my mother.

I add an excerpt from a personal conversation: "Naturally, I'm disappointed," father grumbles. "I won't deny it, Brock. But I'm also worried. The Directorate lacks insight. I fear that your generation will continue to fight a war we can win today. War is devastating, son. Societies can't flourish when their primary focus is war. I hold a share of the blame, too, for all that's happened."

I am troubled to see him in such low spirits. "How are you to blame, father?" I ask him.

He shrugs. "I should've been humbler, I suppose. Except I don't know how. In the end, though, it's about office politics."

He explained what transpired: "I constructed a plan for victory, but I didn't submit it to the Colonelcy because I knew it would be buried. So in front of the graduating cadets of the war college, I presented it. Weaving, my superior at the time, had an issue with it. I hadn't, according to him, cleared it through channels. In other words, he was miffed because it was not his plan. From then on, he made certain that my ideas, writings or thesis, neither writings nor thesis, would not be part of the academy's curricula."

"Father, why don't you keep a journal, write a paper or book on your ideas," I say. "Tell the people about your plans and about what goes on in the DMO."

I recall that he smiled and mussed my hair. "My good son," he said, "who would read them?"

I would, I thought then.

New Paradigm

Weaving wants another go at the old Banfield strategy, but with a few modifications. He'll draw troops from every military post in Highland. It's doubtful he'll get anywhere. Then that's my opinion.

My field officers, along with Elliot, Judge Wilkes, and I, are in conference. As host, Elliot pours us whiskey. It's a five-hundred-year-old Tennessee, according to him. Wilkes looks at him skeptically but adds nothing else to that look. The conversation begins with Cairo citing the strategic point of the plan. Everyone listens with great interest. I make no comment.

Elliot pours the vintage Tennessee grog into a stout whiskey glass and looks at me from under bushy eyebrows. "You don't think it's much of a plan, do you?"

"It's the same sow except that it's wearing lipstick and a pair of shades this time," I reply caustically.

"So, do you have a plan of your own, Brock?"

"It's not mine," I say.

I go into detail, and I explain Lysander's plan for victory. After I'm done, Elliot pours himself a third drink and passes the bottle. For more than a minute, a deep silence prevails. We drink and say nothing.

It's Judge Wilkes who finally breaks the silence with a– "It's a brilliant plan but…" The rest of his sentence hangs.

Elliot nods, understanding what Wilkes hasn't said. "This is a new paradigm in thinking," he declares.

Cairo looks from me to Elliot and then at Wilkes. "So if it's a brilliant plan, what's the issue?"

"Implementing it, you see, runs counter to the articles of confederation," says Wilkes.

"These articles are sort of a constitution, no?" Cairo says. "Why not amend the constitution then?"

"Good luck there," Wilkes replies. "The Directorate of Civic Affairs will not hear of it. To the point, though, Junipero can't act as an independent entity. Junipero can't sign treaties or form alliances."

"Should we be concerned with what the DCA has to say about this?" Elliot poses. "If Fay'dorn is willing to accept what Junipero offers, it's a done deal. And, well, it's a good deal too."

Surprised to hear this, Felix Montoya turns to Elliot. "What about the military directorate, uh, Weaving, and the rest?"

"What about them?" Elliot responds.

Felix continues to stare at the abbot, further confused. "But isn't one of the duties of the military to protect Highland's constitution? What is being proposed, Abbot Madigan, is in violation of the Articles of Confederation. Junipero, Glenn Cross, Kirby Baja, and the others are bound by them, no?"

Wilkes cuts in. "Um..." He begins filling his pipe with tobacco. "Um, uh, yes," he continues, then paused again. "Uh, what you say is correct, but only to a degree, captain. Highland is not a nation but a confederation. Junipero Heights and the other states enjoy a broad measure of self-governances. In Glenn Cross, where the broader government seats, the DCA, holds sway. Whether it can impose its power beyond Glenn Cross remains in question. But then why should the DCA or DMO be opposed to Junipero bringing an ally into the fight?"

"Still, we'll have to convince Fay'dorn that it's in her best interest to join the fight," Cairo put across. "That's no easy task."

"Quite right," Wilkes agrees. "Well simply have to find the right man for the job."

City by the Bay

Life laughs behind your back. You don't say the right thing when you ought to. Opportunities open, but you hesitate and fail to gain an advantage. You choose the wrong mate or the wrong profession. In the end, all you've done is make a fool of yourself. I am, if you've not already guessed, "the right man for the job." These are my thoughts as I travel to Mon'tre, Fay'dorn's capital.

~~~

A tall fellow wearing a wide-brim hat greets me at the station. His gray eyes peer, evaluating me for a moment before he offers a slight, stiff bow and bids me welcome to "Faye's City by the Bay."

"I am Bartolus," he says by way of introduction. From his dark cloak, he draws a packet and hands it over. It includes a dozen or so pages that I should read–his suggestion–also a folding map to help me navigate the city. All this is supposed to acquaint me with "Faye's" culture and local customs.

We drive in an open, motorized coach. My attention is drawn to the smell in the air. It doesn't take me long to realize this is what a large city, not a township smells like. Of course, I've been to large cities before, Aguijón was one, but the prevailing smell there came from the smoke of burning buildings and decaying bodies. I feel very little RSE too. I must have muttered that because Bartolus turns his head halfway in my direction and says, "The Rift Effect disperses most of the negative energy north of Alturas, ambassador."

Bartolus is an odd fellow. I don't know that I care for him. He has a high estimation of himself, or maybe he just considers me a Highland Trog, as a Hexas would. He's to escort me to Parador Posadas, where I'm to be lodged.

"Parador, eh?" I say aloud, finding this usage unusual for these parts.

I have to delve into a bit of geography here to clarify what I mean by "unusual." Between Fay'dorn and Terra Solana lies Freeds Land, thousands of square miles of unincorporated land, the Dunes of Deseret, and the vast Bajadero valley. It's a span of area larger than Lower Icenia. I also know from Felix that Solanos aren't enthusiastic about Fayeans. That's his delicate way of saying Solanos don't care for the "opinionated women" of Fay'dorn. But to the point, Solanos call a high-scale hotel a Parador, while an inn is referred to as posada.

Bartolus sends a glance over to me. "I believe the term used in the Mosaic is an inn," he says in answer to my remark.

"Thank you but I know what parador means. I also know what a posada is," I add. The tone in my words is devoid of anger, even though I am annoyed by the man's haughtiness.

The coach rolls into a porte cochere, and Bartolus announces, "We have arrived." He steps off, turns to the driver, and instructs his "Downer" to gather my luggage. I'll explain the term Downer later on. Parador Posadas was once a fortress. Now it's merely a luxury hotel. Brick columns support long spans of wide wooden beams. The courtyard and entryways are laid in hexagonal paving stones.

Meanwhile, Bartolus assails the concierge with a line of rapid-fire demands. His voice is low, and it carries, oddly, a nuance of threat.

The concierge is a young man, early to mid-twenties. He was going about his morning tasks before Bartolus' unwelcome presence changed his mood. So, he greets Bartolus with a nod and a level stare. "There is a reservation for the guest, Tekno Bartolus," he says, turning and smiling pleasantly at me.

"Welcome. Our best room is yours. You'll find a magnificent view from the west-side window."

"Satisfactory," Bartolus declares. "It seems we have no repeat of our past dealings, Concierge Dulaine. I am pleased to see your service has improved."

It is evident from the exchange that neither man cares much for the other. As Bartolus signs the registry, the concierge's attention is drawn towards me. No doubt he's not seen a "Highland Trog" before. However, I doubt if the term trog is used in Fay'dorn since Fayeans, like Highland people, are Natives.

"May the ambassador's stay in Mon'tre be a pleasant one and also productive." With that, Bartolus offers a cordial bow and departs without further comments.

Concierge Dulaine shows me to my suite. His name is Cágg. That's how it's written on his nametag, except that he pronounces it "Káché."

So Cágg or Káché talks endlessly, saying nothing. He violates my personal space, verging too close as he speaks. I don't know if I'll ever get used to his Fayean ways. I'll say this, though, "Káché," the concierge is accommodating. He explains things thoroughly, and he agrees with the suggestion from Bartolus. I should acquaint myself with the city, and he's eager to help in that endeavor if I wish.

Fayean Speak

Mon'tre, the City by the Bay, as its residents refer to it, is a fabulous place. Mind you, I've newly arrived, a first-time visitor with not a germ of an idea of what this place holds.

My first surprise, one of many that day, is the way Fayeans speak. It's peculiar to hear Cágg or Káché jabbering in odd-sounding vocabulary, but it's an eye-opener when everyone I hear around me is talking the same way.

Subtle pronunciations have crept into our mutual tongue. People from the Upland, and the broader Highland, have a different accent from those in the Mosaics, but Fayean English is different. I have decided to call it "Fayean Speak" and not Anlish as these people refer to it. Their form of English omits many expressions used in Highland. It also places accents on vowels and especially on words ending with an e or an o. Spoken are baffling terms. There were times when I heard a word that was utterly inappropriate in context. I understand what is said, but I've yet to figure how this remarkable change has come about in such a brief period. However, my mission in Mon'tre is not to speculate on its people's quirks or Fayean Speak but to persuade the Fayean government to become an ally. I have an idea of how I should go about it, and Elliot, Wilkes, and others have instructed me how to as well. But I'm not one who practices much. I say what comes to mind. However, given the importance of my mission, that might not further Highland's aims. I know I should self-edit, polish what I have to say and how I need to say it. The problem is, I find it impossible.

Journal of Allen Brock

The day following my arrival I rise early. The sun is just forming a golden crown over the east when I leave Parador Posadas. I make my way to one of Mon'tre's wide avenues. As I visit a place and then the next, I marvel at the abundance of the city. This is a wealthy place, nothing like Southaven, Allentown, or any Central Mosaic townships. Glenn Cross in the Upland comes close, and some of the avenues in Aguijón had a similar grace; that is until Tallos Bay reduced that city to a pile of rubble.

I buy lunch at a café and give the young waiter a generous tip. He went out of his way to be cordial, beamed with smiles, and made me feel welcomed. Indeed, the men I run into are friendly. They smile frequently and greet each other amiably. The women, however, act differently. Their manner gives the impression that they are disinterested in everything around them. They seem arrogant. Another disturbing quirk I notice or imagine is that in Mon'tre, from the stocks in stores, advertisements, and the news, all seemed tailored to women's interest. Keg, that's how I'll refer to Káché/Cágg Dulaine, tells me that women in Fay'dorn are referred to as Landers.

Because you see, the word "woman" relegates that gender to a sublevel. Though used in other parts, the term woman has been deleted from Fayean Anlish entirely.

In Mon'tre, the people are homogeneous. A large number of them are fair-haired. Oddly, the blondes outnumber the brunettes, and there are more redheads than would be expected given that recessive gene. In summary, I see little diversity in this place, no wavy-haired Piccolos, no Solanos, or a single Paisan from the Isles of Perdida, or Purdue as Fayeans and also Hexas call that archipelago. In fact, I saw only two Hexas femmes walking the avenues, two among hundreds. The men look healthy but are not muscular like those in the Highland or wiry-whip strong like Solanos. I find Fayean men unmanly, in fact. This is troubling. We men of Highland are rough, not dandies. Compared to the groomed lot in Mon'tre, we would be deemed unkempt because we bear scars from a lifetime of war.

On the third day, "Keg" informs me that a message awaits the Ambassador's attention, handing me a large envelope with embossed lettering atop, which reads: "The Offices of the Matriarch welcomes Ambassador Benitez."

The envelope's content doesn't say much either, other than the usual diplomatic spiel and that I would be contacted within twenty-four hours.

I decide to spend the day touring Mon'tre streets once again. It's my intent to study and learn the social behavior of Fayeans. As I've written in this journal, I was educated in the field of biology. Biologists, no matter their area of expertise, are trained to observe behavior.

From the look of it, Fayean males are active, always up and about at all hours. They're either pedaling on bicycles or, if in a rush, hop hand-in-hand with a partner unto a carriage.

These carriages are called barouches. They're fancy street vehicles, like the one I rode in with Bartolus. Barouches are primarily used by the well-to-do. A less elegant three-wheeled taxi is a more common way to travel the streets, avenues, and grand boulevards of Mon'tre.

I can't say yet where these pretty men rush in so high an emotional state and enthusiasm. I suspect, though, since their togs are always finely tailored, that they're headed to festivities.

The costumes Fayean men wear are garish and inappropriate, in my opinion. Their tunics are white or beige. The pants are crimson, fitted and smart with a tailored cut to amplify a "bulge" at the crotch.

Ruthian Faye

Two charming fellows receive me in Chambers. The first tells me that he'd never seen an "Uplander" in the flesh. The second one takes my hand and informs me, "I'm to escort you to the Matriarch's office."

For a moment, I think he's a girl until I noticed his Adam's apple. As he takes me up the long staircase leading up to the Upper Office, he remarks that I am ferociously handsome. I think of increasing the distance between us then, but I can't, not discreetly or without giving offense.

The Matriarch's last name, Faye, has no relationship to the country's nickname, which also happens to be Faye. It's one of those strange coincidences.

So, there I stand, in a magnificent office, studying its outlay. The interior design is tasteful, with padded furniture cut from leather, walls adorned with stylish prints. A silver sculpture of a female form stands beside one wall. On a separate wall stretches a frieze that seemed to have been stamped onto sheets of bronze. Its footing is decorated with calligraphy. It had grown a thick patina; no doubt this work of art had been there for some time. One scene alludes to a group of women on a hilltop overlooking a rugged, untamed wilderness. I can't begin to imagine the meaning, though. I know that's in opposition because women prefer the indoors, not the wilderness, where danger lurks.

Ruthian Faye's face is pleasant looking. She's not tall of stature, but neither is she short. Like nearly every other woman in Mon'tre, she's a blonde. Her eyes are remarkable. I'm not sure if the purple–

blue effect of her eyes is natural or the result of eye lenses, not that it matters. However, her eyes show no warmth towards me.

"Welcome to Mon'tre, ambassador," she says.

"Thank you for seeing me on such short notice, Matriarch."

She nods, and I'm made comfortable. The formalities now behind us, I begin to explain the reason for my visit.

"Ah, yes, I was told that your proposal would benefit Fay'dorn," she states haughtily.

I shake my head decidedly. "No, I'm here to convince the Matriarch that an alliance between Fay'dorn and Junipero Heights will benefit both parties."

"I see," she says politely this time.

After I'm done, she tells me, "Hexas have a powerful army, Ambassador Benitez. Fortunately for your people, they have the uplands and mountains to fight behind. Fay'dorn, however, has only the green hills of Alturas to bulwark an attack." She halts, offers a vague smile. "Furthermore, I don't consider our neighbor to the north, Hexas Junot hostile to Faye."

"With due respect, Matriarch, I don't see why you shouldn't." I was careful not to say she was wrong. "The Hexas, under Meres Ma'tann, are more of a threat to Native cultures than ever."

Unlike a diplomat, I don't mince words; instead, I go straight to the point. "Matriarch, the people of Highland and Fay'dorn have a common enemy. It's that simple. Hexas are strong, granted. They are calculating, enterprising, and knowledgeable. They have become a threat because we have allowed it. There is no cohesion, no union among the Natives, and Hexas have capitalized on that fact."

She leans forward, tells me, "Alliances create problems of their own, ambassador."

"What if Meres Ma'tann decides to cross the Kol'bien and annex Alturas as he did to the Upper Mosaic?" I lob back. "What will Fay'dorn do?"

"Meres Ma'tann would not dare," Ruthian Faye declares. "Besides, the Prince has shown us no aggression in the past. Why should he do so now?" She pauses, searches my face for a second. "Do you know for a fact that this is Meres Ma'tann's plan?"

I smile, but without guile. "The Prince of Faldiss hasn't talked to me about it but that's what I would do if I were in his position. Fay'dorn wants to expand to the north and east peacefully. Meres Ma'tann intends to expand into the same areas through force. Fay'dorn will oppose him if he invades Central Mosaic. So, in his place, I would launch a preemptive strike from Junot, take the Seaward Seaton coastal plain, cross the Kol'bien, and occupy Alturas. Having done that, I've essentially bottled up Fay'dorn into the southern bank of the Bajadero. Taking the Seaton coastal plain gains him Freedom Corridor and cuts off the Central Mosaic from its only access to the sea."

I give a shrug. It's a common-sense strategy to me, except maybe Ruthian Faye doesn't see it, or does she? She sits back and falls silent. Could it be that the undeniable fact that Fay'dorn is vulnerable is sinking in?

At this moment, though, I am about to call my mission to Mon'tre a dud. My argument stands on solid ground, but what did it matter? Countries won't go to war when they should but will fight when they shouldn't.

At length, Ruthian Faye speaks her mind. "Faye has an army, and it's a strong one. Faye needs no allies. Her cadres of Landers and fadettes will protect her integrity. Furthermore, Ambassador Benitez," she adds with what I see is smugness. "You, in fact, are not representing the Directorate of Military Operations of the Highland, but Junipero Heights."

She just lobbed pie to my face, eh? Well, then it is time to return the courtesy and hurl a cream tart of my own.

"Wasn't the Colonelcy of the DMO who sent troops to Aguijón," I say firmly. "Wasn't Colonel Weaving who sent Hexas forces packing from Hunters Lodge but Juniperos and Solanos. When the Matriarch dismisses Junipero Heights' efforts and her sacrifices, don't let her forget that if Baron Tallos Bay had met with success in Terra Solana, Fay'dorn would now be facing a Hexas threat from the east."

Again I say, I appreciate the time she'd taken to see me despite her busy schedule. Then I walk out since I had nothing more to add. I stroll through Mon'tre's main boulevard for a time, thinking I might find something different or new. I don't, so I head to Parador Posadas to pack my one bag.

"Heard through the Grapevine"

In the morning, I enter the Parador's lobby, and immediately Keg hauls me by the arm and takes me aside. He's breaming with excitement.

"The news is fantastic, ambassador, absolutely!" he gushes. But I'm used to his ways.

"Your boldness is the talk of the streets, ambassador. Rods are hurling their studded collars at Landers." He halts, seeing the befuddlement on my face. "Uh, that's a saying," he explains. "A show of defiance."

"Ah, I understand," I say, realizing the intended meaning. "Um, Keg, have you called for a barouche, by the way? I'm leaving today, left my notice in the reception counter."

Keg finally grabs hold and looks at me awkwardly. "The ambassador just called me Keg, not Káché," he says. He repeats the name, pronouncing it the way I did. "By my hairless armpits," he declares, laughing. "I like the ambassador's twist of accent. 'Keg' has bravura, vigor. I will be called Keg. Yes!"

"Settle down," I say before he goes further into another emotional fit. "Tell me what you're trying to say in Highland English so I can understand."

Keg grabs hold if slow in coming. "In Mon'tre it's about the 'know', what you know or don't know. Your reputation depends on it. That's why it's wise to keep an ear close to the grape vine, so to speak. Everyone is talking about your meeting with Ruthian Faye. Mon'tre's continues. "Mon'tre's *Daily Expositor,* that's one of the media outlets here, led with this headline: 'Highland's Ambassador minces no words. He tells Fay'dorn's Matriarch that if Faye does not fight the Hexas alongside the Lofty Highlands today, she will have to fight the Hexas alone tomorrow.'"

He draws a deep breath then continues. "Ambassador Benitez, people are saying you are what Faye needs, a splash of cold water on her plastic face. Fayeans deny, although they know that Meres Ma'tann is a villain intent on doing harm. Fay'dorn is a small nation with a tiny military. Your presence in Mon'tre tells the people of Fay'dorn that they have stalwart Uplanders on their side should Meres Ma'tann try to move against them.

"Keg, the Matriarch has dismissed me. She'll hear no further words."

"No, no, no!" Keg shouts excitedly. "Don't you see? The Landseer will not have it. You are to stay. Ruthian Faye will have to listen to the rest of what you must say."

~~~

Keg is proven right. The next day a young fellow is waiting for me in Posadas' lobby. He goggles at me in wonder, as though I'm a strange sight like a giant meteor just crashed into the Parador's swimming pool. Ah, but I am used to looks of awe. He is there to escort me to the office of the Matriarch.

When I meet Ruthian Faye a second time, she seems less confident. She fidgets and fusses over some of the items on her desk; the penholder, a brass timepiece, and notepad are shifted and moved around. When done with this, she looks at me, and the corners of her lips dip slightly. I construed that as a frown. She isn't happy to see me.

"First, let me say that this office disclaims the allegations in the *Daily Expositor* that Fay'dorn's participation in any direct or covert action during the conflict in Terra Solana."

That is all rubbish. I know that factions in Fay'dorn had, in fact, helped the Solanos with arms and supplies.

"Franx is not our friend," Ruthian Faye stresses, lifting her eyebrows and seeming to look down her nose at me. "Pico, as Franx prefers to be called, is a criminal."

Fayeans and Highland people are Natives, but they can't be further in their way of speaking, in ideology, or mannerisms. I had to correct her. "I beg to differ, Matriarch. I know François Franx very well. He's a man of honor."

"Allow me to explain my point," she says. Pico Franx and his supporters seized power in Guahataki. They overthrew the elected head of state, and now rule Terra Solana through a military junta. We know about Pico's ambition, and especially about his antipathy toward Faye."

Her point is groundless, and I tell her so. Am I being crass? Possibly. But I figure since my mission is a wash, I'll call things as I see them. "Are Pico Franx's designs worse than those of Meres Ma'tann's, Matriarch? Pico only wants Fay'dorn to stay out of Terra Solana. On the other hand, Meres Ma'tann wants far more from Fay'dorn."

She lets that stand and goes on to explain the reason why she called for me a second time.

"I reviewed our meeting, ambassador. At first, I thought, well, Faye shouldn't be entering into an alliance. She needs to be free to find her destiny without encumbrance."

How meaningful is that? I think. Say, for example, you were drowning, and a person tossed a line your way; would that be an encumbrance on you? Indeed, Fay'dorn doesn't stand a chance against Meres Ma'tann's army. Even their weakest Barony can knock Faye's front teeth with not too much trouble.

I'm instinctual, and I feel what people think of me when we first meet. Ruthian Faye believes she is superior to me.

She blathers on. "My advisors, however, say that we should examine your ideas further."

Oh, is that so? Well, I am not going to let her slip out so quickly. If she thinks herself a cut above my people, or me I will disabuse her of such a notion. I ask her point-blank, "What about you, Matriarch? What's your opinion? That's the only one I'm interested in hearing."

She remains haughty. "Fayeans are unique people, ambassador. We have a vision; a great destiny lies ahead of us."

Oho! I'm not putting up with any more tripe. "Matriarch, I'm through listening to nonsense about the exclusivity of certain Natives. There's no difference between us. My eyes are as blue as yours, and when I'm cut, my blood flows red just like yours. When a Hexas lashes me, I feel the sting just as you would. I hate my enemy, Ruthian Faye, and I will do anything I must to break him over my knee. I will shred every vestige of him from the Earth. Our Highland spirit will not be tamed or broken by Hexas aggression. I came to Mon'tre to determine if Fayeans would join us in the fight against a mutual enemy. I presented my argument, explained my reasoning. These are dangerous times, Matriarch. We can't afford to be idealists."

Drawing back, she says, "I meant no insult, ambassador. The fact is that Fayeans admire the unbreakable spirit of Highland's people. They are heartened by it, in fact, particularly now because of your visit."

I think this woman seems to be speaking from both sides of her mouth. Her hand goes to her console, and she keys for a half second. What's now? I wonder.

When her hand comes up, the twin doors behind her desk slide open. A young woman enters the office.

"May I present my assistant, Ambassador Benitez?" Ruthian Faye says, "This is Lilit Oberon."

The first thought that enters my mind is that Lilit looks anything but Fayean. Yes, I know, I've been in Mon'tre only a few days, yet I hadn't expected Fayeans to look like her. Lilit's looks are different from those of the people I've seen in the city's streets.

I present my hand somewhat hesitantly because I've been told my hands are rough. I greet her. "Please to meet you, Lander."

Lilit takes my hand in both of hers and shakes it firmly. "The pleasure is mine, ambassador. I've always wanted to meet someone from the Highland. To my good fortune, I now meet one who is also famous."

"Famous?" I had to laugh. "Lander Oberon, I lay no claim to fame," I say, meaning it.

"Ambassador Benitez, please call me Lilit."

Sunrise Over the Bay

From the balcony of my suite, I gaze at a fantastic view. To the east are terraced vineyards. This scene stretches as far as the eye can see. To the west lies the bay. The fleecy clouds above it disband under a brisk wind while the rising sun behind me touches off golden tints over the blue water. The "City by the Bay" is being "crowned" at the moment.

I slept well, arose early, and I feel energized. I am to meet Lilit, but it will be later this morning, so I'm in no hurry to groom myself. Nonetheless, I should look presentable, no?

Seeing myself in the mirror, I know that I don't fit in Mon'tre. I have a large head. The bridge of my nose is slightly off center, and also, I've been told, I have a crooked smile on account my teeth are large. In other words, I know I'm no dandy.

In the dining area, Keg sees me and hurries my way. He looks me up and down. I figure it is his reaction to the way I am dressed. That is part of it, I'm sure, but instead, he begins to fume about the newly arrived guests.

"The Northern Fayean trash has invaded Posadas," he complains. "They're like locusts, ravenous, ready to consume every scrap of food that is placed before them. They demand nonstop service, service, more service! They've been attracted here like moths to firelight and because of your visit, ambassador."

"What do I have to do with any of it?" I ask, genuinely surprised.

"Everything!" he replies in turn. "You are the big story–the Uplander from the lofty hills of Junipero who gave Tallos Bay a drubbing. Everyone has come here to see the Matriarch eat crow, so to speak. Ruthian Faye's popularity is not as widespread as she supposes."

Later that day I find myself strolling the streets of Mon'tre with Lilit at my side. As I've mentioned, she's unlike other Fayeans. Although she's fair, her hair is almost jet-black, and her eyes are amazing. They're as dark as chalcedony. She's not stunning, but her looks aren't plain either. There's elegance in her manner, and she has a warm smile. Her laughter is contagious, makes you want to laugh along with her. I wish I could laugh the same way, openly and without reservation.

"If I may be so bold to suggest, Ambassador Benitez might think how best to blend in," she adds tactfully. "Then he can walk the streets free from notice. Fayeans like to gawk."

I understand now why Keg looked at me the way he did at breakfast. Obviously, I look gauche. My attire is not in fashion. I look tacky, graceless, and out of sync.

"Unfortunately, Lilit, I only have an Upland wardrobe," I explains.

"I can help Ambassador Benitez in finding a new ensemble," she says. Her eyes sparkle then. "Would my assistance be acceptable?"

I am hesitant. "Uh, well." Knowing not what else to say, I shrug. "I suppose that would be all right," I say finally.

"Oh, it's no trouble at all," she assures me. "I find shopping immensely rewarding. It will be interesting finding just the right clothes to smooth out the ambassador's Stiff Rod appearance."

By the Blood Stones! What the devil could she mean? I had to ask. "What is a stiff rod?"

Seeing my puzzlement, she realizes her faux pas. "How unthinking of me. The term is a vulgar one. Do forgive me. I should have phrased it differently."

She flashes a charming smile again, but I see by her look that she rather dismisses the matter.

I press the issue. "Tell me what it means, regardless. I'm in Mon'tre to learn stuff like that."

She's blushing by then. "It's a term applied to a dull person, particularly a male."

I laugh heartily. "Heck, Lilit," I say to her, still laughing, "I've been called worst things."

My laughter dispels her embarrassment, and her laugher blends into mine. Needless to say, Fayean speech has more than its share of double-entendres, and whether intended or not, a stiff rod conjures multiple interpretations in my mind.

In the Uplands, we have fine mercantile outlets, but they pale by comparison to what I see in Mon'tre. Maybe it's because the boutiques, chi-chi retailers mainly cater to the upper crust of Mon'tre. Nonetheless, they are replete with everything one might fancy. The restaurants and bars are a cut above those in Central Mosaic, being more stylish and directed to a sophisticated clientele. The word chic comes to mind.

I am made aware again why Fay'dorn is free to spend vast amounts of wealth on the frivolous. Elliot said it once. They don't have to maintain a strong military. The people of Highland are doing the fighting for them.

Only the Best for Faye

Lilit and I continue to explore marvelous places in the City by the Bay. I feel ridiculous, dressed the way I am. My trousers are too tight around my crotch and buttocks if loose around my legs and thighs. My belt is wide, studded, and maroon in color. It has a silver buckle. The belt matches my shoes and their buckles, yes, shoes with buckles match my belt. I wear a loose-fitting shirt, off-white in color with a stiff collar and tight cuffs around my large wrists. I have to unbutton them. My shirt has a puffy placket, like some of those worn by a stage poet. Oh, and I refused to put on a red ascot and epaulets that came along with the ensemble. I will not look like the Hurdy Gurdy Man's monkey.

Lilit tells me I looked absolutely stunning. Naturally she's being sociable again because, I assure you, I looked like a clown. If anyone from Junipero sees me dressed this way, I don't know where I would hide my face.

As we walk along, Lilit confides that she has to put up with her co-workers' petulance. I don't know why she's telling me this; maybe it's just small talk, a way to pass the time.

"They complain if they have to run their personal errands. After all, shouldn't someone be doing that for them? They object to having to pay so much in utilities and rent since it's not subsidized. They feel they are not paid enough. They grumble because they have no domestics to clean their apartments or personal chauffeur to drive them around. They are convinced they live the life of serfs."

It's somewhat amusing hearing her side of things. Ah, but Lilit has many more issues to air.

"In my position, I'm called to deal with public affairs. There are times when I have to meet with Sennists Sacerdotes. These are the people responsible for all the public disobendience in the streets. Sennists are a headache, a big problem for Faye."

I see then a mite of anger flaring in her eyes as she tells me all this.

"The last citywide demonstration was in reply to our supposed unfair labor laws. Ambassador, the fact is that Fay'dorn compels no Downer to do a job they don't want. Yet Sennists don't see it that way. They claim that Faye treats Downers as through second-class citizens. They demand legislation against a situation that, frankly, doesn't exist. To hear Sennists spout nonsense about class distinction is unbrearable at times: 'Down Folk should not perform this or that other demeaning task. Downer Folks aren't peon for privileged Landers to exploit.' and so on and nauseam."

Downers in Fay'dorn–I meant to explain this meaning previously–are people of the Lower Class, laborers, drivers, farmhands, and such. At any rate, what Lilit was describing sounded like a labor situation wrapped around a social issue. Were Sennists political activists, I wondered. I didn't pursue the matter, actually, focused as I was on her. Throughout the day, she was gradually drawing physically closer to me. There was an instant while we browsed the boutique that her breasts brush against my shoulder. She smiled and offered what I think was an apology. In retrospect, I think she did this on purpose.

Just then, a bevy of splendid-looking girls in glad rags strolls up the aisle. These teens chitchat with each other in a loud yet comfortable manner. I hear a few of them use familiar idioms. Others in their entourage, which I see are mature females in uniform, immediately correct them for speaking this way.

Noticing my frown, Lilit says, "Those are Purple Whips there," pointing to the older females. "A Purple Whip's task is to turn recruits from the Mosaics into Fayeans."

Confounded once again, I turned to her and say, "I'm not following what you mean."

"Faye recruits young women from all the Mosaics," she explains. "We select the best females and indoctrinate them to the way of Faye. Only then will they become fadettes."

Although I have more to add, I have to end my entry at this point. I have little time to devote to my journal while here. Late this afternoon Lilit handed me a ream of printed pages in a binder. It's a compilation of what Fay'dorn is about, what in fact the country wants to accomplish. It's a "must-read," according to her. I read parts of it but find it an impossible task. Other things concentrate my mind more forcefully tonight: Lilit's wonderful scent, the sound of her voice, and the flashing of her dark eyes.

Of Sennists & Rods

It seemed I had only dozed off when the alarm clock startles me to wakefulness. Doesn't matter, I tell myself, so I lie in bed for half an hour longer. I have no appointments, and so there I lie thinking of, you guessed it... Lilit.

Going about my morning routine, showering and grooming, I decide to eat breakfast in an outdoor café. It's then that Keg, my snooty pal, intercepts me before making my way out.

"How does this morning find Highland's ambassador?"

"Not as refreshed as I hoped," I say, speaking the truth. "Sleep was hard to find."

Keg is up earlier than usual, and I wonder why. "I thought your management chaps slept in on weekends."

He gave a short laugh. "Chap? That's an old term for males ambassador. In Fay'dorn, males are referred to as Rods. You have Lower Rods and Middling Rods, and then, well, there are Prime Rods."

"As always, Keg, you leave me baffled," I admit. "What are Prime Rods exactly?"

"That, my noted ambassador is the top cut," he declares with significance. Then he turns a narrow-eyed glance of suspicion across the lobby. Keg has that habit, I've noted.

He explains the reasons for his feelings. "Downers would be swabbing the works everywhere, in domestics, on the grounds, and in the kitchen if they don't see me doing the rounds. The cooks could care less if breakfast for the guest tastes like frakk. Downers are all malingerers, pilferers, and liars too. If the gambling machines in Posadas' Casino weren't bolted down, they'd steal them."

"There's a saying in Mon'tre: Give a Downer fifty doubloons worth of credit, and he'll go Downer Rich. He'll get drunk every day. He'll troll Downer Downs for a dock-side tunny, if you follow my meaning. By the end of the day, he makes his way to a casino and blows whatever remains in his pocket. Meanwhile, the roof over his hovel leaks, the plumbing needs repairs, and his two children, if he's been permitted to have any, could do with a new set of clothes. Ambassador, Downers are congenital idiots. They're a waste of DNA, and that's the reason why they need a permit to propagate. There's an element in our society; in all societies, I think that no matter how much effort is brought to bear to raise them from the dregs, it will not work."

"I understand that the–See–Nitz–Sacerdotes," I give the term the same pronunciation Lilit does, "champion them."

Keg offers me a sad smile. "Ambassador, you must be educated to the Fayean way. Sennists are not part of a religious order, although it may appear so. Sennists don't hold to a crazy doctrine of an afterlife. They are philosophers. Hence, they explain the reasons why Downers commit so much crime and are more prone to violence. Sennists say that for a society to have an upper class, a lower class must be created as its underpinning."

How interesting, I think. So I ask, "Can you tell me more about these Sacerdotes?"

"I can speak volumes about them," Keg professes. "First of all, Landers can't stand their sight. Sennists are masters of the Mentalics, which I have no way of explaining. Landers know that Sennists are not afraid of them, say like Rods are. Sennists can be spooky too. I saw one stop a crazed Downer from committing murder. It was a strange scene. The Downer thug was going to kill his Downer mate for cheating on him. It only took two words from the Sennist Sacerdote- 'Do not!' The Downer drops his knife and falls to his knees, begins to sob. The Sennist places his hand on the Downer's head and tells him to forgive the female, return home and be faithfull."

"When a Sennist's hand touches you, 'he connects,' becomes instantly aware of your nature, hence the spooky part of Mentalics.

He knows the source of your anger, the sum of your fears, and the rest of the baggage. He feels the extent of your lust and envy, your greed, and, well, the sack full of deadly sins you tote along. Even though Landers aren't religious, they go out of their way to avoid Sennists. Sennists are like the carriers of the plague to them."

"Why exactly?" I ask.

He looks at me with a kind smile this time, as though I was a child asking if Old St. Nick actually exists. "Ambassador, Sennists feel what we Rods know, that Landers are creatures without a heart. We Rods hate them, but Sennists pity them. They pray for the day Landers will find their souls."

Keg is good-looking by the measure in this land. He has blond hair and blue-green eyes. His facial features are pleasant, and his physique, though not muscular, has potential. He sports an Haute Style haircut. This is a term I learned from Lilit. Generally, that's a rectangular cut, neat and tight on the sides. His clothes are spiffy. He wears a light gray tunic with a banded collar, black pleated slacks, and leather loafers.

My plan to breakfast elsewhere is put on hold because Keg has ensnared me. The man's ability to do this is uncanny. I get him to talk about himself. At first, he's hesitant, then he lets it out.

"No Lander has found me," he tells me. "Despite that, I'm a happy Rod. I'm free, but a Rod without a collar usually ends up in Downer Downs, cassé."

That means broke, living in a rundown, flea-beatin flat. "So, you don't fear ending the same, flat-out broke?" I ask.

He shrugs and admits that sometimes he feel that's a possibility.

I empty my cup of tea. "Keg." I begin, "do you know how to fight?"

"I've never been in a fistfight," he admits. "I practice pugilist moves in the gym, though."

"I'm talking about war, Keg. Have you fired a shot at an enemy?"

"No, but even if Faye enters a war, I doubt they'd employ me, being a Rod and all."

Point made, I figured, since Rods are conditioned to be peaceful. "Keg, have you ever used a weapon?"

He laughs. "Why would I ever own one? Weapons aren't permitted, not in the hands of the average citizen."

"If you had one, would you kill a rabbit, say, maybe a deer?"

Keg's eyes widen. He's shocked by the suggestion. "Absolutely not," he sputters.

I cradle my hands. "Keg," I say carefully, "have you ever thought what you might do if you had to kill someone?"

"Faye's tunny, of course not!" He utters, then apologizes for his profanity.

Tunny is a word variant of a disparaging nature for either Downer female or female genitalia.

"No need to apologize, Keg. Highland men are fond of cussing. So, what if a man is trying to kill you, Keg?"

I provide him with a scenario. "The enemy is coming at you with a Logan lance, intent on skewering you, taking your life. You have a loaded shot pistol. You lift it. Your hand trembles, but you'll have to pull the trigger and put a hole in his chest before he does the same to you. Can you pull that trigger, Keg?"

I watch as he rubs his clean-shaven chin for a second or two, and then I hear him mutter an, "Umm." He thinks for a moment longer, then says, "I'm not sure, ambassador. I don't know what I would do until I find myself in that situation."

Fair enough answer, no?

Hook Line & Sinker

I can't shake off my obsession. Lilit captivates me. I fight this feeling to no avail. As you might figure, I'm in a down mood now. Here I am, in a strange country, having a good time while my people are in hardship, grinding away in the cold, rocky hills in the Uplands, fighting the Hexas. Meanwhile, the Fayeans have no stomach for the fight.

When Lilit and I meet for dinner later that day, the first words out of my mouth, other than a greeting, are, "Why's the matriarch delaying a decision? First, she says no to an alliance; a day later, she calls me back and informs me her advisors have told her to reconsider my proposal."

Lilit's look shows her bewilderment. "I don't know what's in the matriarch's mind, ambassador."

"I'm not trying to be rude, Lilit," I say, "But I feel like I'm on a treadmill, walking but getting nowhere."

Her eyes search mine for a moment. I am sure she understands my point, yet she's not willing to share what she knows. "So, Lilit, how long do you suppose the process takes? Is it two days, four days, a week?"

"I have never been called to serve at a top-level meeting," she says. "The ambassador must understand that the political process in Mon'tre grinds slowly. A decision like this—"

I interject before she can finish. "I want you to call me Brock. You've known me long enough, so let's drop the formalities."

She smiles beautifully. "Brock, please be patient. Give the matriarch a few more days."

Her words sound sincere, but my suspicions are hard to brush aside. I'm not suggesting she's leading me on either. I just don't know.

Here's what I think I know, though. Lilit was made my liaison for specific reasons. I've noted that she's as keen as a Highland dirk. Also, she let out very little about the nature of her function as "Assistant to the Matriarch."

I tell myself that maybe one day it'll be Lilit traveling to a foreign land to rally its people against the enemy stalking the countryside. They'll let her know they're aware of the danger, and they worry. They wring their hands and dish out platitudes. After a while, she realizes they're leading her on. They'd prefer for someone else to do the fighting, make the sacrifices.

Would these people be considered cowards? Possibly, or it could be they lost the will to fight. Lilit would then come to the same conclusion I just have—they won't make good allies. Yet for Lysander's plan of victory to work, a second front has to be created.

Pico Franx and his Solanos aren't strong enough. Terra Solana is devastated. Highland has faced the brunt of Hexas arms virtually alone. When Abo Hassa was around, his hassims posed a problem for Junot and Chetsí, so the Hexas had to keep an eye on him. They devoted two of their best legions to that. This eased some pressure away from Highland. Now Abo Hassa is gone.

At length, Lilit says, "Matriarch Ruthian Faye takes your mission seriously, Brock. I can tell you what I know, which by the way, is very little. The people of Fay'dorn want closer ties with Highland. The matriarch's advisors tell her that Faye should, at the very least, post a military attaché, preferably in Glenn Cross. You come here, not from Glenn Cross, but from Junipero Heights, which the members of the Sororan regard subordinate to the Directorate of Military Operations in Glenn Cross."

"Sororan?" I say, not having heard the term before.

"It's the legislative body of Fay'dorn, much like Highland's Directorate of Civic Affairs," she explains.

I grow interested, and so next I say, "Does the Sororan have veto power over the Matriarch?"

Her reply sweeps all other questions aside.

"Why don't we spend the night together, Brock? I'll hear your concerns, and you can lend an ear to mine."

Timeless Whisper from Bon'aire

The morning light filters into the room to find Lilit and me in each other arms. It's terrific when you awake next to a woman. The soothing warmth of her body, scent, and the feel of her skin is ecstasy. So, we lie together, enjoying this moment.

Lilit turns her eyes to me. They sparkle as she smiles. "You're still thinking I look different from most Fayeans, aren't you?"

She is right again. Why isn't she like so many of the blonde Landers walking the streets of Mon'tre?

"Brock, there is a reason why I'm different," she hints.

"Not just in looks but also in name," I point out.

She laughs. "That too is the case. The shade of my hair and my eye color are qualities passed to me by my father. My looks make a contrast here, in the city. Yet, not all Fayeans are cast from the same mold. My first ancestor on the family record, which goes back hundreds of years, is Hernando Diaz Obregon. He was a gaucho-but also a scion of worth and value. Hernando was born in the southern continent, a place called Patagonia. He named his estate Bon'aire. That's the place where he established a dynasty.

"The Obregons were explorers, driven by a lust for adventure. That's why I'm here today. Hernando's sons traveled far and wide. I'm told also that I am a throwback. I have a remarkable resemblance to Hernando Obregon Nevado. His hair was black as the night, as were his eyes."

She springs from the bed, and I marvel at her body. Lilit is not slim, but she isn't hefty either, not by far. Her body is subtly muscular but with outstanding feminine lines.

"The name Obregon was dropped when Hernando's descendants settled in the northern continent," she explains. "Obregon became Oberon. Except that the family didn't entirely break from their past or their traditions. My extended family still hears faint whispers from Bon'aire. That's why I was named Lilit de la Nevada."

A Prince in Court

No doubt Meres Ma'tann's agents in Mon'tre have made him aware of Junipero's envoy to Fay'dorn. Hexas have spies everywhere, and Fay'dorn is no exception.

Before I arrived in Mon'tre, I read an interesting account from one of Highland's agents. She's our mole in the Hexas Court. Although she works in the kitchen supposedly as a proxy, she was called to waitress duty. This is one of her accounts that day: "The Prince hosts his guests amid splendor. Ostensible wealth is all around. Gilded artworks encrusted with jewels, ancestral statues carved from semiprecious stones stand at every entrance. There's a massive frieze of a satyr pursuing maidens, and it's the point of attraction for men. There's filigree metalwork skirting the foot of every wall."

That's to say Meres Ma'tann's Court is princely in every way. She goes on with her report: "As in every 'Princely Court,' this one has a jester. This jester wears neither harlequin's costume nor a coxcomb hat. Maestro is his name, and he dresses in a green-gray cape when in Court. His manner is collected, doesn't seem to care about much. He offends everyone, including Meres Ma'tann. This doesn't bother the Prince. In fact, Meres Ma'tann encourages it.

Maestro is a gadfly, and strangely, a favorite of Court. Young Master Edourd Ností is a court's favorite also. Apart from being a mass murderer, Master Ností has other talents. He's an excellent orator, and he vies with Maestro for the attention of the Prince. Since Meres Ma'tann enjoys poetry, Eduord Ností delivers poetic lines expertly."

And wouldn't it be just so? Ah, but I digress. I'll narrate more of what our brave spy reports. Here's a snippet of Maestro speaking to Meres Ma'tann: "My Prince is too fond of the Logans, particularly of Quogör Millor, the latest rough gem carved from Mirren. Faldissi fret, saying, what have we come to? The Knights in Bruins and Smithies of Nomis ponder the same. Will Logans become Icenia's seventh barony?"

Meres Ma'tann adds his own theatrics. He rises and gestures with open hands: "What would occasion such troubles in the hearts of my kindred, dear Maestro?"

Maestro yawned, seeming from boredom. "Oh, that the Prince, in a rare stroke of genius, might decide to move his Court to Mirren."

The Prince of Knaves clasps his hands and says, "That's a wonderful idea. There on the foot of the glacier, yes! It's an excellent location, Maestro. I'll have you know I'm invigorated by cold mornings."

Seemingly unconcerned, Maestro shrugged. "Unfortunately, I am an endotherm, not cold-blooded like the Prince."

To Maestro's biting wit, Meres Ma'tann throws back his head and laughs raucously.

Another excerpt from the report reads like this: "Prince, these violins are bothersome to my ears." That's Maestro's complaint. "The sounds are like the squeals of small animals being slaughtered. Equally bad is the gavotte en rondo there, in the ballroom. Are those people, or are they marionettes on strings?"

"So, what would you suggest, Maestro?" The Prince asks.

"A livelier dance, say a dozen doncellas from Aguijón a-pacing. I prefer them in ankle-length ruffled skirts, swirling to Terra Solana's Flamenco."

"Meres Ma'tann laughs loudly. "Damsels? Ha! I fear, Maestro, that they are hard to find these days in that arid land."

"So correct, Prince. Uncle Tallos saw to that, didn't he?"

"Maestro, you are a villain," replies Meres Ma'tann jovially. "At times I think I should send you to the guillotine."

The jester isn't troubled. His reply to Meres Ma'tann: "The Prince can do so, but it would yet add another mistake to a long list."

Ah… I am done with drinking my morning tea, which tastes flat. My temples throb, having had too much wine the night before. Yesterday slipped away from me. Be that as it may, I've yet to hear news from the matriarch. Headaches don't visit me much, but this morning it seems that one is knocking at the door. And speaking of that, indeed, there is a knock at my door.

I open it, and to my surprise, I find Lilit standing there. I immediately perceived something is wrong. She's in uniform, the first time I've seen her in one. The uniform seems more fashionable than practical. The blue tunic has a high collar with purple piping around the shoulders. The pants are a deeper blue shade, while the shoulder tabs are brown, and so are her ankle-high boots.

So, what's this now? We're not to meet until evening. Something's afoot because I see the look of apprehension on her face. Her eyes are in turmoil, and the pink blush that usually glows on her cheeks is absent.

"May I come in?" she requests. Shutting the door behind her, she quickly makes her way to the center of the room. Her manner is tight. "Dire news, I am afraid," she says quickly. "It reached Central Security Concerns about an hour ago. I came as fast as my duties permitted."

I stare at her, saying nothing, well, because I didn't know what to say.

She begins hesitantly, "Brock… the Directorates were holding joint session when an explosion occurred."

I am so stunned hearing this that a minute passes before I can utter a word. My mind runs through the gauntlet: confusion, horror, and fear for my people. Finding my voice, at last, I say, "An explosion?"

She explains. "The government of Highland was decapitated yesterday. Central Security Concerns received the information this morning. Our analysts don't have a full picture yet, but the situation, I assure you, is dire."

At first, my mind doesn't register what she has said. I retreat from the door and drop onto the nearest chair. It takes me a moment to push the fog away.

"Decapitated"–meaning heads were lopped. This can happen in various ways, by the sword, by shooting, and by several other means.

Journal of Allen Brock

Glenn Cross is where Highland began; her military and civil Directorates preside there. Now those Directorates have been taken out.

I lift my eyes to hers. "Are there any survivors?"

"It's unknown," she says. "We're in the dark."

Finally, I rise to my feet. "I have to wrap up things here, Lilit. I need to be in Junipero."

Her eyes grew wide with alarm. "You can't. Don't you understand?"

"No, I don't. What else am I supposed to do, sit here and twiddle my thumbs?"

She interrupts. "Listen to me, Brock. You've yet to hear the rest. Junipero's courier was found staggering along the roadside by a Downer teamster. By the time the medical emergency personnel reached her, she was dead. We have no idea who has done this. Central has declared a red alert. Is Meres Ma'tann going to strike Fay'dorn under cover of this confusion? It's been suggested that more assassinations might follow. Brock, you must remain here in Mon'tre until all of this is sorted out."

"The hell I'll stay," I storm. My anger is near a boil by now. "It's not Fay'dorn Meres Ma'tann will strike, but Junipero Heights."

She shakes her head several times. "No. No. No! It is you, Brock, who the Hexas wanted to kill. You're forgetting why you've come here. Please listen. This is the time to drive your point. Go before the Sororan, convince the Landers of the threat to Faye just like you've convinced me."

I'm confused by all the information that's hurled my way. It's coming too fast and it's making no sense.

"Brock, listen," she says, drawing back my attention. "I know you're under stress, but what I have to say is important."

She kisses me. Her soft hand runs down my cheek, and her dark eyes search mine. "Highland's ruling Directorates, the DMO, and DCA are gone," she points out. "Highland's constitution, in the Articles of Confederation, to be exact, makes it clear. If the head or heads of government fail to carry out their duties or are no longer capable, the military's chief will assume power. Allen Brock Benitez, a great responsibility has been placed on your shoulders today."

Tread not on Faye

Lilit planned a trip to the outskirts of Mon'tre. We have time to kill before the Sororan is to convene to hear my words. You can say that Matriarch Ruthian Faye has passed the buck, or so Lilit alludes. Perhaps the matriarch didn't feel comfortable making the decision on her own.

I have time to collect my thoughts. How was it that the assassin responsible for the bombing executed his plan so perfectly? The Colonelcy, all DMO's personnel, are security-minded. Yet, someone managed to penetrate that hardened layer of security without much trouble.

By mid-morning, we head out to the country, traveling in a fancy barouche. We cross a forest. Maples and oak trees give way to rolling farmland, orchards, and vineyards.

As we travel, I ask Lilit why animus exists between Terra Solana and Mon'tre, given that Hexas are a threat to both. She doesn't forward an offhand reply. That's one of her qualities; Lilit always reflects before answering my questions.

"I will say this much, Brock. Fay'dorn and Terra Solana share a porous border, and in between are unincorporated areas. Freeds Land should belong to Faye. However, people from both sides live there. They come and go as they will. No border guards patrol Freeds, the Dunes of Deseret, or the Valley of the Rivers in the Bajadero bend. However, politically there is a clear line of demarcation. The Sororan has declared that François Franx's territorial expansion into those areas must cease. François, who is cleverly referred to as Pico because of his sharp nose, thumbed his nose. In the last warning to the junta, the Faye's government demanded the return of democracy to Terra Solana a year ago. They wanted Pico Franx to set a time frame for elections. Pico Franx paid no attention to it. The truth is Fay'dorn has no quarrel with Terra Solana; in fact, we recruit young females from there. Terra Solana has vibrant DNA, and Fay'dorn wants to acquire the best people from everywhere. Unlike the Hexas, Faye wants a diverse gene pool. The young females you saw at the emporium the other day were from Freeds Land and Terra Solana. They were wholesome, no?"

Heck. I can't say for sure what those young women looked like exactly. I did recall the event.

"You were in Terra Solana for a time," Lilit says next. "Is it true that in the summer fiestas in Aguijón, the doncellas are bolder than the males?"

Lilit spoke of Terra Solana's custom during the spring and summer fiestas when young men and women court brazenly. The ladies there are open about it, much like the young women from Highland.

"The ladies I saw in Aguijón resemble you, Lilit," I finally say. "But I don't care to discuss that at this time. I want to know why Pico Franx, who fought Fay'dorn's enemies, is despised by everyone here?"

Bothered, she tosses back her hair. "Why must we talk about Franx?"

"Because I need to know," I insist.

After a time, she lets out a sigh, a long, deliberate one. "Brock, to you, Pico Franx is a hero, but to me, and to Faye, he's an ingrate. With the help of right-wing federales in Guahataki and Púa, they carved a country for themselves. Understand this, Franx is Fayean, and he deserted Faye. To us that's the same as treason."

Coeur d'Faye

When a vacuum is created, it draws in everything, and idiots like me are the first to be sucked in. So again, I travel down Coeur d'Faye, and this time with Lilit.

Coeur d'Faye or Faye's heart is the name for the vast, tree-lined boulevard leading to the Chamber of the Sororan. This boulevard is via celebrant, seemingly as holy as Jerusalem or Mecca. "It's the way to Fay'dorn's heart."

The term is laughable. No government, particularly one run by a gaggle of elite women, is the heart of a country. The people are; it's the men and women who get up every morning to work, the soldier who stands guard, the families who raise their children to be responsible citizens. That's the heart of any society, not politicians.

After a cordial welcome, Ruthian Faye gets down to business. "When Ambassador Benitez arrived," she begins, "the Sororan made inquiries as to the nature of his visit. I explained to those Sororans Highland's proposal."

What a load of manure, I'm thinking as she blathers on. My thought is not kind. I figure that only a mentally ill electorate could have placed a harridan like Ruthian Faye into office.

That she thinks herself bright, and I the dunce sitting in a corner, rises to mind. Refusing to hear any more, I say. "Matriarch, I'm not interested in which direction public opinion swings, only in getting results. Junipero in the Highland means to destroy the Hexas military. Is Ruthian Faye opposed to that? Are the people of Fay'dorn?"

Ruthian Faye sets her jaw firmly. She takes a drink from her crystal flask before parrying, "You are unusually blunt for a diplomat."

She's wrong; I am no longer a diplomat. I am Highland's leader.

Sororan

Lilit is waiting outside the dress-room as I emerge. She inspects me closely and says, "You look perfect in that ensemble, Brock."

"Are you talking about the way I'm dressed?" I ask, blushing. Lilit nods, confirming that she's delighted by my clownish costume. Let me explain. I'm dressed in a dark tunic, night jacket with a single row of buttons, cummerbund, and ascot, which again I refuse to wear. My trousers are pleated, once more they're too tight around the crotch. The white shirt is complemented by a thin, red bowtie. The shoes are black, with inch-high heels, and remarkably comfortable. Thankfully a hat is not part of the formal dress. I detest men's hats.

Lilit hands me a document and says, "Read this with care."

I look at the loose-leaf page and ask, "What is it?"

She seems surprised that I don't know. "What you must say to the Sororan assembly, of course. Are you able to memorize this in a short time?"

I read the page, fold it deliberately, and then hand it back. "No one puts words in my mouth, Lilit."

"Brock, the matriarch insists," she explains.

I'm patient only to a point, and Lilit had crossed it. "Thank Ruthian Faye," I say deliberately. "But explain to her that I'm capable of delivering my message without her assistance."

The Sororan is the legislative branch of the government in Fay'dorn. It hosts two wings, one the House of Purple and the other the House of White. Lilit explains that the difference between the houses is mainly ideological. The House of Purple is imbued in traditional values, ostensibly. While the House of the White promotes a progressive agenda, meaning socialism, or the government's taking of money from people who work and distributing that money to whomever it pleases.

To the point: I stand before the Sororan. Several steps above the Sororan semicircle is a dais. It reminds me of a throne, large and imposing. Its base is lined in fiery garnet stones, while its back is inlaid in gold leaf. From this lofty perch, the matriarch gazes from right to left to the members of the Sororan. On the flanks of the "Matriarch's Seat of Power," rows of seats are arranged. They are few in numbers, no more than ten on each side. It's from this venue that the public sits to listen to the proceeding during open sessions. Today, however, most of the seats are empty, except for the first rows to my right, where several dozen women are sitting. They are finely dressed. I don't have to ask Lilit who they are. From their manner, I get a sense these are the top members of the ruling class of Fay'dorn, the Landseer.

Formality is observed during the proceedings. No session is to commence until the matriarch bangs the staff on the floor. Lilit again explains this won't happen today. That's to say, Ruthian Faye won't get a chance to use her stick.

My eyes shift shift back the matriarch. Ruthian Faye holds the bejeweled staff in one hand. It's like a scepter, I suppose, a symbol of power, except hers resembles an ornate quarterstaff.

This reminds me that Meres Ma'tann has a baton also, although shorter. I don't care for royalty. The members of the Hexas ruling class fancy themselves royals. It's claptrap, really. Nonetheless, since Fayeans are Natives, I am tolerant of their ways.

My address to the Sororan is brief. I mince no words, come to the point straight off after my greeting and expressions of thanks. I'm thinking too that Glenn Cross' tragedy is not why I'm being heard in the Sororan. No doubt they think I am a disgruntled clan member. Circumstances, however, dawned a new reality over Fay'dorn.

"Junipero will depart from DMO's doctrine," I state, modulating my voice not to strike an echo. The chamber is capped by a copula outside, forming a rotunda. "Junipero's strategy will be different."

The members of the Sororan and the Landseer sit before me. They listen intently. A pin drop could be heard.

"Obviously I'm not going to go into detail as to how we will defeat Meres Ma'tann. But let no one be mistaken. Meres Ma'tann's power will continue to grow if we don't stop him. Hexas nature is predatory. Hexas' tenets are predicated on this fact: subjugate the Natives. So put yourself in the place of the people conquered by the Hexas. Everything about you, your literature, your art and works, your entire culture is made to disappear by decree. Your lineage is erased. In the Upper Mosaic, Hexas satraps make serfs of those under their heel. Even the Prince's jester says Meres Ma'tann wants to make the Native-born his commodities. They are to be expendable, a resource to exploit no matter the human suffering. Think for a moment, Sororans, what designs does the Hexas Prince have for Fay'dorn?"

I am speaking from the heart here, hoping to reach these people and stir them from their stupor.

"Not once, not even after setbacks, have I surrendered to thoughts of defeat. Hexas will never lord over the Highland, Terra Solana, or Fay'dorn."

So, I am done with my brief message. I'll admit I'm no great orator or a slick politician with a crafted delivery. I'm a man of the lofty hills of Highland, a proud man, not one who is doubtful or timid. I am the son of a greater man, Lysander Benitez.

The Recruit

Once more, Tekno Bartolus enters Parador Posadas, this time to send me on my way. I can feel Keg's quiet disdain for the man. Then he won't have to deal with Bartolus on my behalf.

By mid-afternoon, I'm packed and ready to return home. It's a relief, really, but I'm not sure if I've accomplished what I came to do. I gave it my best, though. Lilit is standing beside me. She was cordial with Keg, but I know she disapproves of his decision to leave Faye.

Keg Dulaine, the disaffected Rod, has decided to come with me. "I will seek a new career in the Uplands." Those are his words.

I must enter another event in my journal that I believe is significant. As Keg and I begin to board the Alturas Transbridge to the Banfield, Bartolus approaches me.

"In time," he says, "Ambassador Benitez, you will hear from one who bears a signet ring. He will bring news of interest to you."

It takes half a day's travel to reach Castleton. From there, we pay a private Mo-wag hack to Kirby Baja and a second one that drives us up all the way to Junipero Heights. There is to be no disclosure of who I am or what I'm about. For security, I'm a private citizen going about his business.

Brother Elliot and Cairo meet us. I introduce my traveling companion. "Here is a recruit, a Fayean who wants to fight the Hexas. His name is Keg Dulaine."

Cairo looks at Fayean Keg from head to toe. "You've got the makings of a soldier," he declares.

I had to laugh. Keg's second career was about to take off.

The faces of the men of Junipero's council are grimmer than ever. I study them. I see these men are determined to carry on.

"No chaos to report as yet," Cairo assures me. "It's a dicey situation either way. Hexas are moving all across the west."

He rolls the board map across to me. "Meres Ma'tann has launched a two-prong offensive. His cetrons are going for Glenn Cross again. The Knob is also also under threat. Meanwhile, Logans are rampaging across the Lodge."

I address Elliot. "Run me through this decapitation of the Directorates. How was it done? I've thought about nothing but that, yet I come up with a blank."

"The explosion took place in the meeting chamber outside the tower," he says.

I'm baffled still. "If the meeting didn't take place in the usual location, how was it that the Hexas knew where the Directorates were going to meet?"

"It's a mystery," Judge Wilkes interjects, entering into the conversation for the first time. "Hard to figure, don't you think? First, why were the Directorates meeting in a joint session to begin with? I can't remember the last time there was a call for a joint session, do you, Elliot?"

Elliot nods his head in agreement but adds, "Unless they were to discuss what to do about Brock and his mission to Fay'dorn."

"Could be too that Hammering Matt was fixing to arrest all of us," Cairo suggests. "Except he couldn't, not without consensus, meaning the DCA had to be brought along."

"If that's the case, why would Meres Ma'tann take them out?" Felix poses. "Directorates would have been doing him a favor, no?"

"Obviously, he didn't know," Wilkes replies. "Still, the question remains, who's his agent? Hard to imagine a man from Highland betraying us."

"What about the explosive? Do we have any clues? I'd been thinking about this for some time. It had to be a mother of an explosive to overcome the negative energy of the RSE."

Cairo answers with, "We only know that the explosive agent was unusual and that it detonated precisely as the RSE ebbed."

There it was, two factors acting in tandem, the Dampening ebb and the explosive nature of the device. But as I digest these facts, I'm suspecting we've missed something vital.

At length, I had to ask, "Do we know the type of explosive that was used?"

"An RSE resistant compound," Cairo says simply. "That's the answer I was given by the bomb disposal unit. Evidently, it took only a small amount of the stuff to do the job. The largest piece of debris was no larger than a man's thumb. They're calling it a nano-nuke for lack of a complete explanation. In other words, they don't know what it is."

"Exeunt the old Directorate of Military Operation," Elliot declares theatrically. "Enters Junipero's New Directorate."

I ponder on that for a moment and say, "Why not call it Staff instead of DMO? Why not bury the Directorate of Military Operations along with what remains of Hammering Matt and his cronies."

Strategy

We're in a huddle in the planning room. "Huddle" is the term we use when a group of officers is called together to make a decision in haste.

Cairo runs his finger across the map from Kirby Baja to Hastings as he speaks. "As I read the field reports, I'm thinking that Meres Ma'tann is going all out. His plan is to throw everything he's got at us, including Logan Mercs."

I have to take time to explain additional details. For reconnaissance we use Snoop-kites referred to as SKs. They are simple aerial devices, drones actually, borne by wind currents. They have a camera with a signal relay. SKs can be steered, but this ability is limited.

So let me return to what Cairo believes is our enemy's plan. Meres Ma'tann's target is once again Hastings. What better time to go for the prize? He's decapitated Highland's government and its military directorate too.

Moreover, Hastings is Highland's industrial heart. I'm not sure if I've mentioned that. Hastings, by the way, is divided into two parts, Inner and Outer Hasting. It's also Highland's most remote township. Our high-tech labs and weapons shops are located there. I've always felt it's the wrong place for them.

I turn to Cairo and say, "When this is over, I want every science personnel in Hastings, every industrial manager, foreman, metallurgist, and technicians, the whole works, moved to Junipero. Junipero Heights will be Highland's new center of science and technology."

He gawks at me for a moment. Is he thinking that I've gone off my rocker? Well, maybe I have. Moving hundreds of men and women and their families is not something you do with the snap of the fingers. Yet Hastings is not the place I want Highland's best minds to live and work. I worked there, lived there too. Hastings is a cold, gray land and a place where people dwell because they have no other choice.

Cairo says, "I'll get right on it, Chief."

I shake my head. "No, that's no job for you. Get the new Civic Council to do it, and let the councilmen know I expect it done straight away."

In the coming battle, Highland holds advantages. Her terrain is one, as I've explained. What's important is how people view their new military. Do they trust us with their future? No army can win a war without the support of its people.

Every man in Highland, from the age of sixteen, is trained to be a soldier. To some degree, women are too. Women are Highland's second line of defense. Don't misconstrue that statement; Highland women can fight as savagely and fiercely as men when the hearth is threatened.

"We'll have to stop the enemy in Knob Noster," I say, looking at Cairo. "I'm thinking we should begin by sending two companies to Kirby Baja. Lt. Lawson will hold them in reserve."

"I've already sent them, Chief," he replies.

I say nothing else, except I should have apologized because I had told an experienced field captain what to do as though he didn't know better.

So here's the reality. I have Highland's forces to command. I instinctively know what to do, but how to go about it is the question. I spent the entire night thinking about that and more. As you might recall, when Lysander was passed up for promotion by the DMO, I told him he should write a book. Instead, he left a journal on military tactics.

One distant day Dagne was about to toss my father's journal into the fireplace. I stopped her. She said, "Brock, your father told me all his works would be turned to ashes. I'm carrying out his last wishes."

The mule-headed Finn hadn't understood the meaning of Lysander's words. I snatched my father's work from her hands and kept it.

Carbines and rifles are necessary weapons in a fight, but most firearms become unreliable given a high RSE index. I've explained this before, and I'm mentioning it again only to provide continuity.

I'm familiar with two close-combat weapons, the knife and the tomahawk. I was taught how to use them as a crag-rat scout and then as a Highland soldier.

At this time Cairo and I are sorting through the rows of weapons in the armory. He tells me that combat soldiers should upgrade their weapons at every opportunity.

I agree, so I'm there to choose weapons for the upcoming fight. Earlier this morning, Elliot rebuked me: "By the Blood Stones, Brock, you are the Chief of Highland. You have no business going into combat and risking your life."

As I started to say, at times, firearms are unreliable. A revolver has a better design to deal with the RSE, but a shot pistol outperforms it because of its less complicated mechanism, three barrels, three shots, no cylinders, no magazine feed, or springs to put a jinx on the function. We have broom-handle pistols with magazines, too, but again they can jam or misfire.

In our armory is any weapon a soldier could want. I select a three-barrel shot pistol with removable sixteen-inch barrels. It's bulky but well crafted. A particular weapon draws my interest. I find it in the bottom rack. It's a long poniard, almost a sword. I study it closely, running my eyes up and down its gleaming blade. Its handle fits perfectly in my hand. The overall weight is just right, balanced perfectly. When I let it slip from my hand, it twists to the pull of gravity, and its tip bites into the floor with a thudding stab. I let it fall several times, and every time it lands upright. In bold designs, symbols are engraved into the clean metal on both sides of this weapon's length. These aren't kanji symbols, not ancient runes or cursive Arabic lettering like those you see on fancy swords. These characters draw the light. They look alien, yet I know the weapon was forged here in Highland. I make it mine and christen it, Lysander.

On my way back from the armory, I see my recruit, the fair-haired Keg Dulaine. His face looks as red as the backside of a lobster.

Evidently he's been put through rigorous drilling. For a moment, doubts assail me. I regret having brought Keg along. Should former "Prime Rod Dulaine" be here? I wonder? Highland is a dangerous place, especially these days.

Keg is dressed in basic officer uniform, with head-cover but no insignia or shoulder tabs yet. He's standing at attention as the training instructor rails at him because he was slow during the double-time pace.

I pass by, not greeting him because he wouldn't want that. On our trip from Mon'tre to Junipero, he explained that I should neither assist nor favor him over others. He left Fay'dorn and had no qualms or regrets: "I am in Junipero to find my worth as a man."

Tactics & Feigns

Junipero's armed force is fully mobilized. From Easting to Glenn Cross, northwest to Kirby Baja, northeast to Junipero Heights, Heron's Landing, and south to Pitt's Caldera, we muster. Anyone who can shoot a weapon, including senior fellows and young women, stands ready. The fact is we have more volunteers in the militia than weapons to arm them.

I stand on top of a Mo-wag's cab and shout at the assembly of citizen soldiers. "Meres Ma'tann's grenadiers have laced their boots," I declare. "They are certain they can take Hastings. In fact, Meres Ma'tann has announced victory already. It's only a few days off, he claims."

The soldiers in assembly are in good humor; everyone knows Hexas will never take a part of Highland. They'll have to kill every last trog on a hill, behind a boulder, and on a mountaintop.

Since the demise of the DMO, the people of Highland have gained a different mindset. They realize we can win this war. Optimism pervades Highland. I don't need to explain to Cairo that an advancing enemy can't be strong everywhere.

"We need to exploit this fact." Again, I needn't have said it because Cairo knows all this.

"Understood," he replies.

"That's good to hear because I'm promoting you," I inform him. "You're in charge of the Highland army, Colonel Coalman."

I hand him Lysander's writings.

Cairo looks at the slim journal with wonder. "What's in it?"

"A blueprint for victory. It was written by a captain of infantry, a soldier very much like you, Cairo."

~~~

Cairo unfurls the maps he's reviewed time and again. He has ordered his field officers to imprint it inside their heads.

"We can't fail in any phase of this plan, gentlemen," he tells his officers. "We will demonstrate to the doubters, those who need a victory before they enter the fight, how to defeat the Hexas. This will be a fight of rapid movements and of tactics and feigns. Our mobile artillery will support the ground forces."

The moment to explain has arrived. Staff has experienced officers from the old DMO. However, Cairo is going to break with tradition. He tells me he wants officers who have fought alongside him to lead this battle. I have no issue with it.

Colonel Coalman turns to Major Montoya and says, "Felix, I'm selecting you as my pivot man. Any sign of disarray, you fix it. No confusion, no misinterpretation of orders, a drive begins to falter, you fire that manager and take over. Got that?"

"Understood, sir," Felix replies smartly.

Cairo's following selection is Captain Raylock, who gained promotion like the rest of the officers. "Chuck, your skills are indispensable in this coming fight. I need every Molly, armed Caracal, and mortar squad ready to roll within forty-eight hours."

Caracals are armored personnel carriers with two repeating mollies on its turret. Like it's namesake, caracals are fast, robust and deadly.

Lysander's plan: "Bold Tactics & Feigns," employs aspects of simplicity and complex moves. What would seem like folly, a counterattack in the face of a strong enemy, for example, is one of its stratagems.

Since Meres Ma'tann has marshaled his strongest army yet, we use our wits to deal with the fact. We have set up vital points, two of which are unknown to the enemy. When our center of defense begins to crumble, as supposedly it should, the Hexas will ramp up their drive. Yet, they'll be suspicious of our rapid response teams. So, our reply "must fail," and therein is the ruse.

When the enemy is assured that we can't stop his drive, that it's "victory under sunny skies," Meres Ma'tann will commit the rest of his forces. It is then when the deciding blows are to be delivered. The strong points, our hidden flanks will swing out, and like a pair of pincers will close around the enemy.

Banfield Rout

Meres Ma'tann's forces strike Kirby Baja's knobs, the series of high hills to the west. Maniple elements, grenadiers, and regular infantry under Eduord Ností cross the lower Cumberland and attack the Citadel at Glenn Cross. His plan is straightforward enough. He's going to threaten Junipero Heights from the west and from the north. He will crush the nascent government of Highland in Junipero and also the forces of Staff.

To move this large number of forces at a quick pace, Meres Ma'tann uses the Banfield Trans-rail. Once more, he's violating the Banfield Way Accord, but so what? Who is there to tell him he shouldn't? Is the spineless Mayoralty going to oppose him? Of course not; they're nestled in their splendid villas, getting wealthy by slurping bribes. Is Ruthian Faye going to mobilize Fay'dorn's "vaunted" army? Hardly. Only one other group of people besides Highland has the will and the spine, the Solanos under Pico Franx.

We've deployed three strong forces, Army Group North, south of Hunters Lodge; Army Group Center in Junipero; and Army Group South in Pitts Caldera. Soldiers have slogged it on foot for days. Caracals, our armored fist, churn alongside. Within forty-eight hours, unbeknown to the enemy, a Highland regiment has crossed the Cumberland. It advances west through the narrow neck of the Upper Mosaic. The plan is to lay pontoons over the River Tone, which separates Hexas Hœff from the Mosaic.

To the point, fighting is heavy at Glenn Cross Citadel and Kirby Baja's Knob Noster. It's the type of battle that increases ferocity with every passing day, yet the Citadel and Knob Noster hold no matter how many grenades are lobbed at the Citadel's glacis or at the Knob.

Meres Ma'tann, with unlimited numbers of troops and the weapons capacity of Faldiss, doubles down his effort. He means to win this one, and he's got the forces to do it.

Logans have moved south from Mirren, but they don't attack the Lodge. It's uncertain what they'll do, or if this time they've fallen in with the Hexas. Their leader is Quogör Millor, and he's a crafty Logan.

The overarching question is: have the Hexas committed all of their forces? Our informant can't tell us.

"We'll just have to go on instinct, Chief," Cairo declares.

Once again, I see how he's studying his tactical maps and the plan of operations. I don't think he's left the building in the past twenty-four hours or whether he's slept.

"Army Group Center is taking a pounding. I don't know how much longer we should hold," Cairo adds.

I'll take an aside. I'd just returned from Kirby Baja, one of Meres Ma'tann's main objectives. The town itself hadn't taken much fire, but all of her knobs, Gideon Knoll, Bullrush Crest, and especially Noster, have. Highland soldiers defending Kirby Baja's knolls are taking a pounding, sure enough.

I study Cairo for another moment. The demands of command don't seem to have worn him any. He looks sharp. He's clean shaved, and his uniform is spotless. I ask, "What's your gut telling you?"

His reply is: "Risk everything—Go for broke."

When the RSE gauge drops, the theater of combat reacts. Cairo launches an offensive from Easting. Mollies blast the Hexas northern lines around Glenn Cross. On the Mirren shelf, a mobile Logan force is reported. We don't know its intent.

The cetron in command of Ností's left flank in the north sends a sprinter–Hexas term for field messenger–to his Command Post. Eduord Ností reads it, considers its merit, and, ever the ham, tells his adjutant that the cetron in command of the north is seeing trogs under his bed.

The antagonism of the people in the Upper Mosaic for Hexas is a matter of course. First of all, they are subjects of Icenia, and once again, their land has become a battleground. Hexas soldiers are billeted in their homes. They are disrespectful, and they take what they want, including the women. Stasa's mistreatment of civilians in the Upper Mosaic is customary. They can be robbed, or they can be shot for an infraction. To behave otherwise is not in style.

Yet the civilians aren't necessarily helpless, and in retaliation, a Proxy auxiliary squad was recently "massacred" on its way to the Banfield. Grenadier columns are fired upon from concealment. No cooperation from the locals is expected. The areas of the Upper Mosaic bordering Chetsí are on the verge of insurrection.

On the River Tone, Highland's gunboats fire across into Hœff as elements of our SP Wolverines Battalion infiltrate. Piney Hurst, Chetsí's capital, is gripped by panic. Cantos Kier, Chetsí's baron, is worried. There's fighting around Allentown, Southaven, and even in Midlothian! Midlothian is a large township in the Upper Mosaic, very close to the homes of Hexas apparatchiks.

"Our force needs to be brought back to defend the Barony," Cantos Kier demands. That's from an intercepted dispatch. Ah, but there is more. The Prince confides this to his aide—Ah, I'll use his exact words: "Cantos is without exception the most boring person in all of Chetsí."

Leopard II is Highland's newest armor vehicle. Like the caracals, it deploys medium size Mollies on a turret. I've seen them in action; their rapid, thud, thudding of twin Mollies inspires dread. Leopards are long and slick in design, with a low profile. They can carry a five-man infantry team.

Lysander's plan is executed. Army Group North swings toward Glenn Cross. Armor and mobile infantry are unleashed. The Hexas spearhead is turned aside and reels from the counterattack. They need to dig in, but they've been on the offensive, and they've not had the time to establish a fallback line.

I have to make my entries brief. I'm on the battlefield. Thus far, no one has dared to tell me I shouldn't be here. My stomach grumbles. I remember eating yesterday, but not yet today. My discomfort is unimportant in the scheme of things. A man can go

Journal of Allen Brock

without eating for days, a week, or longer, and he can still kill his enemies.

Hexas lines are harassed from every direction, are forced to shift and reform. However, despite our northern success, the Hexas occupy Gideon Knoll, Bulrush Crest, and Knob Noster.

Hexas Entor Raoul Boski, commander of the war theater, is put to task. His drive has stalled in Kirby Baja; moreover, he finds himself in a situation, not to his liking. His supply lines are stretched, and he's told that a Highland Army Group has hurled from Caldera and is coming straight for him. Is it another ruse?

The fact is the enemy infiltrates his front lines at night. During the day, mounted infantry harasses the lines. The front is reinforced, and troops are dispatched to engage these raiders. The pursuers are ambushed in the hills, in the boulder-strewn heights, and in the brush.

This continues non-stop. It's a constant grind that chews up equipment, exhausts troops, and degrades morale. His reach for Hastings is by no means a drive but a "snail's dash."

The Fog of War prevails. Ností is under the impression that Quogör's Logans have taken Hunters Lodge. He's secure in the notion that no threat exists to the north and that Boski is still driving east. His understanding is that Entor Boski's troops are to link with his in Highland's eastern flats, and there, this combined force will take Hastings.

The fact is that Quogör was made to retreat. The wily Logan saw infantry reinforced by armor coming his way, and by no means could his mounted force oppose it.

The following day, Cetron Ností receives the news. Highland's Special Forces, Wolverines, are hammering his left flank around Glenn Cross. He's on his own. Where are the Logans? His aide-de-camp explains that Highland Trogs have chased them off. This news staggers Ností. He calls for reinforcement from Boski, except that Boski has problems of his own. The fighting on his flanks has intensified. His reply to Ností is to hold at all costs or lose the fight. At the same time, Ností's scouts inform him that "Highland Trogs" have launched a counteroffensive. They mean to sweep him aside. That they're deploying armor, artillery, and thousands of troops.

Again, he requests assistance from Theater Commander Boski and this time in the strongest terms. He won't be able to hold the northern flank without significant reinforcements.

Unfortunately for Ností, Raoul Boski has none to send. The primary objective is not Glenn Cross but Hastings. And sadly, he's nowhere near Hastings. He orders Cetron Ností to counterattack.

When Ností hears this, it's reported that he went into a spate of hysterical laughter and then into a rage, followed by a state of depression. When he recovers, he draws a moment of calm by quoting Latismo, a most celebrated Hexas poet and playwright: "Let the thunder be heard far when the lightning bolt strikes."

A close look at the tactical map confirms Boski's worst fears. If he doesn't draw in his flanks, his forces in the center will be encircled. Following that observation, he receives a grim directive from Faldiss-a-Main. Meres Ma'tann expects him to continue his advance. How would that be possible? He's practically at a dead stop. Meanwhile, his flanks are folding under a renewed attack by the enemy. Trogs are nipping at his heels. Continued resistance is not an option. If he doesn't pull out, he'll see his army destroyed.

After agonizing over a decision, the illustrious Entor Raoul Boski makes up his mind. That Hastings will not be taken is obvious. No matter his personal cost, he will save his army.

His forces in the center begin a gradual pullback. His flanks are drawn in, and they too begin a retreat west. This leaves Cetron Ností, whose cohorts are fighting in Glenn Cross Citadel, exposed to Juniperos rushing up from the south. Ností is not fully aware of the dire situation. Entor Boski has sent orders to break off the siege and turn his cohorts west over the Cumberland. Those orders, we're told, never reached Cetron Ností.

The report of our agent from Hexas camp reads this way. When at last Ností hears that no link-up is to take place, he drops onto his field chair, opens his mouth to scream, but nothing is heard. He's mentally and physically broken. His arms and legs go into spasms. His jaw sets hard, and he's driven into a condition resembling lockjaw.

Onward to Victory

Never was there a battle like this. I don't lead; Cairo, my extraordinary field commander, does. He's made possible what everyone, except Lysander, thought impossible. After Entor Boski is made to halt, the heat of battle is fanned into a blaze. I'm with the men driving at the enemy. It's an ongoing fight, demanding the last bit of energy a man has to give. It's fatiguing to the point where you think you're broken. Somehow, I can't say where I'm able to draw the energy.

There is no halting, no respite, not a minute in between to grab a bite to eat. Light cavalry gallops ahead, infantry sprints behind, and Caracals, Leopard II also shed their tracks. No longer do they run on rollers but on eighteen metal wheels. They bully on, firing their last rounds while running on fumes.

North of Glenn Cross is where we break the spine of Ností's cohorts. Hexas Cetrons of grenadiers muster and dig in for rear-guard stands. We bypass them, or our armor plow over them. At the end of a two-day-long struggle, Ností's cohorts are ours. We bag in a thousand men, scores of armored maniples, and tons of enemy supplies.

How I manage to hang on, I still can't figure. I have lost fifteen pounds in weight. Ha! I still look like a trog. I climb down from the top of the leopard's turret, and I feel immense joy.

It is dawn. The morning sun rises over the eastern hills, and the five men team: driver, loader, and gunners gather. As we see Highland's spangled flag flying high over Citadel Tower, we shout in triumph. Its colors are silver, blue, crimson bounded by gold trim, and as it flutters in the wind, its colors blaze. At the sight, a lump rises to my throat, and my eyes begin to mist. Why is this sight significant? Hah, I must once more delve into our history.

I'll be brief. The Citadel in Glenn Cross is the stronghold of the Masons. Masons were the founding fathers of Highland. Lysander Benitez was a Mason.

Everyone in Highland knows the history. Centuries ago, Masons fled from the chaos and settled in the "Uplands to the East." Here they built Glenn Cross, a city, and then a citadel to guard it. It was in Glenn Cross where Highland was born.

The fighting isn't done. We'd crushed the Hexas northern army, but the Hexas army in the center, pulling back to the west, remains mostly intact. We launch another offensive and chase Boski's army into the Central Mosaic. We gain the upper hand there. Now we deliver everything we've got in order to destroy that army.

Raoul Boski is no amateur. Why should anyone think otherwise? He's Entor Magnus, the head of the Hexas army. He is very skilled, knows how to make a tactical retreat happen.

Consolidating his units, Boski command his cetrons of grenadiers to higher ground, where their weaponry can be more effective against our assault. Except this is Native territory, and we know every inch of it. Raoul Boski, no matter his military skills, is outmatched.

As the Entor Magnus continues to retreat, we wonder where he's headed; is it Chetsí or Junot? Let me explain this moment. We're gathered in HQ. After days in the field, there's a reprieve. The men eat a warm meal, clean their weapons, and load up on ammo. We're prepared to complete the third phase of the plan.

Captain Raylock makes a point. "With what support are we to manage that? Our mobile artillery is worn. Its tires are chewed to the rims. The tracks of our armor are tinfoil thin!"

Out of fuel, our vaunted armor force shudder to a halt. The drive has outpaced the supply lines. Yet our infantry is still on the chase.

Cairo curses. "It's not over," he exclaims. "Boski is not fleeing to Chetsí or Junot. He's headed for Castleton."

"Damnation!" I let out a blistering curse, realizing the implication of Cairo's words.

We could've bagged the entire army, except we didn't think of securing Castleton! Thousands of Hexas troops will board the trans line at Castleton and head for the Hexas garrison in Salton.

Here's irony at its cruelest. Days later, it's confirmed. Entor Boski escaped to Salton Basin with half his troops. He wasn't victorious, but he outplayed us. He saved his army, which was about to be destroyed. When he arrived at the garrison in Salton, he's received by no other than the butcher of Aguijón, Tallos Bay.

Tallos congratulates him. "It was a brilliant slight-of-arms," the would-be Duke of Hœff declares. Slight-of-Arms is Hexas term for a brilliant military maneuver.

After making sure his men are tended to, Raoul Boski, Entor Magnus of the First Hexas army, repairs to his quarters. There, he draws a warm bath of hyacinth perfume and injects poison into a vein. He floats peaceful to death, unlike so many of the men he led into battle who died in the blood-soaked hills of Highland.

Prince of Knaves

This is another of those few reports Staff's intelligence section in Junipero received from Faldiss-a-Main. It has nothing to do with military stuff I've been writing about, but I think it's worth mentioning.

Meres Ma'tann introduced a new style of dress this spring. His Court applauds his refined taste. It's the Prince's preference to wear snug-fitting trousers. These pants sport a codpiece with a zipper. Looking at a picture of it reminds me of the clownish outfit I wore in Mon'tre. Meres Ma'tann's pants have a different purpose in mind, though. He would show the femmes how well-endowed he is. Some Hexas say, in private, naturally, that their Prince is a sex addict. Oh indeed, if only that were his only sin! But let me continue with what was sent our way.

Young femmes from Lower Icenia and from the Mosaics are paraded before him for his "judging." It's a sort of beauty pageant. Some of these girls, in fact, volunteer for the "Grand Viewing," as it's called. As contests usually go, the participants await a prize after their performance. It's usually money. But for the winner, there's the promise of more than Faldissi doubloons. Will she be invited for a night to Meres Ma'tann's quarters, perhaps? Might she possibly join his seraglio?

This is my opinion. No matter where women come from, they are drawn to Alpha males. This is an instinctual drive in the female, regardless of how liberated or empowered she claims to be. Given the opportunity, a woman will give the boot to her current mate to favor one with more resources. No? Have you ever heard a woman complaining to another about her current boyfriend being always broke and also unexciting? "My dear, you can do better," is the standard reply. With women, it's about resource extraction. They always seek the man who will provide them with more. This is not misogyny. It's called monkey branching, going from one relationship to the next until you find that man who sits higher on his wallet than all the rest.

To the point, then, the Crown Prince casts the deciding vote. Ah, but which young femme, or Native girl, has the commensurate body type and facial lineaments?

Again, Meres Ma'tann is known for his supposed prodigious sexual appetite. This is the reason scores of unacknowledged children are his. Oh, but they are hardly unwanted. The members of Hexas Royal Houses avidly seek these children of "value" for adoption. These bairns, supposedly, are perfect specimens, that is, according to Hexas standards.

The seasonal pageant, or a cavalcade of debauchery, as Jester Maestro refers to it, was not postponed this season, even when Hexas soldiers were desperately fighting to hold the lines in a war the Prince started. This shows you another facet of the narcissist called Meres Ma'tann.

A grammatical explanation is required here. When referring to Meres Ma'tann's title–Prince, that word is always capitalized, whether his name is used or not.

Dubious Prize

Regardless of the Prince's assertions, his military design to take Hastings fell flat. I'm writing at night by candlelight, composing the events that led to victory. I served in an eight hundred men battalion. It was reduced to six hundred-nine by the time the fighting was done. To a man, the survivors bear wounds, sprains, contusions, and broken limbs. War is hell. I don't understand why mankind is so committed to it.

Cairo apologizes for his late-night visit. He brings me exciting news, but it's not the news I expected or welcome.

"Who captured him?" I ask.

"Mullins sent out a detail to an abandoned farm near Cumberland's west bank. That's where they found Verbal Eddie and two of his men. They were waiting for nightfall to make their getaway. They didn't put up a fight, just gave up."

Let me add this. Verbal Eddie is none other than the notorious Eduord Ností. I ask, "Did you question him?"

Cairo says no. "We asked the man only his name, rank, and his unit, you know, the sort of stuff prisoners expect. I figure it was best if SID, Staff Interrogations Department, had a go at him."

Having heard so much about Ností's good looks and his verbal dexterity, I ask, "What's your impression of him?"

"Meaning no discourtesy, sir, Ností is arrogant and is a Hexas inbred like all the rest."

Cairo looks exhausted, wrung out. His usual ruddy face seems drained. The skin around his cheeks is drawn tight. His eyes have a hollow look.

In other words, he's a man who's been in the fight for too long. As a result, Cairo looks like a walking corpse. I imagine I look the same to him.

My throat feels raw, and I'm dog-tired. I want to sleep, but my mind won't let me. I quit my room and roam the abbey for a time. After a while, I find a sofa and rest my head on its cushioned armrest. There I drift off.

I awake to find I'm covered by a blanket. Elliot is standing over me, and hands me a cup of warm liquid. "Drink this."

I feel shaky, but I manage to drink it. After a moment, the fog lifts from my mind, and I feel rested.

"You slept for eighteen hours," he tells me. "Your bladder must be full."

Indeed, it was, and not having eaten, I was hungry too.

In the afternoon, Cairo returns to report that JAG has questioned Ností. Verbal Eddie admitted to all the charges, and no, he shows no remorse.

"He declared, though, that in a war, people die," Cairo adds. "Oh, and no, he doesn't recognize our authority or our reason for questioning him. His imperturbability, uh, that's Judge Wilkes' phrase, by the way–is astonishing."

Judge Wilkes has the authority to pass a different sentence. Eduord Ností, as you know, was the cetron in command of Hexas troops responsible for the massacre in Marlton. But in my opinion, Eddie Ností is not altogether right in the head.

"Hexas Ností," Wilkes begins, "Do you have an excuse for your lack of leadership in Marlton Township? Any words of regret for the massacre you could have prevented?"

"But war is a criminal enterprise, my good fellow," Ností responds. "That's why soldiers are armed, so they can kill other soldiers and civilians too if they get in the way."

Wilkes bangs his gavel on the sound block and says, "The former sentence stands. Eduord Ností, you are to walk the scaffold, and there you will hang."

Staff

As you are aware Junipero's Military Command new name is Staff. It's official now. I suppose we've buried the Directorates, and that's a good thing. Its military side was staffed with aging prima donnas, while its civilian counterpart was riddled with political hacks. For example, to become a DCA councilman or councilwoman, you had to be part of the system and know someone on the inside. I call that corruption. Basically, it was no better than the Mayoralty in the Mosaics. But enough of that old dribble.

Today Highland troops enter Midlothian Township in the Upper Mosaic amid stirring music. My heart swells with pride as I hear Bagley's National Emblem play and as our troops march smartly. We have liberated not just this large township but also Freehaven, Allentown, and others. The Upper Mosaic is ours.

People cheer and wave pennants and banners. The Spangled Glory of Highland's flag is paraded through the streets, and the people recognizing it, cry tears of joy. The Hexas tyranny is over.

Staff has accomplished a remarkable feat of arms. It's to the courage of the partisans that the Cross of Honor is presented. The fight for Midlothian inspired us. I saw a boy, thirteen-fourteen years old at most, lob a hot grenade back at the Hexas grenadier, a woman, with a baby strapped to her back, hurled a Molotov cocktail at a Hexas maniple; and an old, rail-thin woman, fire at the advancing enemy with a vintage Garand rifle. When the Natives laid eyes on Highland's battle flag, insurrection swept throughout the Upper Mosaic, and Hexas reeled before its fury.

With our help, the Hexas were thrown back across the River Tone. However great this all is, Highland is fighting alone, and as a consequence, it can't exploit this victory to the fullest. After the series of battles, Highland's army is spent. We can't press on to Faldiss-a-Main. The men are exhausted, their equipment battered, and munitions at the lowest level. Yet, there's an upside. The mighty Hexas offensive across Highland is shattered!

Elliot said that the old ways were given a fond farewell with the Glenn Cross Blast—no pun intended. It's not for the first time I hear the abbot employ a play on words.

Indeed, the mighty DMO Colonelcy and venerable Directorate of Civic Affairs lay in the past.

As to the investigation of the bombing, it's ongoing. There's a well-found suspicion that Cora, Hammering Matt's mistress, played a hand in the plot. How extensive, whether she planted the explosive or guided the assassin, is still unknown. Cora Quinto, if indeed that's her actual name, is wanted for questioning. She has vanished.

The Upper Mosaic is Highland's now. The Lower Legas members tried to escape; most of those rats were caught, tried, and sentenced.

Unfortunately, decades of Hexas occupation degraded Upper Mosaic's industrial and agricultural capacity. It will take a long time to restore this once prosperous area. What's important is that our victory reverberates. It's the talk across the breadth of the Mosaics. It's heard all way to the chambers of the Sororan in Fay'dorn.

Eno Kelvin

A visit to Junipero Heights by a Fayean delegation was not expected this soon. What's equally surprising is that it consists of men. During my mission to Mon'tre I saw only women conducting affairs of state.

The man who steps from the vehicle looks oddly familiar. Maybe it's how he's dressed or perhaps his manner, but I am sure I've never seen him before. He wears dark garb, a long-sleeved coat with a wide collar. Bartolus, the unsmiling Tekno I met in Mon'tre, dresses the same. Maybe therein is the similarity.

I study the visitor more closely. He wears dark gray trousers and black ankle-high shoes too. His high collar tunic is also gray with a row of black buttons. Maybe he's a guru of Science and Technology, in other words, a Fayean Tekno. Lilit always pointed them out when we strolled through the streets of Mon'tre.

Brief introductions are made. We sit and, as customary, offer them refreshments. After drinks, we serve a feast of roast pork, rack of lamb, stewed chicken, freshly baked bread, yams, asparagus pickled in garlic and green beans. Drinks are set to their preference: hard cider, beer, or wine. We people of the Highland are generous hosts.

The envoy's name is Eno Kelvin. In appearance, he is very much the Tekno: tall, narrow of form, with large, round eyes. His eyebrows are bushy and create a coppice over his gray eyes.

Coming to an agreement with his fellows in a brief conference, Eno Kelvin nods to Enif Kent, sitting to his right, and says, "Since you are the delegate of the Sororan, Sennist Kent, you will open this session."

Aha! So Enif Kent is a Sennist, interesting that. Perhaps Sennists are more than Lilit alleges. Here I draw from the knowledge I gathered while in Mon'tre. Enif is a member of the politico-spiritual group whom Lilit condemns as troublemakers.

The man, Enif, that is, wears a thin cape the color of saffron. Underneath is a white tunic, deep burgundy trousers, and what resembles Aladdin's footwear during a carpet ride. Enif is older than the others: gray-haired, peaceful of countenance, and has luminous dark eyes. His bearing is exulted yet humble, strange contradiction, no? Is he a monk on a mission? Actually, I can't think what motivates Sennists.

"Fay'dorn will enter the war, Highland Chief," Sennist Kent states outright.

He has a surprisingly soft voice, the type you don't mind hearing even when he's saying nothing worthwhile. He is a Sennist, of course, and that's the point.

These sacerdotes are different, and they have a commanding manner and a voice that draws you.

Sennist Kent proceeds. "The Sororan is prepared to issue a formal declaration of war. Therein will be explained in precise detail why Faye is entering into war with the Hexas war machine. To speak plainly, the hostility displayed by the Hexas toward their neighbors is unacceptable to the people of Fay'dorn."

Why is that such a startling revelation now? But I wait until he's done with the fatuity. Then I say, "You mean you will make war on Meres Ma'tann. A war machine is a concept. It's not a concept that Highland's people have been fighting for decades, but thugs and Hexas grenadiers. A criminal named Meres Ma'tann leads the Hexas. The would-be Magnus Royce has repeatedly thumbed his nose at treaties and accords. Under the pretext that Terra Solana owed Faldiss vast sums of money, he sent Tallos Bay, another criminal, to Terra Solana. Fay'dorn doesn't side with fellow Natives, Solanos, because of her dispute with Pico Franx. In Púa, Logans and proxies under Tallos committed grievous crimes. Statistics speak for themselves, Sennist Kent. Thousands of young women in Terra Solana were raped, and hundreds of young men in captivity were murdered."

I didn't want to go into a rant but couldn't help myself. "Logan soldiers will rape the women they capture. It's just their way, Sennist Kent. A Hexas soldier usually doesn't. They go about this in a different fashion: persuasion, coercion or charm. Then what can a woman do when she has no kinsmen to protect her?

"Stasa proxies are thugs I want to kill, too," I continue. "I vow to apprehend every man and woman. Yes, women are accomplices too. I'll march them all to Novo Ceres. There, in that belching fiery Hell, I'll cast them."

Call it a fantasy, but its anger born out of frustration and outrage. I had made my point.

"Is Fay'dorn willing to enter the fight, Sennits Kent?" I ask. "Are your people prepared to die for a cause? That's what it's about. Either Hexas dominate this land, or we do."

Kent's lips lift slightly. I can't say whether it's a facial gesture, a tic, or a smile. "The Fayean people will support the decision of the Sororan. They are also aware of the risks inherent to any armed conflict."

He had said nothing. That's what I heard, nothing, not even a hint of commitment. I figure the fellow wouldn't or couldn't, for some reason, answer so simple a question. Keg's words came to mind then. Landers, meaning the women of Fay'dorn, don't take physical risks. That's what Downers are for.

Kelvin motions to the man on his right. "Tekno Navarro," he calls to the man, "deliver your point as succinctly as possible."

"Highland Chief, there is a vote coming up in the Sororan," Navarro informs me. "The Chief is aware of this legislative body, of course, having delivered a rousing address before its members."

Here he pauses for emphasis then goes on. "The matriarch's office, which I have the honor to serve, cannot dictate to this legislative body, but, fortunately, in this case, Matriarch LeNoire is in complete agreement with the Sorora. Highland Chief, it has now come to this. Faye is looking at Highland as an ally and also as a protector. The Fay'dorn's matriarch has the authority to mobilize and direct to action Fay'dorn's army. It's an executive privilege of one hundred twenty days duration. Ruthian Faye has ordered Central Concerns,

Faye's security, to seek Staff's advice. Fay'dorn has never fought a war. The people of Highland are skilled in this craft. The forces that the matriarch must contribute should be equally accomplished. Staff, your center of military strategy and tactics, can achieve this through vetting and training Faye's cadres. The training of fadettes and the integration of Purple Whips to lead them into your officer corps is an absolute necessity. Matriarch Ruthian Faye requests an exchange of military attachés. Will the Chief agree to this?"

I'm nursing my red ale, avoiding drinking more. My mind must remain clear. So, Faye–clipped name for Fay'dorn–wants her troops trained, eh? That's a tall order. It takes on average twelve weeks to train a regular soldier, longer for a ranger, an infantry scout, and especially for a Wolverine or Snow Ghost. Specialists in reconnaissance, engineering, demolition, armor, and artillery take longer still. The matriarch's executive privilege would have elapsed just about when her troops are ready for action.

The Matris

On the morning of their scheduled departure, Eno takes me aside. "Bartolus spoke to you before your departure, yes?" Eno asks another unexpected question. "What are your thoughts on Mon'tre, Highland Chief?"

I have to think for a moment, not wanting to offend him. Yet, I have to speak plainly. "Mon'tre is a beautiful place, Eno Kelvin. Its neighborhoods are neat and well maintained by Downer peons. The cobblestones of her streets sparkle in the sunlight. Crime is rare, but Downers are imprisoned for the slightest offense. Outwardly, Mon'tre's people look happy. I find the way men behave very odd. I don't care for the manner displayed by Fayean women either. That is, except for one."

"Lander Oberon, perhaps?" He poses.

Doesn't surprise me he knows about Lilit and me. So, I ask him what had long been on my mind. "Lilit is part of the Landseer, isn't she?"

He doesn't answer the question directly; his gestures do. He pulls his shoulders back and, for the first time, the look in his eyes changes. "The Landseer is comprised exclusively of females, Chief. There's a belief that a Lander's thinking is, uh, unclouded that they have the patience and compassion males lack, and therefore can govern more effectively."

I look into my empty teacup. My mind is cluttered with thoughts, and some are disturbing. I've also known, in fact, several women in life with no compassion whatsoever. I suspect, however, I am missing an essential part in all this, but I can't put a finger on it. Highland could continue to fight, but we would never gain victory, not without the second front Fay'dorn can provide.

Journal of Allen Brock

I find it curious when he declares, "What does the Chief know about the Salton Project?"

Oho! Eno obviously knows about my past. I've never told anyone, except for Elliot, that I worked in Salton. While in Salton I had always asked myself, not sharing the thought with others, of course, why the Hexas are so determined in this project. It has nearly bankrupted Faldiss' treasury, which is why, I think, Icenia had to expand to pay for it all. The cost of building the complex is enormous. For instance, an entire underground trans-line, paralleling the Banfield Way, is dedicated to the project.

The Salton Project has a central operating system called Matris. Its workings are wrapped in mystery. The implication, if the rumor of its potential is correct, is frightening.

"I know what the opinion of our Science Wizards is if that's worth anything to you," I say to Eno.

Eno examines my face for a moment. I think he's not convinced. In the end he says, "Hexas claim that the Salton Project is a blessing, a breakthrough technology, potentially capable of providing unlimited power and mineral wealth and all the rest. The fact is, Highland Chief that the Matris is a weapon. Bartolus said that you would be hearing from us, and now you have."

"This must mean that you're a member of the Signet Ring Society," I say to him.

"We go by different names, Highland Chief," Eno replies. "What's important, no matter what name we choose is our aim. The finalization of the Space Rift Matris must never come to pass. If it's completed, then it must be destroyed."

"Destroy the Salton Project?" I say, puzzled. "As a man of science, Eno, wouldn't you consider such action a violation of your principles?"

He looks at me as though trying to read in my face what's on my mind. "Highland Chief," he tells me after a moment's pause, "Every weapon invented by people, no matter how horrific, has been used by its makers on others."

As I pour more tea, I share another thought. "What if," I begin slowly, "What if the Matris was in the hands of the Landseer? Would that threat be mitigated given the fact these amazing Landers are reflective, risk-averse, and sharp as tacks?"

His reply is interesting. "A matter of perspective, Highland Chief. For instance, would you want the Landseer to mold our future?"

The question is rhetorical, and once again, Eno shows that vague Tekno smile that expresses his point better than words can. Clearly his mind is outpacing mine. He locks his fingers together and draws his shoulders back. "Might the Highland Chief have an idea as to the location of the Matris?"

"I dislike being called Highland Chief," I tell him, adding a cordial smile. "It sounds like a title of a self-important jerk in a kilt swinging a Claymore. Address me as Chief or Brock. Look, I'll answer your question as best as I can. Yes, I knew where the Matris was located. Hexas think they're smarter than anyone else, and that's their weakness. I never worked in the main compound, but as everyone knows, safety drills are practiced twice a week, sometimes every other day. It's during those events that the Matris' core is moved to various locations. This is a waste of time because coolies always know where the thing is being moved. So, if your people want to know all there is about the Matris, they should be asking coolies. And if the Landseer intends to take the Salton complex, there's another factor to consider. The Hexas deploy a legion of grenadiers and two cohorts of maniples in the Salton Basin. Tallos Bay is the commandant of that post. It's called Fortress-a-Bay. The Salton Basin, Eno, is militarized."

The Quahog

The people of Highland have battled the Logans since my grandfather was a boy. Over a decade ago, we drove them from Hunters Lodge and chased them back north.

We lay siege to Mirren. We could have destroyed the city but decided not to. If DMO's intent was to send Logans a message, the Logans didn't receive it.

Mirren was built at the foot of a glacier. Mirren is Logans' largest city and has significant historical and cultural importance.

Logans want to expand south. Unfortunately for them, Highland people live there. Logans seek warmer lands. They have a burgeoning population, and the pressure to push south continues to grow.

I'll crimp short a long story. The Logans experienced bloody clan wars for years. In the end, a man named Quogör Millor rose to prominence. He united all the Logans under his banner.

Quogör is a brute, but he's crafty, which is a nature that has served him well. He dispatched his opponents, not with murder but by arranging accidents. It's a practice he has in common with Meres Ma'tann.

In summary, Quogör, as stated, united the warring clans and now is the Lord of the Logans. It's this man who Meres Ma'tann has been courting. Staff is told that Meres Ma'tann has promised the Logan Baron all of Easting and Glenn Cross. These will be his prizes, but only if Quogör helps him.

Logans know Quogör by a moniker–Quahog. The Strongman of the Logans has no problem with the name. Quahogs are abundant in the mudflats of Kordova Lake tributaries, including the River Quark. Logans consider the meat of this hard clam a delicacy.

More facts, Quogör/Quahog, rejected Meres Ma'tann's offer. Yes, they have a common adversary, but no deal. He tells Maestro, the Prince's emissary, that he wants lands in the Mosaic by the River Tone. Logans demand access to the sea via this large, navigable vein as they once had. But that was long ago, way before Hexas annexed the Upper Mosaic.

Logans are raiders. They used River Tone to access the sea and pillage the coastal towns and cities south of Novo Ceres. By the way, Logans build excellent shallow keel sailboats. So if they gain access to southern waterways, they would ply that trade again.

As always, I deviate from the topic. So to the matter at hand: Meres Ma'tann has little choice but to accede to this Logan's demand. Quahog knows this, given the trouncing Hexas army received at the hands of Highland. Hexas need the Logan forces, no other way to put it.

Quahog is willing to show his worth; that is only after a Hexas-Logan pact is signed sealed.

With a potent strike force, the Quahog has promised to take the field and wreak havoc on Highland. When Logans seize a Highland hold or small township, it is looted and burnt to the ground. The men are shot, and the young women are taken as spoils of war. So, as Chief of Highland, I must stop this plundering, Logan.

Lander Oberon

In the late afternoon, my orderly rouses me from meditation, the reason, an envoy from Mon'tre is waiting in the abbey's courtyard. That's odd, I think. Eno Kelvin hadn't mentioned a subsequent visit. Then that's the way it is I suppose, no respite from the grind. I'm resigned to it all, so after a weary breath, I go out to meet the guest.

When I see whom, I had kept waiting, I feel like a heel. In the courtyard, standing tall and smiling is the woman I thought I'd never see again.

Lilit walks toward me and, in un-ambassadorial fashion, hugs me before everyone. Then immoderately, she plants a kiss on my lips. It isn't a modest one either.

Elliot and Wilkes are there, also several officers from Staff. They bid welcome to the Fayeans, and food and drinks are served. After talking with the delegation members for a suitable period, I draw Lilit away.

"I have missed you," Lilit tells me when we're by ourselves. "As you prepared to leave Mon'tre, I wanted to tell you to remain and stay with me. Of course, I knew that was impossible, but such is the nature of my feelings for you."

"And I have missed you, Lilit," I reply, making a confession too. There is truth in that, I guess. But then why am I getting involved with a woman again? Had I not learned from the last time?

"I have good news to report," Lilit says, her face lighting up with a smile, "It is official. The votes were cast and the Sororan has decreed publicly that our two peoples are now allies in a war. Highland and Fay'dorn are now official allies."

"Hurrah!" I shout with joy. Despite my former reservations, there's no overlooking now that Fay'dorn will be our southern front. We'll have Fayean forces strike Junot, and Solanos will lay siege to Fortress-a-Bay in Salton.

"First, I want to bathe," Lilit declares, undressing without modesty in my quarters. "The trip here is unbelievably awful, Brock. We have got to find a different route. I have been rained on, tossed around inside an armored Troika like a beach ball. Yesterday I was pie-faced by mud flinging up from churning tracks. The trip was arduous, plain awful."

I gaze into her incredible dark eyes. Suddenly, tears welled in them and coursed down her cheeks. "What's wrong, Lilit?" I am alarmed by her distress. She has sublimated from a state of joy to misery.

She wipes tears away, shakes her head. "I think I'm going insane, Brock. I occupy every waking moment making plans. Faye is in danger; all of us are. I find myself here, in the lofty hills of Highland, and I don't know what more I can do."

"Stop it," I tell her. "Nothing good comes from thinking that way."

She caresses my face then kisses me. Her eyes, like glassy obsidian in the light, reflect desire.

"I've dwelt on our first encounter," she whispers. "When first I saw you, Brock, I was anxious, felt I was lost. I was thinking, this is a fierce Uplander from a land a thousand miles away. Warrior masons founded Highland. Her people are as hard as steel. We Fayeans have never fought. I was asked to trade ideas with you, Brock. One of them-will you allow Faye to follow her destiny?"

Honestly, I have no idea what brought that about. Highland has no designs on Fay'dorn. All we want is to defeat the Hexas.

"There's no way to see the future, Brock," she adds. "Tomorrow brings changes, as it always does. On my way here I had a dream. It was an awful dream. I dreamed I slept peacefully in your arms, but when I awoke, I found an empty bed; you weren't beside me."

The rest of her words die off. All I want is to be with her.

Bursa Pastoris

Lilit's embraces are a wistful memory. Tonight, I huddle in a tent under the light of a dim bioluminescent lamp. I write in my journal. We've been on the hunt for Quahog's force for two weeks.

Let me digress for a moment before I go on with this present narrative. A problem has arisen. Pico Franx refuses to join in a tripartite alliance unless Mon'tre recognizes him as Terra Solana's head of state. It's up to the Sororan and Matriarch LeNoire to solve the impasse is my way of thinking.

Elliot said, "We have our plans, and God has his. Yet, we can't lose the Solanos in this fight. We'll have to exert pressure on both sides. From what I've heard, Pico Franx is a reasonable man."

I happen to agree. The problem is the Landseer. Those women are unreasoning. To the point then, Fayeans have declared war. They call their fighting units coteries, hardly a military term. They've engaged in skirmishes with Junotine grenadiers in the plains of Takk. It's nothing of much significance. It's Staff's opinion that Meres Ma'tann is testing his latest enemy's worth. The initial plan is to lay a combined Fayean/Solano siege of the Hexas garrison in the south. But it appears that's not going to happen. The irony is that the Solano army is deployed a few miles from the headwaters of Bajadero. Fortress-a-Bay is commanded by the newly conferred Duke Tallos Bay. Tallos was freshly minted, that's to say, granted the title of Duke of Hœff, and also of Børth, Førth, and Høfur. These are Hœff's westward islands.

Meres Ma'tann has not moved to retake the Upper Mosaic now that the Fayeans are Highland's ally. His finely tuned army is fighting a two-front war now, and it's one of the reasons he has reinforced Tallos Bay's garrison in Bajadero. This is done by sea, with troops and equipment rushing up the Bajadero.

We're in summer, but the northern weather shows its intemperate side, nagging us with high winds and thunderstorms, especially in the foothills. However, this doesn't slow our pursuit.

"If you don't surge over your enemy, it's a certainty he will overcome you, making your life a misery." Those are my father's words. I marvel at times how right he was about things.

Looking back at history, DMO and DCA presided over a disaster. They were, particularly the DMO, for the most egregious lack of foresight in our times. How was it, I've often wondered, that these men made such a mess of things? The annexation of the Upper Mosaic, the subordination of the Central Mosaic's Mayoralty, Highland's isolation, and the destruction of the best cities in Terra Solana lay at Weaving's doorstep. We are fighting this war today because of yesterday's disastrous policies. Thinking about this leaves me numb of mind and spirit.

Today Lysander's son is the leader of a people besieged by war. It's an odd situation. I'm thirty years old, and inherent to that time of life, some might say, I lack tenure. They would be wrong. I learned to overcome hardships very early in life. I have bested my enemies and prevailed despite difficult circumstances. I'm not crowing, far from it. Yet on sober reflection, I've confronted facts. Rookies make mistakes, and I fear I've already made several.

Quogör Millor and his mercenaries are still at large. When I find this "Quahog," I'll cut off his head and send it back to Mirren. Except that wish is not easy to fulfill. Quogör is a cavalryman trained from childhood. In Logans, horsemanship is valued. In that land of narrow roads and frozen plains, a well-fed horse can take you where a vehicle can't. Here in the open grasslands and forests of northern Highland, Logans can go where they will, strike any community, and evade capture.

Journal of Allen Brock

During our long chase, we've not come close to surprising him. When we rush to where Logans are reported, they've high-tailed it, leaving behind wreckage and death, of course.

Quogör Millor started out with supposedly a force of seven hundred cavalrymen. That's an estimate because we don't know the actual number. On the other side, Staff has allocated close to six times that number of men searching for that bandit. Moreover, Quogör has tied down an entire brigade of Highland's army. Again, Meres Ma'tann's designs are evident. Furthermore, the Logans' land has tens of thousands of young men eager to join "Quahog's ranks."

I break away from those awful thoughts. In my tent under the luminescence, I study my long poniard. It lays on its edge on a woolen wrap. It gleams under the glow, and its sight brings me solace.

~~~

According to the meteorological assessment, the weather will clear and is to remain so for some time. Given the downpour and lingering clouds on the horizon, I find the report questionable. But I feel a light breeze over my head; it might be a descending thermal layer. If so, that would dissipate the RSE and work to our advantage.

Cairo is a proponent of L.O.S., the low observance scouts we call snoop-kites. I've mentioned those recently. These are self-propelled low-flying kites with solar gathering ability and cameras slung on their undersides. They travel with the wind and are not easily steered.

SFC. Mullins spits a chaw out of his mouth and says to Felix that Cairo might as well use astrology for what it's worth. "Maybe when the moons of Jupiter align, we'll find that…"

It's best if I don't add his colorful expletives. But Mullins is no doubt chewing Oja. Oja, by the way, is pronounced O-ha. In Guahataki, it's spelled with an h–Hoja. Be that as it may, Oja or Hoja–silent h there–is a thick gum paste impregnated with coca leaf resin. The leaves are gathered from the high mountains of Fin-de-Terra and smuggled into Puá. Our Solano allies introduced it to the Highland. It keeps the mind sharp and focused, also increases energy, but it can be addictive. It should not be used as a recreational drug.

By late afternoon I'm feeling the same way as Mullins. Seems that for weeks we've been chasing ghosts. Wispy trails evaporate with no sign of the Quahog.

At dusk, the first photos arrive. We sift through the digital images. I see nothing striking in them, and I'm thinking we've just about run out of places to search.

"Shepherds Purse is the place," Cairo says with assurance. He grins, "It's a simple process of elimination, Chief. We've been to just about everywhere but."

I'm skeptical and tell him so. Bursa Pastoris, meaning Shepherd's Purse, is a region mile west from Glenn Cross. I go back to my study of photos. Not one provides a clue. They are worthless, as far as I can determine. But there's a photo showing disturbed terrain. It could be an encampment, then who knows? The area is flat, green with blackened circles. They might be campfires, but what of it? This could very well be the result of transhumance, for that matter. Sheepherders from Easting and ranchers from Glenn Cross move livestock as the seasons change.

Cairo believes this is the place. Then why would Quahog chance discovery? Bursa Pastoris is flat ground with few trees; his presence could be easily detected from above. Then maybe he has no choice since he needs to rest his mounts and replenish after his long murderous tour de force across Northern Highland. There was another possibility, though. His presence at the Purse could be a staging area for a strike at Glenn Cross.

Argh! It's maddening, all this guesswork. You have to appreciate my frustration. Quahog recently attacked two towns by the Cumberland River. To trek all the way to Shepherd's Purse will take time and effort, and, well, Quahog may not be there. No, I need more proof before I commit our forces again.

Another day passes, a second, and then the winds die. The snoop-kites are unable to loft. What do I do now?

Journal of Allen Brock

Returning to Junipero empty-handed is unacceptable. Indeed, Meres Ma'tann has come up with a brilliant tactic. Highland is besieged from the inside by an armed bandit! Now Magnus Royce, free to act, can launch an offensive from Junot against Fay'dorn untroubled. He knows too that Pico Franx won't lift a finger to help the Fayeans.

Meanwhile, in the back of my mind is the Matris. We must take the garrison guarding the Salton Basin Project, and this must be done soon. Ah, the list of needs and the must-do-now is a long one.

I'm keen on seeking advice from my officers because I know I'm not the military genius Lysander was. So, I call for a Huddle. After hours of deliberation of back-and-forth discussion, the decision is made. Felix Montoya reads it: "We ride to Shepherd's Purse."

Capsella Bursa-Pastoris is a plant with seeds that resembles a purse, and so goes the name of this particular area, Shepherds Purse. This medicinal plant thrives there. Ah, and there's another inference. The location, as seen from above, resembles an old fashion coin purse.

Justice

I'll set a moment aside to give you an update on our notorious prisoner of war, Eduord Lyon Ností LeBey. Oh, there I go again, giving Verbal Eddie his full name and title. I'm not going to erase it. I write in ink. Have you been wondering about Ností's fate?

Before leaving Junipero, I meet with the man. Sergeant Mullins captured him in the Cumberland. Cairo could have executed him in the field, given that Ností was sentenced to death in absentia by Judge Wilkes. Ností's men massacred civilians in Marlton and elsewhere. Instead, Ností was taken to the provost marshal in Junipero. This jail is not a bad place, actually. Ností is provided with a bed, clean linen, a toilet closet, and three warm meals a day. Up to me, the punk deserves a cage or tied under a lean-to in a paddock.

Our meeting went like this: I enter his cell and introduce myself. Don't know if he realizes who I am or why I am there. Either way, he doesn't care; one Native is the same as the next to a Hexas. He assumes my visit is tied in with the ransom he presumes is being asked for his release.

"The Prince will meet whatever price is demanded from you people," he says. He doesn't call me trog, so I guess he's being polite this time.

Ností is confident, though, that he'll be ransomed and released. He is also under the misunderstanding that we follow the directives of the former Directorate of Military Operations. The DMO had an exchange policy, captured Hexas soldiers for the release of Highland prisoners. It never balanced out. Hexas, when led by a Stasa officer, opted to shoot prisoners. This is one of the reasons why I'm committed to the destruction of this murderous apparatus.

So I study the notorious man. In height, Ností is slightly above average, but he's not imposing. His hair is dark brown. He has a sturdy jawline, clearly defined features, straight eyebrows, and dark brown eyes.

"Staff doesn't ransom prisoners, Eduord," I say to him. "You've been judged and have been found guilty of war crimes. Do you understand what that means?"

"Uplander, you will address me as Hexas Eduord Ností," he declares haughtily. "I am a royal heir. My uncle is the Duke of Hœff."

There is nothing else to say I decide. Ností has failed to understand the situation. But I see no reason to make him the wiser. Maybe if he expresses regret, it might go differently. Judge Wilkes could reverse the sentence, possibly? I'm not sure of that, though. Then I remember saying this before, so let me go on.

Before I leave him, I ask if he needs a hierophant to hear his last words. Hexas hierophants and priests serve a similar function. Ností scoffs at the notion.

A day later, he swung from the gallows. I didn't witness the execution. I was told that the look on Eduord Ností's face was one of astonishment. His fate had at last crystallized in his mind.

Drawing the Strings

Valdemar Romo, one of Montoya's scouts, returns to field post sooner than expected, and he looks no worst for wear after traveling through hostile country. It's a large area to scout while trying to remain under cloak. Logans, too have scouts outliers looking for their counterparts. Romo is swarthy and slim, also handsome. He likes to flash a smile to the ladies, except there aren't any with us today. But his smile coveys a different inference this time. He outrode Mullins, the man who trained him. To the point, then, Romo confirms Cairo's hunch. Quahog has set up camp in Shepherd's Purse.

Mentioned before is that the area of Shepherd's Purse is shaped like a pouch. It has a narrow neck or entry with a more sweeping inner expanse. Most of it is surrounded by high limestone formations. It's excellent grazing land, the perfect place for horses to replenish. Shepherds Purse, however, has only one entry with no other exit point. Unless you can fly over the limestone cliffs and overhangs, you go out the same way you went in. Quahog had made a mistake–or has he?

Cairo shrugs. "It's possible," he suggests. "Crafty Quahog could be laying a trap of his own."

He's right. This Logan is brutal, canny in the way he goes about business. Quahog has animal-like instincts for survival. Maybe there are more Logans north of us, waiting, and if we go into the Purse, we get bagged instead.

I turned to Felix and ask for his opinion. He is quick with his reply, "Chief, neither Mullins nor Romo spotted a second Logan force."

I look from Felix across to Cairo, next Bartlett, and finally to Cavalry Capt. Guilfoyle. They stare back, remaining silent, which means that they're expecting me to decide.

Quahog has traveled far. He'll rest his soldiers, feed his horses, and leave Shepherd's Purse as quickly as he possibly can. There's no question in my mind that once he's rested and rearmed, he'll continue his campaign of murder and rapine. I can't allow that to continue.

~~~

Before the Logans awake to their bitter morning brew, blasts from mortars make every man in the camp jump from his sleeping bag. As they run wildly, trying to find safety, our carbines fire down from opposite sides of the overhangs. The way out of the trap is through the entrance, but it has been blocked.

More mortar fire rains down, killing men and beasts. No safe place is to be had. Logans die, but hardly enough, I think, not close to the numbers of Highland people murdered by Quahog's men.

Some of the Logans manage to snare panicked horses, climb on them, and attempt to escape. It's futile. Crossfire from the limestone above, and the infantry at the entrance bring them down.

We rush down from the rocks and put an end to the remaining Logans, shooting, slashing, and stabbing them. We spill their entrails on the green pasture. In scores of Highland towns, these men pillaged, slaughtered, and torched. Now it is their turn to die.

Quahog's personal guard doesn't break and run. It stands firm at the end of a mossy backdrop where the lack of sun allows a wall carpet to grow.

On a battle pennant, a flying arrow traversing a red maple leaf symbolizes the Logans. Today it flutters gently in the morning breeze. Deciding the time has come to put an end to the carnage, I call out.

"Logan Millor, I see your flag but not you. Are you hiding?" I shout. "This is Brock Benitez, an Easter calling you out. Are you cowering under Highland moss, eunuch? Come out and drop your furred breaches and prove me wrong."

I was taunting him. Quogör Millor may be a psychopath, but he's no coward. I soon hear his reply from the cavern on the rock face.

"I know you, Brock," he shouts back. "Yours is the yowl the Hexas fear. Ha! I dunnah fear Highland hounds, not from Easting or from Junipero."

"You should be afraid, Quahog!" I fling back. "I mean to put you six feet under."

That's a challenge Quogör Millor, a proud Logan, can't ignore. He emerges from the cavern and takes his position among his men.

"Crowing Chief of the Highland, come out from behind your men and face a Logan with a pair of balls."

I'm with the men, not behind them, and I go to face him. His guards part aside, giving us space. With my long poniard, I rush at Quahog and we clash. It's like hitting a wall. Quahog is immovable!

He slashes at my head with his dirk, missing. But knocks me with a headbutt, and I go down. He sends a kick, but I roll away just in time and spring to my feet. A fury burns inside me. I don't care what happens next. I'll do all I can to kill this man.

Quahog's fist hurls my way. On my feet, I'm faster than he. I dodge the impact, yet I feel the air displaced by the power behind his fist. His next blow I can't avoid. It lands square on my left shoulder and nearly spins me around. He pivots and swings his ax at my head. It swooshes by, and I'm saved by a hairbreadth. Again, I scramble to my feet. I realize then I might not be able to kill the man. From top to bottom Quahog is a mountain of muscle. He crackles with energy, and his reflexes are lightning-fast. I gaze at his eyes. They are as blue as the sea of Arctica. His hair is long, chestnut color, which he wears loose, like a mane.

"Brock of Easting, you're a jackanapes," he scoffs, in a brogue. Slashing with his dirk this time. Its tip graces my forehead. "You're not worth killing, monk." He grins. "In Mirren the crones would spread their slits and piss on a buggering Highland monk like you."

"Boom! Boom! Boom!" Three loud blasts ring out.

The ax Quahog wields drops biting the ground. Oddly, Quogör turns his head momentarily, looks toward the entrance of the moss-covered cavern. His dirk slips from his hand, and he pitches over and surrenders his life.

It was Cairo who came to my rescue. He blasted at the Quahog, putting three slugs from his shotgun into the Logan.

Amen.

Quilty

A wounded soldier doesn't feel the pain of injury until after the flow of adrenalin subsides. I can barely stand after my fight with the Quahog. My head throbs, and my ears are ringing. I grab Cairo's outstretched hand. He hauls me up to my feet.

One by one, the surviving Logans drop their weapons. They came from very far, did us harm. Now their great leader is dead. We can kill them all; that's what they deserve, really. But we're not that kind of people; we don't murder prisoners.

So, the Shepherd's Purse drama comes to a close. Before I end this entry, though, I'll add a brief postscript.

A boy walks out of the limestone cave toward the bivouac's fire. On his feet he wears moccasins, a woolen blanket drapes his shoulders. It becomes clear now why Quogör Millor had turned his eyes toward the cavern.

Felix cuts a piece of meat from a skewer and tells the Logan whelp to help himself to it. The boy eats ravenously, tears at the meat like a starving animal.

"Hambre Canina!" Felix exclaims, amazed by the boy's hunger. Solanos are generous people, and they love children. This boy has gone without food for a spell, and Felix realizes this.

The evening of our victory, we bivouac in the open. Cooking fires light the camp. It has been a while since we had the luxury of a warm meal. Logan prisoners, in dismal spirits, watch us eat. We'll feed them last.

"Should we toss this wee one in the fire pit?" Mullins says, assuming a Logan brogue. His wink is hidden from the boy.

"Hmm... You know, I've never eaten Logan's liver," Guilfoyle declares, grinning under his wide rust color mustache. "They say it tastes best when seared over a bed of red onions."

"I understand Logan's meat tastes just like chicken," Bartlett says objectively.

Cairo jumps in with, "You mean tough old rooster."

My officers are in good spirits. We didn't lose many men. Logans did the dying today.

The boy's eyes widen, but I'm not sure if it's from fear. I study him for a moment. I figure he's around seven or eight years of age. I ask for his name.

"Quilty Gaines Millor," he says proudly.

"That's a fine name," I tell him. "Why are you here, Quilty? You're not old enough to be a soldier."

The boy stands straight. "Logan be born soldiers." His frosty eyes storm. This is followed by a spate of Logan brogue that's nearly impossible to decipher: "Need nah say, Quilty, be afraid to die. I ken, indeed, and thank ye, Uplander. He works noh intent toh undo me."

I have no reason to kill you, Quilty," I assure him. "You've not lifted a weapon against the Highland. You're not my enemy, so I'm sending you back to Mirren."

Reproached

My lovely has returned to Junipero and I rejoice. Seeing Lilit again buoys my spirits. There is more reason to rejoice. Uplanders have rid Highland of a menace, Quogör Millor. The Logans are now fighting amongst themselves. I'm sure another brute will rise to prominence in that forbidding land, but it will take time.

Ah, but a lot has happened, no? We trounced Meres Ma'tann's forces, brought down Hexas haughtiness. We executed the criminal Eduord Ností, sending a clear message to the Barons of Icenia–tread carefully from now on. Lilit, however, is not always in agreement with the way we do things in Highland.

"Never again take the risk you did in Shepherd's Purse, she admonishes. "You had no business getting involved in Bursa Pastoris, Brock. You're no longer a soldier but Highland's head of state."

I shrug. "Leaders come and go."

She doesn't want to hear that. "Another thing, the execution of Eduord Ností was an unwise move. A ruler has to weigh the pros and cons of every decision to be made. Brock, don't you see you could have used Ností as a bargaining chip?"

I remind her of the facts. "Lilit, first, I didn't pull the gallows lever that sent Verbal Eddie to his death."

"Verbal Eddie, quaint moniker," she remarks. "A pity there because Eduord Ností was a talented orator. It was within your power to commute his sentence."

We are in my quarters, talking privately. I don't want to go on about any of this. I'd prefer that we be doing something else.

"What's not wise, Lilit is to overrule Judge Wilkes in judicial matters," I tell her. "Highland, Like Fay'dorn, is a democracy. There is a division of power."

She draws a deep breath and lets it out slowly, giving up, I guess. Finally, she drops onto the small sofa. I watch her. She looks marvelous, yet she wears no makeup. She unpins her bun, and her long dark hair drops to her shoulders. Her eyes close for a moment. Never was a woman I've known as comfortable with herself as Lilit. She's here not just to rebuke me but to go over the planned offensive. She has studied it, yet she needs more reassurance. After a time, her eyes return to mine. She asks, "Will the new offensive be successful? Will it gain us what we need?"

I assure her that it will. But her concern remains.

"Central Security has learned that Faldissi Command has reinforced Junot," she confides. "Junotines are armed with more Belchers. In the fight, will our casualties be high?"

I won't lie, so I level with her. "Expect the worst. It's always the best. That way you're not surprised when the numbers are tallied."

She cringes at the thought. "The Landseer," she says in a whisper, "does not want heavy casualties, especially as the worthiest of fadettes will be put in harm's way."

I couldn't find anything else to say but this: "That's war. Men die, women and children too, towns are destroyed, and the land is ravaged." I could say more, sound like a philosopher or a college professor teaching ethics, but where's the good in that? This is our reality, and we can't change it unless we fight.

As to Ností, not that he's important to me, I've thought for some time that if the idiot would've shown understanding, had he been able to see our point of view, I might have come up with a compelling argument to commute his sentence.

"Your candor is refreshing, Brock," Lilit tells me. "You communicate the feelings in your heart like no one else I know. I'm afraid for you, Brock."

That's a sobering statement, I think. So, with that, this journal entry is done.

Goodnight.

Plains of Takk

The battle begins. Fayean Central Security Concerns sends her covens, battalion size army units, east across the Kol'bien River in Freedom Corridor. Their forces have to drive east into the Valley of the Rivers and establish a bridgehead over the Bajadero River. The objective is to isolate the Hexas garrison in the south.

Cairo informs: "Central Concerns says it will not go further. Fayeans can't fight the Hexas where the Banfield Transline surfaces. The fortifications all across Bajadero are insurmountable, they claim. The only way they will fight is if Staff lends significant support toward that effort."

"We've already sent two infantry battalions to stiffen their spine," Bartlett grouses. "How many more soldiers do we send to hold their hands?"

So that's another impasse, another set of difficulties I have to find solutions to. Junot, Icenia's southernmost Barony, is the long way to Chetsí, our objective. But with an attack on Hœff, we can cut off Lower Icenia from Faldiss. However, Central Concerns is not sure it can commit sufficient forces to drive into El'athea, Junot's capital. There's the Plain of Takk, an arid, rocky stretch to cross. Junotines will be waiting on the higher ground.

Cairo expresses his frustration. "Armies are mobilized and ready to strike, but the women in Mon'tre want us to pave the road to El'athea for them. It's unbelievable."

I share his sentiments. Fay'dorn has to attack Junot, and it's not up for debate.

Journal of Allen Brock

Staff's top officers are once more called to a Huddle. I don't know what to say. I've gone over the maps, the tactics, studied the situation; frankly, my mind is numb from thinking.

The conversation continues. "Light a fire under their heels, and watch the Landers hop," says Lt. Areu, referring to the Fayeans. "We tell them this is the way it's got to be."

Raylock replies by saying, "What if they dig in those heels, 'hot foot' or not. What then, lieutenant?"

Guilfoyle reminds everyone of the distances and the terrain, thinking like a cavalryman, naturally. "From Alturas to the Plains of Takk is a trot, but from there to El'athea, it's an uphill slog. First, the Fayean force has to cross the Barrens. Then travel hundreds of miles through the Junotine Plains of Takk to get to El'athea. All the way there, Junotines grenadiers will be hurling their grenades."

In the Huddle soldiers continue to exchange ideas and suggestions, but it seems there's no solution to our present dilemma, getting the Fayeans to move. Not even a swift kick in the rear seems enough.

I have to compress tonight's narrative. So much has been happening every day that it's impossible to record it all.

It takes time and effort to muster army units, not to mention the need to rehearse tactics, techniques, and procedures. This is what we've been busy doing for several weeks. Thankfully after a time, I'm able to disengage from all that and leave, but only to find Judge Wilkes waiting for me outside Headquarters.

"We've received news from Ruthian Faye," he informs me.

No surprise there, Fayeans have been nagging us with demands from day one.

"What does the matriarch need this time?" I ask.

"It's best if we discuss the matter in Ad Council," the excellent judge replies.

I dislike meetings, but I guess I have no choice but to attend this one. Before I provide the gist of the meeting, I'll give you the skinny. Ruthian Faye, Matriarch of Fay'dorn, doesn't give two bits about how many Landers, fadettes, or Downers are killed in this coming offensive. With her it's all about political leverage. It has developed that the Sororan is concerned about violating neutrality, rather the fear of retaliation by Central Mosaic's Mayoralty if Fayean troops cross the Kol'bien into Freedom Corridor.

Oh, suddenly they're concerned, eh? I want to curse, except this is serious stuff. I detest Ruthian Faye; as to the members of the Sororan, why should I take them seriously?

My opinion is that the mayors of Central Mosaic are worthless; maybe Ruthian Faye's estimation runs along the same line of thinking. For instance, are these mayors going to raise an army? Will that army march onto Mon'tre and kick Matriarch Ruthian Faye off her pedestal? The mayors remained silent as mummies when Meres Ma'tann violated the Banfield Way Accord and invaded Terra Solana. The only thing the mayors care about is lining their pockets.

I'll move on from my feeling of outrage and to the facts of the meeting. Judge Wilkes, the councilman below Elliot, explains that when the war is won, Fay'dorn is requesting a buffer zone on the north bank of the Kol'bien. Ruthian Faye also wants a protectorship over the western part of Freeds Land, hence why she will not alienate the Mayoralty.

It takes me a moment to digest that. I tell the Civil Council that what the Fayeans want is our approval to grab more land.

Freeds and Freedom Corridor are autonomous areas, you see. If it's a change in the status of these lands Fayeans want, it's in the hands of the people who live in those areas. I think that at the very least, Fay'dorn should begin to convince the people living in those areas why a change in their status is needed.

After the meeting Elliot takes me aside. "Did Lander Oberon mention that Fay'dorn would be making territorial demands?"

No, she hadn't, but I wish the hell she had! Naturally, I don't phrase it the same way, not to Elliot. I have immense respect for him. I perceive, though, that my darling Lilit left me out of the loop in this one.

Osprey

West of the River Tone, Hexas grenadiers fight tooth and nail to prevent Highland's Wolverines from gaining a foothold. Wolverines finally gain the upper hand, and the defenders of Hœff, fearing they're about to be flanked, pull out, and establish a new defensive line further to the west.

Baron Lanthos Moc I, the new Baron of Chetsí, is a punk. I can't think of a different term to peg him with. His is a new dynasty in Chetsí, as the old Baron who governed prior was a palsied wreck of a man who left no heir. So Lanthos is trying to gain a reputation, that of being a badass. To go into specifics would take this narrative in a different direction.

Let me be succinct. Lanthos Moc knows nothing about war because, like most of the Hexas Barons, he's a dilettante, concerned with looks and fashion. In other words, he's superficial and as shallow as a gutter run in a drought. His ministers press him. He should keep his army in Chetsí instead of aiding Barco of Junot in the south. "The Junotines will do just fine without us," they advise.

Lanthos takes his ministers' advice. It's a blunder, though. Without the Chets, Baron Barco can't launch a counteroffensive against the Fayeans.

I'll give an overview of Operation Osprey. Fayeans began by pressing Junot's defenders from the south, but the Junotines fought stubbornly. We come to the aid of Fayeans, support them with our Wolverine units, and overwhelm the Junotines. It is, to date, one of the most intense battles for the Fayeans. Both sides take heavy casualties. After two weeks of action, battered and bruised, the

Junotines pull entirely out the Takk. The battle for the Plains of Takk ends, and the fight for El'athea, Junot's capital, begins.

I traveled there, to the Plains of Takk, and spent some time with the Fayeans. Our ally had suffered heavily. I'll relate a conversation. It's between a Fayean and me. But I'll skip my part and go directly to hers.

"It was devastating, Highland Chief," the fadette tells me. "We were blasted; blast after blast rained on us. The awful belching sound of the Junotine guns was heard after every round. We lost over two hundred fadettes and four times that in Downers. I saw when the Whip leading III Coterie was tossed into the air by an exploding shell. Not one piece of her was found. Faye! Without your Wolverines, we would have folded. It was their courage and skills that kept us in the fight."

She was very young, eighteen or so, sandy-haired with large blue-green eyes. It was difficult to meet her gaze. She reminded me so much of Bristol. I say Kudos to those brave Landers and to the Highland Wolverines in support.

At last, we launch the second offensive–this time from Mountboro. Fayeans sent a strike force from the island of Fanlo, landing west of El'athea. On paper, the operation has merit because El'athea would be threatened from the east and from the south.

The Junotine Baron Barco, who's armed to the teeth, repels the attempt at a beachhead. Hundreds of Fayeans are killed or captured. That's the nature of war. Some strategies work while others fail.

Is winning the war predicated on the number of battles one side wins? No. Lysander said that winning key battles wins wars, not the side that scores the most victories. War isn't a game of checkers.

Highland army units cross the River Tone into Hœff. The northern offensive is timed to maximize Fayean advantage in the south. Despite recent setbacks, they are inching closer to the Junotine capital.

The capture of El'athea is absolutely essential. Unfortunately, Meres Ma'tann wants to crush the Fayeans inside Junot, and in a fashion, they won't soon forget. He tells Barco, the Junotine Baron, to extracts the maximum number of casualties from the Fayeans. For this, he provides Barco with heavy Belcher cannons, a cohort of grenadiers, and two units of maniples. Then he orders Baron Lanthos of Chetsí to get up from his rear and help the beleaguered Junotines. As for the Fayeans, they have to slug it across the Junotine plateau, and like the fighting in the Plains of Takk, it's not going to be a cakewalk.

Lander Gly

Fighting is raging on all fronts. Fayeans are eighty miles south of El'athea, and that's the best news yet. Logans in the north are stirring trouble again. Twice we repel their assaults on Hunters Lodge. Logans make the worst of neighbors.

There is an aspect of the war that isn't going according to plans. I'm referring to the situation in the Salton Basin. Staff is concerned, including Elliot.

"There's evil afoot there, Brock," Elliot says. "Hexas are building Satan's machine to undo God's good works."

Eno Kelvin mentioned something similar, if less ecclesiastical. Ah, but today I have exciting news to report. Lilit is in Junipero. She is with her adjutant, a Lander named Garnet Gly. Gly holds the rank of over-Lead, equivalent to Staff's rank of captain. Gly, you might say, is a military attaché. Lilit lets me know that and hopes that Lander Gly will be of help.

Garnet Gly seems young. I don't know her exact age, but that's not important. The color of her eyes is frosty gray, glacial, and without warmth. Their cold stare reminds me of those of Ruthian Faye.

By Lilit's look and manner towards Gly, she doesn't seem to be fond of her. Is that to be expected? Absolutely, because I observed during my stay in Mon'tre, Landers are suspicious of each other. When I question Lilit about it, she shrugs, saying, "You need to understand, Brock, that in Fay'dorn, Landers compete with each other at every level. What's important is that when we need to come together, we do."

Journal of Allen Brock

I'll hurry on now. Seems that Lander Gly, the attaché, provides only brief comments, with no positive suggestions on improving the situation in Junot. She tells me that Fayeans fighting there need more help from us. In turn, I make it plain to her that we have none to give. I won't mince words or lie to anyone about the facts.

"Fayeans will have to fight and die if need be, just like the men and women of Highland are doing," I tell her. "What needs to be done immediately is for Ruthian Faye and Pico Franx to bury the hatchet. I want a combined attack on Fortress-a-Bay in Salton."

She is staggered. "Sal, Salton?" For a moment, Gly can't find the words. "Why, uh, Central Security Concerns is not ready to open a new front, not when the fighting for El'athea continues to exact so steep a price. Fortress-a-Bay is a hardened target, Highland Chief. The Banfield Transbridge resupplies it. We can't outgun that fortress into submission."

"Then the Banfield Alturas route in the Banfield Bridgehead has to be taken," I suggest. "Logistically, Fayeans are in better shape to do that than we."

Her jaw drops. "We tried taking the Banfield line on the Kol'bien and couldn't. The Hexas are their strongest there, and they are determined to hold their position."

I wave that aside. I don't want to be reminded of failures. It wasn't necessarily Fayeans at fault, not that time. There were simply not enough troops to do the job. But damn it, if Fayeans can work with Solanos, they'll be able to take the Banfield line and Fortress-a-Bay too!

I can go on with the particulars of this meeting, but what would be the point? Salton is what matters. It has to be taken.

Lilit breaks in, speaking to Gly. "We'll have to find a way to convince Pico Franx that it's in his best interest to join the fight."

Gly is about to say more, but seeing Lilit's look falls silent. It is obvious who is in charge here. There's this other observation I'll mention, the look that crossed Lilit's face during that moment. It was furtive; I almost missed it. That look told Gly that she would permit no further word of contradiction. I'd not seen that look on Lilit's face before, and I didn't like it.

Tragedy

The fighting continues. Hexas reel at the pounding dealt by Highland Wolverines south of El'athea. Wolverines and Fayeans are slugging it out with Baron Barco's Junotines. Barco's troops are disciplined and tough, well-armed by Meres Ma'tann and bolstered by fellow Hexas, the Chets.

Now would have been the best time for a third front, for Pico Franx and his Solanos to attack across the Salton Basin. Ah, but that will not happen because my trusty friend, Pico is dead.

Across the cities of Aguijón, Púa, and Guahataki, people are dressed in mourning. Pico Franx, the patriot, is dead. He was benevolent, incorruptible, and just. Solanos beat their chest and raise their fists in anger. Their voices clamor for justice because they know Pico was murdered. They want to lash out at the perpetrators. Yet, according to his physician, Pico died in his sleep of an unspecified heart ailment. The people don't buy it. They suspect he was poisoned, and they demand his physician conduct a thorough autopsy.

Here's an interesting observation. Keg thinks it was Pico Franx's doctor who murdered him. "Maybe Pico rejected her," he suggests. "Doctors know how to deal with death better than anyone. She decides to do El Flaco clinically if you follow me. Women are not beyond criminal behavior when scorned. Or..." he adds after a meaningful pause, "she was ordered to terminate El Flaco."

Seeing our look of skepticism, Keg says, "Not all doctors are benign. Does anyone here know anything about this doctor? You see, Chief, when there's a murder, which the Solanos think this was, the usual suspects are close friends, a significant other, and so on."

Keg is analytical and sharp. That's why he is part of Staff. During my time in Terra Solana, I recall seeing a woman strolling with El Flaco along the shores of Bajadero. She was tall, with lighter colored hair than most Solanos. Then Terra Solana is inclusive, poly-ethnic, actually. The woman could have been Solana or from any township in the Mosaics. Could she be, I wonder the doctor in question?

I'll put Keg's conjectures, curious as they are, away and speak instead about the battlefronts. Meres Ma'tann knows that if El'athea falls, it will send a chilling message to Lower Icenia–to Junotines, Hœffians, and Chets—and he is correct.

Staff is planning a different offensive, a psychological operation on enemy soldiers and the civilians supporting them. The conduct of war isn't solely about the battlefield; it's also about "working" on the enemy's mind. Psychological operations (PSYOP) are planned operations to influence the enemy's thinking and reaction. Staff wants to promote misperceptions, convince individuals at the front, and the people at home, that they're in a heap of trouble. The purpose of PSYOPs is to put an end to objective reasoning.

Piney Hurst, that's the capital of Hœff, is in Ma'tann's mind. If we capture that city, then we'll be able to strike at Faldiss-a-Main across the Beaufort. Then Meres Ma'tann will be forced to divert his support of Junot to protect Faldiss. Like in chess, if the king is taken, the game is won.

Junotines and Chets give ground under the fury of a renewed Fayean assault. Blazer cannons, an artillery piece very similar to the Hexas Belchers, pounds the Junotine lines. Fayean fast-moving Troikas, lightly armored vehicles with 22 mm cannons, blast away. Alongside are Highland officers and NCOs. They urge the fight, bolster morale, and instill esprit-de-corps. Downers and fadettes respond and fight harder still.

Days pile on, weeks pass, and fighting goes on until one day we gain victory!

The guns fall silent, and as the smoke in the battlefield clears, the soaring towers of El'athea appear in the distance. The sun is sinking, and its rays are reflected from those towers. It is a magnificent sight.

Cairo sends me a brief, mentioning that Lander Lilit Oberon led a Fayean unit in the fight for El'athea; to what extent he didn't know.

So Lilit is a combat officer, I muse. I admire her all the more.

During my time in Mon'tre I saw her in uniform once, but I'm not sure why she was so dressed. Reading Cairo's dispatch, I kept thinking, why would Central Concerns risk a Lander like Lilit by sending her into a battlefield? Ha! I'm taken by a spate of laugher after a moment. Hadn't Lilit posed a similar point of view about my involvement in Shepherd's Purse?

The list of casualties in the Junotine plains and before El'athea is substantial. Downer units suffered greatly, as did many "Coteries of Fadettes." Scores of Landers in field command were killed in the taking of the Junotine capital. This war has become an eye-opening experience for the people of Fay'dorn.

Philo Grünfal

Our informant relays a somewhat humorous event that transpired during one night in Faldiss-a-Main. Late in the evening, as our spy walked to the square, she heard shouts. The curses were those of none other than the so-called Magnus. Hearing of the rout in Junot, Meres Ma'tann was, she relates, drunk at the time. He staggers to Faldiss Square with a bottle of Gineff in hand.

A commemorative obelisk carved from obsidian stands in the square to honor the great Hexas philosopher Philo Grünfal. Grünfal's philosophy is one of the pillars of Hexas culture. Philo, a scholar, was guided by higher principles. Although Hexas don't believe in a Higher Being per se, they honor their ancestors' achievements. They're not into Shintoism, nothing like that. Hexas Grünfal, instead, was an interpreter of arcane mysteries, a man of great intellect. His teachings are revered.

Meres Ma'tann takes a long pull of Gineff and empties the bottle. Then he pegs it at the obelisk and proceeds to urinate on the monument. This amounts to blasphemy, not in a religious context, but as an insult to Hexas culture.

The hierophant, whose function is to maintain the square's tranquility, is outraged. He confronts the drunkard, tells him to leave the enclosure immediately.

"Grünfal is a fraud!" The magnus of the House of Royce shouts at the keeper of the square. When the hierophant admonished him again, the newly minted magnus lifts the man over his head. Meres Ma'tann is a towering man, strong and quick to anger. But this time he shows restraint. Maestro, who has followed him, is amused. He tells Meres Ma'tann that he's behaving like a royal ass.

As always, Meres Ma'tann listens to Maestro. So instead of hurling the hierophant into the obelisk as he intended, he brings the man back to the ground and straightens his disheveled robe.

"Grünfal has other pearls of wisdom, hierophant. Do you know this one," says the Prince of Knaves: "'A community in amity produces a bounty?'"

The hierophant shows no fear. "I know it, you wretched gent," the keeper of the square replies, still unaware that he is talking to the would-be Magnus of Icenia.

Meres Ma'tann motioned to his jester. "Will you tell this cleric, Maestro, what I want?"

"Gladly, Prince." Maestro turns ands says to the hierophant that Meres Ma'tann, this sod before you, demands an appeal to higher forces. "The, uh, Magnus of Icenia would have you and your devotees call for the opposite of peace."

The keeper of the square gasps. It's unclear whether it's because of the unorthodox request or that he realizes the drunkard is Meres Ma'tann.

"The Magnus wants your convocation to raise an appeal to Gaia," says Maestro. "Call on her to rain her fury down on Mon'tre in the form of a tsunami or earthquake, say. Have your fellows concentrate their prayers to bringing about twin calamities, a massive earthquake, first naturally, and then a giant tsunami to sweep the wreckage away."

"I am of the mind to send all these shamans to the snows of Prudo Crown," Meres Ma'tann raged. "There, they can lick frozen frakk from the rears of caribous."

I'll remind the reader that the word frakk is the vulgar Hexas word for excrement, oddly used in Fay'dorn, and it seems everywhere in colorful forms and phrases.

Finally broken, the Junotine army retreats north to Chetsí, yet Meres Ma'tann keeps his calm. He's well aware that the threat to him comes not from feminist Fay'dorn but from the "Highland Trogs."

Much as he wants to bludgeon the Fayeans, he has to reconsider. He's a good tactician, knows how to read a battle map. First, he launches an assault on Seaward Seaton from the Hœffian island of

Børth. He has a fleet of dreaders. With those battleships, he has command of the sea.

Staff recoils at this new development. It's the making of a disaster. Ah, how I wish Abo Hassa's sturdy Hassims were still with us. Meres Ma'tann would be nowhere near Freedom Corridor today. Now we can only rely on partisans. They'll fight, but it's going to be bloody.

Meres Ma'tann's war council tells him this is the time to go full speed at Highland. He listens to his advisors this time. A formal alliance with the Logans is finalized. Now he prepares to strike.

On the same day the Hexas/Logan alliance is signed, Logans invade Easting. Who is leading the Logans now? We do not know. No matter, Meres Ma'tann doesn't hesitate. He orders a counter offense across the Hœffian front.

We've been ready for this for some time, and when the fight breaks out, it's horrendous. Hexas give it all they've got, but in the end, they can't break through our lines. We then begin to force Hexas soldiers back across the River Tone. The aim is to keep moving, establishing a ten-mile deep front into Hœff. We're in a position to cut off Chetsí or go straight into Piney Hurst, except the Logans' reentry into the war has complicated matters yet again.

"It appears there are thousands of young Logans from Mirren willing to fight us still," Judge Wilkes declares. "They're lining up by the hundreds to be recruited."

"How is it that those rocky hills of Logans have bred so damn manya thugs?" Cairo wonders out loud.

"'It's what they eat." Elliot answers. "In my opinion their food enhances fecundity."

"Really?" I laugh. "Logans eat what they can scavenge. Anyone would do the same if they lived on the foot of a glacier."

Elliot shakes his head. "Wrong. Mutton stew, rarebit, cabbage soup, and shellfish from Kordova Lake provide the best of nutrients. It is this diet that makes Logans big, strong, possibly more aggressive, and, well, more predisposed to practice sexual congress."

Well, there you have it, the words of a researcher. Elliot is seldom wrong.

A Loss

I don't know where the days have gone. They seem to stream like the waters of a fast river. It's hard to account for time. The war has entered its second year. We continue to advance into Icenia, but it's a hard go. Staff is confident we'll win this war, and so am I. Solanos, thanks to Major Felix Montoya's efforts, have entered the war, so the weight of Logan numbers, so significant before, are neutralized.

A siege on Fortress-a-Bay in the Salton is underway. Fayeans are only miles from Seaward Seaton. If we capture that port city, we might be able to launch an invasion of Hœff's windward islands. In summary, Hœff has been cut in half, and most of Junot is ours. We are poised to invade the big prize, Faldiss-a-Main.

Baron Lanthos Moc was killed in the last days of the fighting for El'athea. He was thirty, survived by his wife and a two-year-old son. Ah, what is there to add, other than he was just another casualty of war.

Meres Ma'tann is worried. The report is that around his temples, his hair is showing a bit of gray. His patience snaps at everyone bringing bad news. He drinks "immoderately."

So there you have it. I've managed to squeeze half a year's worth of events into one page. But I ask, in one of those moments of doubt, how much longer can we fight this way? The cost to Highland and her allies is staggering. My only comfort is that the Hexas have fared worst.

Now to the grim news of the day, I am called to the field hospital in the late afternoon. Captain Josephine Areu has not long to live, so I visit to hear her final words.

I first met Josephine when she was a cadet. She was right out of Citadel Military Academy. A heaviness settles insides me, and soon my eyes shed tears. I hold Jo's slim hand while she speaks. Her voice is frail, seems to come from somewhere else, not from her. Josephine is a Piccolo, born in Pitts Caldera. She's attractive, with wavy hair, deep brown eyes, and delicate features.

She speaks of family events, thinking I'm Rolf Areu, her husband. "It's my fault we don't have a second child," she says. "I was always away, wasn't I, Rolf?"

Jo asks forgiveness for the times she argued and used sharp terms. Then she closes her eyes, and her grip on my hand falters.

To a soldier, the loss of a good comrade is a hardship. Josephine Areu was forthright, a faithful wife, and an outstanding officer. When I attended Pruska's funeral, I felt hurt in my heart, but I shed no tears. The post commander of the Fighting Easters showed extraordinary courage in the face of the enemy. But she was not familiar to me, not like Josephine.

War brings about wreckage, death, and unimaginable loss. I hate war, and I want an end to this one, except I realize it can't end just yet. There will be more fighting, more deaths, and misery.

I bid you good night.

By the Blood Stones!

My adjutant informs me I have a visitor. I throw up my hands. I've been disrupted ten times this afternoon. As Commander-in-Chief of Highland, I want to shout I've had enough! Yet, because I can, doesn't mean I should.

To my amazement, I see Lilit. After all this time, my lovely has returned. Her lips rise to form a vague smile. I take her hands, draw her to me, and she returns my affections.

Realizing we aren't in private, Lilit feigns modesty. "Why, Highland Chief, I am astonished by your outward display." She puts her hands on my shoulders and sets the proper distance between us.

I'll explain. Lander Lilit Oberon is in the company of her ennead, you see. An ennead in a coterie is a military unit comparable to a squad. She's the bearer of good news, however. The Salton Basin is ours, and Fortress-a-Bay has raised a white flag.

By the Blood Stones of the Citadel! I rejoice. The mighty bastion of Hexas power in the south has been shattered! Lilit's news is stirring.

Then Lilit drops her eyes, stares at the ground a moment and says, "Salton was a very bloody battle, Brock. Many Fayeans and Solanos died. The Hexas garrison, especially its grenadiers, fought like demons. Many wouldn't surrender. They knew that after what Hexas did in Aguijón, Solanos would show them no mercy."

She brings up her head, wipes away her tears. "I am to convey accolades from the Sororan. You, Allen Brock Benitez, Chief of Highland, are a hero in Fay'dorn. You guided us to victory."

I disagree. My top officers brought about victory, not me. Felix convinced the people of the Easterly Winds—Solanos—to join the fight again. Cairo's force captured the Banfield bridgehead over Bajadero, choking off the garrison's supply line.

"Now we finish the job," I say with verve. "We take the Hexas cities and make the Hexas Baronies bite the dust. Let them understand at last which group of people is superior."

For the first time, I see Lilit's poise waver. She begins to speak, slowly explains what has transpired in Mon'tre, and I'm left speechless.

She gestures with a decisive sweep with her hand. "All fighting is to stop, Brock. A truce will be declared."

This is unbelievable. We have the Hexas army on the ropes, and Fay'dorn wants to give it a reprieve?

"What the Sororan is suggesting makes no sense," I say. "We have to strike and continue the fight. All of Icenia can be ours. We can make it happen."

Lilit understands my point, except... "Let me explain," she begins. "Meres Ma'tann has extended an olive branch to Fay'dorn's matriarch. He requests a truce, an end to the killing that's gone on far too long. The magnus of the House of Royce is willing to come to the table and negotiate a peaceful resolution to this war."

But I'm thinking past that and say, "Will he give up the Salton Project?"

"That is a must," she says directly. "Equally important, Brock, Meres Ma'tann is giving up. His army is broken! The invasion of Hœff, the loss of Junot, and our forces threatening Faldiss-a-Main made him realize he's done."

I don't know what to think, actually. I am shocked—my spirits wane. We can deliver a knockout blow, but we won't? It's madness. I express my sentiments exactly, and in reply, she says, "I'm sorry you feel this way."

I don't care what she feels, and I tell her that I won't be a party to bringing about a bogus peace. "Any rational person knows that unconditional surrender is what has to be demanded from Meres Ma'tann and his band of thugs. With Meres Ma'tann, especially, we're dealing with a mad dog. The only thing to do with a mad dog is to put it down. I want to get my hands around the Rat Prince's neck and snuff the life out of him. Then I'll have his body strung from that golden statue of his. I'll line up his satraps, the Stasa thugs, and the criminal barons and have them walk the long way to the guillotine. These men have presided over a criminal enterprise that has brought death to hundreds of thousands of people, wreaked untold destruction, and inflicted misery upon millions. Where is the justice if they slink away and don't receive their dues, Lilit? Not to muster the determination to finish him off is cowardice."

She drops her eyes again. It must be from shame this time, I think, but I'm not sure. I can't think clearly.

"Brock…" she pauses for a second, places one hand over my chest, and the other on her breast, "This is a terrible war. If it continues, tens of thousands more will die. Don't be mistaken; Meres Ma'tann will fight to the death if he doesn't find a way out. Do you want more deaths on your conscience, Brock, knowing you could have brought the killing to an end? Fay'dorn has taken tens of thousands of casualties, and your people have lost countless numbers. The cities of Terra Solana lay in ruins. The gutters in the streets in Seaward Seaton are stained red with the blood of Highland's partisans. How much will you ask the people to bleed?"

"For as long as it takes to bring about complete victory," I counter, shedding aside my restraints. I'm livid. "Lilit, tell Ruthian Faye that when people enter into a war to crush the enemy, then that's what they must do. If Fay'dorn's intent is a partial victory, it will only allow her enemy to learn from his mistakes. That enemy will recover and rise up against her once more. The next time, the enemy might just win."

Lilit shakes her head decisively. "That is a primitive way of thinking, Brock. People learn from their mistakes. Maybe the Hexas have learned, or maybe not. But a war fought without a clear political objective is pointless bloodshed."

I'm frustrated. Lilit fails to understand what is at stake. I draw a few breaths and bring myself to a semblance of calm.

"Lilit," I begin calmly, "some people do change, but most don't. Men like Meres can't change. They are egotists. They don't give a damn about appeals to reason. What matters to them is their needs."

Journal of Allen Brock

"Fay'dorn's stated goals were clear from the beginning," she replies. "Take time to remember, Brock. Ruthian Faye never agreed to destroy the Hexas. We don't like Hexas anymore than Highland does, but Faye entered into this war to put an end to Meres Ma'tann's aggression and only that. Together, the people of Highland, Fay'dorn and Terra Solana have accomplished that. Now we enter into negotiations, and as victors, we dictate terms favorable to us."

"Favorable terms, eh?" I say bitterly. I'm at a loss. How, after all these sacrifices, has this come about? I'm not done, oh not by far.

"Where's Baron Tallos Bay?" I ask with growing suspicion. "Staff is certain he was one of your prisoners. You have him in custody, no?"

She draws back, surprised. "I have no knowledge of this."

With every passing second, my misgivings increase. I know that sometimes, vital pieces of information fail to filter from the top down. Maybe Lilit doesn't know, or perhaps someone on the inside helped Tallos Bay escape.

"Tallos Bay no longer matters," she declares.

"Oh, on the contrary, Lilit, he matters more than ever," I say emphatically. "That man needs to join his nephew and hang like the criminal he is."

Her eyes search mine for a long time. Her jawline is firmly set, and her posture is rigid. "So, I see you want to do to Tallos Bay what you did to Edourd Ností," she replies.

"I didn't hang that rat, Lilit. I've explained how it went, but let me repeat it. Our justice system sentenced Ností, and a hangman carried it out. I didn't put a rope around his neck."

"That decision on the part of Advisory Council made Hexas fight more determinately," she alleges.

"I'm well aware our brand of justice is not popular in Faldiss-a-Main," I tell her. "The Hexas habit of shooting our soldiers and their policy of burning entire townships isn't popular with us either. As for Ností, he's no longer around to cane young Native women as he pleases. Justice meted out. He won't cane another Native girl. Odd, don't you think that he never dared to whip a Hexas femme? I say—one less vile Hexas walking on the Earth this day, and I rejoice."

Lilit heaves a sigh of frustration. "The Sororan will hear Meres Ma'tann's offer but will not agree to a separate peace if the Advisory Council or the Guahataki delegation of Terra Solana objects. However, the members of the Sororan and office of the Matriarch are committed to bringing about peace."

It sounded like a done deal to me. I figure too that Fay'dorn would apply pressure on Highland's Advisory Council, throw in a bone, like recognizing the Guahataki junta as an interim Government of Terra Solana. She continues to talk, but I'm listening with only half an ear.

"Hexas will cease all hostilities. That's a precondition," she declares. "They are to relinquish all territorial claims outside Icenia."

"What about the Logans? What do they give up?" I ask.

"I was coming to that, Brock. Logans will be part of the negotiations too, but no concessions to them are on the table. They lose nothing because they have nothing to lose. Logans are Icenia's problem. If they have been promised lands, then it must be carved out from Icenia."

A dreadful feeling settles over me, but I stir my flagging spirits once more. I feel I shouldn't surrender to this. Lilit needs to see, at the very least, come to understand why this acceptance of peace is beyond bearing.

"Hexas Barons are snakes, and snakes don't change their nature," I tell her. "The word of Meres Ma'tann means zero, Lilit. He will give nothing to the Logans, which will make the situation in Hunters Lodge worse than it already is. I say hand over Tallos Bay and his officers to our Judge Advocate General. Let them be judged. It will remind Faldiss what it means to murder our Solano friends. Next, insist— No, demand without conditions from Meres Ma'tann, since Ruthian Faye is so eager to save his hide, to cede Kordova province to the Logans. That'll be showing a spine. It'll convince Meres Ma'tann that your Matriarch has finally grown a pair."

Her eyes storm with fury. "Your words are insulting. Don't forget that I'm Fayean too, Brock. The office of the matriarch and the Sororan are our symbols of nationhood, just as as the spangled flag of Highland is yours. Faye is a female, and you are a man. Never will I dare insult your flag or your gender. Why do you see fit to disparage Faye?"

"At times, the worst enemy is the one you sleep with," I snap. Of course, in the heat of an argument, one seldom pauses to edit exclamations born in a moment of anger.

I heard her gasp. "What gives you the audacity to speak to me this way? Brock, I've demonstrated my love. I placed my trust in you. You are the person I chose as my mate."

I could say nothing, not after those sanguine words. Instead, I lower my head, realizing I have spoken immoderately.

"I apologize if I offended you," I reply softly, meaning it. "I shouldn't expect Fayeans to understand Highland's ways. You see, Lilit, after a century of hostility, Highland can't live with the Hexas next door unless their ability to do us more harm is taken from them. The Advisory Council may accept a truce, but the men of Staff can't. Nonetheless, it will be up to the Advisory Council, the Solanos, and your matriarch to make the final decision. I give you my word, Lilit, that I will not interfere in the Ad Council's decisions or try to influence the outcome."

She draws a sigh of relief. "Brock, I had no idea you would receive this news the way you have; otherwise, I would have put it differently. We Fayeans have not experienced the hardships you and your people have endured."

The look on her face shifts and grows serene. "Why not come with me to Mon'tre?" she proposes. "We can sort out these issues. We'll have time to discuss our differences. I am sure we can arrive at a solution that benefits both our people. Let's be away, you and me, Brock, away from all this awfulness, this strident place so filled with strife."

I nod, agreeing in part. "Highland was different, an idyll, a place full of wonders like Fay'dorn. Then the Hexas made war."

Heck, she might be right, I'm thinking then. Maybe Ruthian Faye is, too, much as I hate thinking that. How much more can I ask of the people? Hexas have been beaten, if for now. Their dominion of the Upper Mosaic is broken. I want to storm the gates of Faldiss-a-Main, of course, but it is not going to happen.

"Brock, Fayeans admire you. Without you, victory would not have been possible."

Those words were meaningless. "Wasn't my victory, Lilit, but Lysander's," I say to her. "My father devised a plan for victory long ago. All I did was execute it. Soldiers like Cairo and Felix, Bill Bartlett, and Raylock—" I count with the fingers of my hand— "Guilfoyle, Mullins, Areu, and Pruska, the last two who like so many are dead, made final victory possible. Without Elliot and Wilkes, and the tenacity and skills of the men in Staff, Lysander's blueprint for victory wouldn't have got off the ground."

She manages a smile. I feel the drift of her disappointment no matter. "Give yourself credit," she adds. "It was you who lifted Highland's people morale singlehandedly, filled the people of the Mosaic with resolve. You fought alongside Solanos, and they never forget you are their friend. You turned the wheels of the rusty war machine to full throttle. Even as I say this, which is the truth, I fear your passions might one day bring you to ruin. I hope I can convince you to be more flexible. Will you join me tonight?"

I don't know why I speak the words. It's hard to explain what I feel during this moment. My desire for Lilit vanishes. Zip! It disappears, just like that! I am drained. Have you ever experienced a thing like that? I see now that she no longer needs me. Elliot would call this spontaneous awareness a seminal moment. I become aware I was manipulated, steered toward a projected outcome. Lilit, whom I'd given my affection, had been the instrument of machination. I stare at her, and finally, I shake my head.

"I can't," I tell her, declining her invitation.

Her eyes study mine in silence; I feel their power. She sees inside me, and she knows I've seen through her. This sounds crazy, like metaphysical stuff you hear in philosophy class. I have no other way to explain it.

"Brock, are you sure this is the road you want to travel?" Her voice sounds distant, as though she was speaking from the other end of the courtyard.

Once again, I express my feelings. "Lilit, you know who I am, what I am. Why would you think I would compromise my core beliefs?"

Her stare is unwavering. "Brock I had expectations," she admits. "I hoped we could reason this out."

"Then you should have told me about those expectations from the beginning. Instead, you deceived me. You contrived an affection you didn't own." I lift my arm and show her the palm of my hand and say to her, "Go away."

Her eyes linger a moment longer. They harbor a look I can't define. Finally, she turns slowly about and leaves without uttering another word.

I watch her slender form retreating down the alameda. Her strides are measured, purposeful. In the distance, the color of her uniform merges with the shade of ivied walls. Just past the archways leading out of the abbey, Lilit disappears from my life.

"Pax Sui Generis"

The guns of autumn fall silent, and within three months, ninety-two days from the day I last saw Lilit Oberon, the peace treaty is ratified and signed.

As a man from Highland, I observe the world from a different coign of vantage. I've always questioned what most people assume is the truth. My nature is not to take things at face value.

Ruthian Faye has become the power broker. Now her emissaries coax and cajole the Advisory Council to hop on the peace train. Terra Solana's delegates, lacking the leadership of François "Pico" Franx, had no choice but to agree.

An unsurprising Staff Intelligence report came across my desk. The Landseer, via Mayoralty, was busy talking to our enemy behind the scenes, even as our two people fought side by side. Again, it comes to no surprise that those women would be nefarious. More to the point, if a hidden arrangement was worked out, it is unknown to us. Then what's to be done?

Today I sit with my officers. They are celebrating the official end of the war. No one celebrates with more enjoyment than those who have done the fighting. But I've decided to limit myself to two pints of red ale, and I tell the man there's no way they can coax me into a third, well maybe...

It's the early evening of a fine day. Outside, the leaves have turned, painting Highland's landscape in various shades of reds and yellows. I wish Josephine Areu were here, but she is no longer with us like so many fine soldiers I have known.

Four large tables are arranged in a rectangle in the hall, and every seat around those tables is taken. There is battering and shouts of joy as would be expected. The officers, both men, and women are in good spirits.

"I found myself in Marlton the other day," says Mullins addressing Keg, who is sitting next to him. "A stature is being erected on the waterfront there, where the Cumberland bends north. It's, by the look of what's been done so far, impressive."

"A statue to rival that of Meres Ma'tann, no doubt," says Keg. "The magnus of the House of Royce will be filled with envy when he hears about it."

I noticed that Mullins is wearing his new uniform. My trusty sergeant is an officer now, a first lieutenant, in fact. Second Lieutenant rank was skipped in the general order entirely. His silver bars gleam under the low-hanging lights, and I think his double promotion is long overdue. Ito Mullins has more experience leading men than anyone I know, excluding Cairo and Felix, of course.

"What's this about a statue?" Says Gioffre Guifoyle putting down his wine glass. "The people there would be better off rebuilding the place if you ask me. Hexas thorough trashed that township."

"Actually, it's more of a monument," Mullins explains, "in dedication to the Chief of Highland. I saw the preliminary sketch. It's a massive work of bronze, to be sure, with a tall granite wall behind it, which I understand is called a frieze. This mural will also show the likeness of all the Chief's officers."

"I'm I one amongst them, Lieutenant Mullins?" Gioffre asks.

"Why, of course, sir, you and all the rest."

"I will have to go there then, insist that my mustache is to be enhanced," Gioffre declares.

"I'm sure it will be, and with a flourish, no doubt," Raylock supplies sarcastically. "Of course, no one here will deny its personal importance to you, Gioffre."

"A big statue of the Chief?" Cairo looks at me and grins. "I wonder how much the headpiece by itself will weigh."

I'm not sure whether he's referring to the size of my head, which happens to be large, or my ego. Sometimes Cairo is subtle. Everyone laughs regardless.

I turn to see Felix Montoya smiling sardonically. In his dark gray eyes, a twinkle of amusement resides. I suppose he's enjoying my discomfort at being the butt of a joke.

I then look at Mullins and say, "Why would anyone erect a statue of me?"

"Why, uh, because the people voted to have a statue of you, sir," Mullins replies. "It's said that yours is the hand that brought justice to Marlton after the massacre. Verbal Eddie, uh, I mean Edourd Ností, hung from the gallows for his crimes."

I chuckle ruefully as once again I have to explain what I told Lilit in Junipero's courtyard. "Gentlemen, I neither captured nor sentenced the Faldissi Poet Laureate. In my opinion, should anyone care to hear it, the statue should be that of Judge Wilkes who sentenced Ností or even Cairo here," I add, nudging my second in command with my elbow. "He smashed Ností's forces in Glenn Cross, making him hightail. On second thought, Mullins, they should erect a statue of you since it was you who captured Ností."

Bartlett stands, brings his large beer mug up, and says: "Three cheers for the Chief!"

Everyone rises, and the shouts are loud: "Hail to the Highland Chief! Hurrah! Hurrah! Hurrah!"

~~~

Returning to Junipero Abbey, I recline on a comfortable seat in the Genius Loci. This chamber is the spiritual heart of Junipero Abbey, the best place to think and to reminisce. So I reflect, thinking of the lost opportunities. One of these is prominent, and it might sound strange to you. Staff should have enlisted Pico Franx help and invaded Fay'dorn instead of Icenia's baronies.

Ah, then from your perspective, I should be enjoying the tranquility of peace, no? I'm unable, however. Instead I am filled with apprehension these days. I know peace won't last. Until the Hexas are made a conquered people and Fay'dorn's ambitions are checked, there will be strife. I can't bring those changes about.

Did I do all I could to fulfill Lysander's dream? Maybe not, yet I can't imagine what else I might have done.

As always, I think about Bristol. I've not stopped looking for her. I've hired professionals to search for my daughter, but it's been a fruitless quest so far. It's as though Zee, her abductor, vanished from the face of the Earth. Zee has no heart, but she's cunning and knows I'm searching for her. If I find her, it will not go well for her.

It's a chilly autumn evening, but I'm in comfort. The aromatic scent of burning cedar pervades the chamber, and the occasional popping and loud crackle compliments the silence. Elliot enters the room and bids me a good evening. It's late, almost nightfall, actually. He's got more "weighty news," but first, he must have a shot of whiskey, then a second. He feels cold and stands near the fireplace.

"Seems I can't shake off the cold these days," he complains, sighing with weariness. He glances my way for a second and then returns his attention to the fire.

"Today, the Ad Council received the official document. I printed you a copy," he informs me.

I glance at it, but there is a different issue on my mind then. "Elliot, I've been thinking of the explosion in Glenn Cross for some time."

"Ah, that..." he exclaims ambiguously—"an episode quite forgotten..."

Elliot is being theatrical, as usual, but I go on. "In retrospect, it's clear who ordered it."

He turns to me. "Well, go on."

"Was Cora Quinto ever found?" I ask. "I've been too busy to follow the investigation."

"Cora no longer exists, so I'm told," Elliot says. "But, who's this responsible party or person you're speaking of?"

"The Landseer," I say. "It was, you see, the Landseer who contrived and to put me in power. And I, like a marionette, danced on the strings for those women."

"Theoretically, no?" But Elliot ponders on that before saying more. "If that is so," he goes on to say, "it seems that in the end, it worked out for the best, best for Highland, that is."

"That remains to be seen," I reply, wondering.

Elliot shrugs. "I suppose, and I pray for the best. But I'm thinking past that. Understand, the members of the Ad Council aren't soldiers, Brock. They share a liberal mindset also. I don't think that's a pejorative, by the way. I'll just say that the people of Highland, unlike its ministers, are conservative. Yet they too welcome peace."

"So its peace signed and delivered for whatever it might bring," I say without spite. It is what it has become, and I realize nothing is to be done about it.

Elliot gets on with the point that brought him. "Judge Wilkes and I were the two dissenting votes," he explains, capping the bottle of whiskey. "Obviously insufficient votes," he adds with a dark chuckle. "Ruthian Faye's proposal corresponds to a Pax Sui Generis. Not even the losers lose." He motions to the folder he placed on the table. "But you can read it all there."

"How eager we are to forgive," I say, hard-pressed not to sound resentful. "Pity how everything is quickly forgotten, the massacres and the murder of thousands by the Stasa thugs, the leveling of Terra Solana's cities." I shake my head in dismay. "Elliot, by the words of your God, Meres Ma'tann should be put to the sword."

"That would be just, yes," Elliot agrees somberly.

"You understand, Elliot, why I couldn't attend the negotiations," I say hoping, he's still not miffed about it.

His following words are delivered with a splash of recrimination–"Because Allen Brock is full of pride."

I know he's not carping but saying what's on his mind. Nonetheless, I have to correct his assumption. "Elliot, it has nothing to do with pride but with conviction."

Elliot downs his whiskey takes a seat, and leans back. "However, I'm aware there is an abundance of that quality in you, Brock," he adds casually, twiddling his thumbs atop his ample belly. "I'll mention the signatories if you care to hear that part."

Journal of Allen Brock

"By all means, Elliot."

"Well, let's see… Lander Gly was Fay'dorn's delegate. I'll start with her. She was in the company of two other Landers, which I presumed were from the Landseer, but I didn't get their names. Wilkes represented Highland's interests, of course. Maestro, the Court Jester from the Faldissi Court, acted on behalf of the Hexas Barony. While a Logan, whose name is Quigley and nephew to the late Quogör, was the envoy from Mirren. The rest of the delegates were Solanos, none known to me. They spoke Solani among themselves, but unlike you, I couldn't follow what they were saying. Felix says they are honest men, while none seemed thrilled signing a peace treaty Fay'dorn is a party to."

"For good reason," I remind him. "Solanos want not just Hexas out of Terra Solana's lands but Fayeans too." I halt for a second, wondering if I heard him correctly. "I'll have you go back for a second. You mentioned Maestro represented the Hexas Barony? How does a court jester assume the mantle of negotiator?"

"Call him what you will, Brock, but clearly, he's no jokester. Maestro is smart as a whip, knew every written line on the agreement by heart. His assistant was emptor of grenadiers by the name of Riis—um, his first name escapes me. Riis wrangled with Garnet Gly repeatedly. He and Maestro want Fayeans out of Seaward Seaton and out of Freedom Corridor too. Otherwise, hostilities, the end of the truce, will resume. Faye must return to her former borders, south of the Kol'bien. Fayeans gave way but then demanded parts of the fertile Valley of the Rivers. So there it is, in a nutshell, as the saying goes."

"To me, this spells trouble," I say to him. "Solanos don't want Fayeans in the southeast, and Hexas don't want them north of the Kol'bien either. Except that Fay'dorn intends to expand her borders and I'm afraid no one in the Central Mosaic is strong enough to oppose those harpies."

Finally, I ask Elliot what's been nagging my mind for quite a while. "What's to become of the Salton Project?"

"The Salton Project is to remain in the hands of the Hexas but under the supervision of Fay'dorn's Central Security Concerns," he replies. "Staff, as you well know, opposed the plan, but Advisory Council was once again persuaded by Fayeans to allow her Teknos and our Sci-Wizards to work with Hexas Technissi instead of kicking out the Hexas entirely. Together they are to harness the power of the RSE for the benefit of humankind."

"What exactly does that mean, Elliot?"

He sighs. "Fiddle-faddle at best or perhaps another obscure plan of Ruthian Faye and the Landseer."

I'm suspicious about it all and tell him so. "I have my concerns. Letting the Fayeans and Hexas, no matter who they are, run the works in Salton is worrisome. In my opinion, it's a mistake."

Elliot shrugs. "I agree that Fayeans need to be watched, but there's no other way with the Hexas. Faldiss has spent too much time and capital on the project to just hand it over. Also, a sizable Hexas enclave has existed in the mountains of the Solani-Austraneés for more than a century. They are not disposed to leave. To try an eviction means population relocation. The Hexas will not have it. The new Governor-General of the Solani-Austraneés, is Patrice Gambetta, who seems reasonable. You've heard of him, no?"

I nod. "Yes, and I understand he doesn't think highly of Meres Ma'tann. I also know his agents were feeding Pico Franks intelligence."

"Nonetheless, Meres will have influence in the Austraneés, the magnus has to make concessions nonetheless. Gambetta's advice is that Faldiss should pay via reparations to rebuild the cities Tallos Bay destroyed. Solanos, who were the most affected by the presence of Hexas military in the region, insist on it."

I know Elliot is brighter than me and no doubt sees the problem here. Meres Ma'tann is getting away with murder, both literally and figuratively. He hasn't lost a thing; in fact, the former Prince of Faldiss is as strong as ever. A primary condition is that Hexas must desist from the use of military force forever. Ha! What a sham. The Magnus Rat won't keep his word. Meanwhile, Baron Tallos Bay, the Butcher of Aguijón, escaped the noose, as did most of his Stasa goons and proxy lieutenants who carried out murders in Terra Solana, Seaward Seaton, and Upper Mosaic.

Elliot continues. "The Hexas Barony agreed to draw their troops north. They'll leave the Seaward Seaton Sound when Fayeans pull their forces from the city. Hoeff is to cede control of the River Tone to Highland. While the Highland army is to pull out of western Hoeff. Fayeans, even after the slaughter in the Plain of Takk, agree to end the occupation of Junot. A buffer zone between the Hexas and Central Mosaic will be created along the Banfield Way. Faldiss will not pursue imperial designs in the Mosaics again, nor will they direct military aggression against any of her neighbors, etc. Meanwhile, Fay'dorn will continue to press her claim to specific areas in the Lower Mosaic.

And as I said before, Solano delegates will object on the same strain. Hence more negotiations are underway. Ruthian Faye proclaims that the Central Mosaic will be freed from its inept Mayoral government."

"Amen," I say. "I know I sound like a broken record, Elliot, but this is a sore point because I deem the Mayoralty an unnamed accomplice in the war. They remain lackeys of Meres Ma'tann, and they'll always be unless we round them up and toss them on their behinds."

"Ah, but here's another note of interest," Elliot adds with enthusiasm. "Fay'dorn calls to the women of Central Mosaic to become empowered. It's a manifesto, eh, a sort of regular rider within the peace documents. Wilkes can explain it better than me."

Despite all the negatives, I am curious to hear it. "So, what new dribble is this?"

Elliot nods. "Dribble it is. The Sororan has indicted all the males in the Mosaics of 'egregious chauvinism.' Supposedly they don't treat their partners as equals. Accordingly, these men are chauvinist, phallocentric, and sexist."

I laugh. "Since when have men not thought with their smaller heads, Elliot? And since when have women failed to control either head, eh? Ruthian Faye makes no secret that Faye will expand her influence, does she?"

"And her territory," Elliot says meaningfully. "On a more sober note, Brock, Highland must have continuity in her military command. It's paramount that your role as Chief of Staff continues. I am hoping you reconsider your decision."

I won't. I know my job in Junipero is done. Two days prior, I promoted Colonel Cairo Coalman to Commander-in-Chief of Highland's army. Lt. Colonel Felix Montoya is his Joint Chief. Together they'll carry on, make sure Highland remains safe. Elliot is obviously disappointed by my leave, but I believe he understands the reasons behind my decision.

"You're obviously too young to retire, Brock. What are your plans?"

I reach for the whiskey bottle and pour myself a drink, and I savor it. I down a second shot, slap down the empty glass on the table, and I say, "I came to Junipero not entirely seeking refuge. I was determined to find out why my life was in such shambles. I was then caught in a whirlwind, becoming the storm's center. I led with vigor. I lent my energies and determination to the cause but managed to change nothing worth mentioning. I make ruins of relationships ... There is fundamentally something missing in me, Elliot. I need to find out what. So, I'll trek to Glacial Streams Mission. Maybe I'll find a sense of purpose there."

SEQUEL
~~~ Journal of Brindal's Brock~~~~

Night Shadows of Brindal

It's deep into the night, and I watch the stars pulsing in a multitude of colors. The red hues of moonlight offset the darkness, drawing the dreaded peaks of gray rocks as a backdrop. This place of exile is as beautiful as it is terrifying.

I, former Highland Chief Allen Brock Benitez, will, as always, listen to my instincts. It's not only my life I'm attempting to preserve, and I'm not sure I will succeed in doing that. It is clear that if I fail to act decisively, not one of us will survive this exile.

How we came to be in Brindal is complicated, a story that will take hours to narrate. In my former journal, I recounted what transpired in the struggle of we Natives to remain free. In those pages, I ascribed neither praise nor glory to myself. I found no reason to attach worthiness to my actions or accomplishments. In my life, I've experienced more fear and doubts than triumph or gains. In reflection, it was my decisions that correspond to my failures and the peril we find ourselves.

It's a remorselessly cold night in Brindal. I know what winter is, the killer of things. I was raised in the snowy hills of Easting, one of the coldest parts of the Highland. Ah, but Highland is no more...

Next to me, near the fireplace, are my two companions, Otto and Túsa. They're my dogs, and they stand equably beside me. In communion, we'll keep vigil. We know the terrifying Night Shadows of Brindal will return.

www.ingramcontent.com/pod-product-compliance
Lightning Source LLC
LaVergne TN
LVHW091536060526
838200LV00036B/634